HUNTING HELENA

HUNTING HELENA

NATALIE CARTER-GILES

FLANKER PRESS LIMITED
ST. JOHN'S

Library and Archives Canada Cataloguing in Publication

Title: Hunting Helena : a novel / Natalie Carter-Giles.
Names: Carter-Giles, Natalie, author.
Identifiers: Canadiana (print) 20220481512 | Canadiana (ebook) 20220481539 | ISBN
    9781774571231 (softcover) | ISBN 9781774571248 (EPUB) | ISBN 9781774571255 (PDF)
Classification: LCC PS8605.A86625 H86 2023 | DDC C813/.6—dc23

PRINTED IN CANADA

MIX
Paper from
responsible sources
FSC
www.fsc.org **FSC® C016245**

This paper has been certified to meet the environ-
mental and social standards of the Forest Stewardship
Council® (FSC®) and comes from responsibly managed forests, and verified recycled sources.

Cover Design by Graham Blair

FLANKER PRESS LTD.
1243 KENMOUNT ROAD
PARADISE, NL
A1L 0V8

TELEPHONE: (709) 739-4477   FAX: (709) 739-4420   TOLL-FREE: 1-866-739-4420
W W W . F L A N K E R P R E S S . C O M

9 8 7 6 5 4 3 2

We acknowledge the [financial] support of the Government of Canada. *Nous reconnaissons l'appui [financier] du gouvernement
du Canada*. We acknowledge the support of the Canada Council for the Arts, which last year invested $153 million to bring
the arts to Canadians throughout the country. *Nous remercions le Conseil des arts du Canada de son soutien. L'an dernier, le
Conseil a investi 153 millions de dollars pour mettre de l'art dans la vie des Canadiennes et des Canadiens de tout le pays.* We
acknowledge the financial support of the Government of Newfoundland and Labrador, Department of Tourism, Culture and
Recreation for our publishing activities.

To Vanessa,
without whom I may not have finished.

If ifs and ands were pots and pans,
there'd be no work for tinkers' hands.

— Proverb

Prologue

I lie here in the corner on the damp and dirty floor unable to wipe away your blood splattered on my face. My hands are still tethered behind my back. I haven't felt them in a long time, and I'm not sure if the circulation has been cut off by the zip ties or if the pain from the gunshot wound in my arm has caused them to go numb. It's likely a combination of both. I wish I could stand and move farther away from your dead body lying next to me, but my feet are bound, and even if they weren't, I'm not sure I could stand. Between the butt of your gun connecting with my head and the bullet grazing my skull, my sense of balance is slightly off, and I think it is better for me to just lie here until someone carries me out of this place.

I hear David yelling, asking if I am all right, but his voice seems so distant, even though I can see he is here in this room, too. I want to answer, but I can't seem to form the words. I can barely take my eyes off of your body splayed out on the rotted basement floor and the pool of blood that is spreading out around you in a black, shiny pool. It is fitting that your blood should appear black and slick; it matches the darkness of your soul and the immorality you carried. There is a commotion beside you as they check to see if you are really dead. I know you are because I watched until your life drained from your eyes. I wanted to watch as you crossed over into hell, and I made sure it was me you saw smiling back at you as you went.

Our game lasted eight years. Eight long years. In the beginning, you nearly won, but I survived, and for the next days, weeks, months, years that followed, I watched and I waited. I prepared and I planned. I grew stronger and more confident. And you came back, just as I knew you would. But now it's finished. It's over. I have been changed forever. You have moulded me into someone I didn't know existed, but I am still me. I do not have to wonder who I am or what happened to the person I used to be—that person is still here. I have merely created a new version, one who isn't naive or unsophisticated in the ways of the world. I know evil exists. I know I will find it where I least expect it. And now I know it is possible to conquer it. I know because evil is dead on the floor beside me, and all I can do is look at your lifeless figure and smile to myself.

I used to wonder what event or events could possibly have led you to exude evil like you did, but I understand now that evil is not always chosen; sometimes it is accepted, sometimes it is forced, and sometimes it is embraced. I believe you embraced it. It may have been forced upon you, but you welcomed it with open arms and a thirst for more. I'm glad you are dead. There was no hope for you. Not because hope wasn't possible, but because you refused it. You gave up, you accepted what was forced and relished in it. You became a monster, and monsters deserve to die.

The smell of your dead body beside me is disgusting. The contents of your bowels and your bladder have soaked your pants, and even the metallic smell of your blood cannot disguise it. I wish for a moment I could stay just long enough to watch the rats come for you, but that makes me sound a little more like you, and in no way do I want to be like you. So, I will allow David to carry me out of here. I will give up my dream of revelling in your demise, but the vision of your dead, soulless eyes staring at me with panic and uncertainty will be the lullaby that lulls me to sleep for weeks to come.

Maybe we have more in common than I care to admit, but the differences between us are astronomical. We have both encountered the devil in all his glory, yet you became a follower while I became his nemesis. I vowed to fight him with everything in me while you succumbed to his charms. In the end, I have triumphed over evil, but I do not know that I am good. All I know is I am not you. But what if things had turned out differently? What if I were the one lying lifeless in a puddle of black blood tainted by my own feces and urine? What if my eyes were dead and soulless?

1

What if?

At some point in our lives, we have all played the age-old game of What If. I remember sitting in my grandma's kitchen while she baked my favourite chocolate chip cookies and playing What If. "What if I clean my room? What if I clean the dishes? Then can I have more cookies?" The answer was always the same. It did not matter what I was bargaining away or promising to do in exchange, her answer was always the same, "If ifs and ands were pots and pans, there'd be no work for tinkers' hands." Who or what were tinkers, and why did they need pots and pans? It took me a long time to figure out what she meant.

When I was nine, What If seemed like the perfect game to garner the myriad of things any aspiring nine-year-old would need. At bedtime, it could squeeze one more story out of my sweet father. All it took was the biggest hug I could muster and a kiss on the cheek. My mother was easily seduced by the game as well. "What if I promise to clean my room?" meant an extra half-hour at the park. "What if I set the table?" earned me an episode of *SpongeBob* before supper. As children we quickly learn the tricks for getting what we want. For some it's sad eyes and crying, for others, tantrums and stomping or just incessant begging. For me, those two little words were the magic that made my life easy and carefree.

Until they weren't.

When I was fourteen, my father became ill. In the beginning, my parents insisted it was a virus. But the flu does not last for weeks on end. When Dad stopped coming to my volleyball games at school, I asked him, "What if I become the team captain? Then will you come see me play?" The answer was still no. He didn't say it bluntly, yet the combination of apologies and excuses still meant the same to my fourteen-year-old ears. It was the first time the What If game hadn't worked for me. I was devastated. I'm not sure if it was because my father had refused to come to my games or the fact I had failed to change his mind. I stormed down the hall to my bedroom, slamming the door so hard I thought I had broken it.

That night my parents sat me down for a long overdue conversation, and in a matter of minutes, the world as I had known it had come to an end. Sitting there stone-faced as they explained that my father did not really have the flu, I was trapped between them, listening as they cried and held my hands. The reality was stage-four lung cancer. Yet all I felt was anger and resentment. I must have asked a thousand what-ifs that night, but there was no bargaining left to be done. No long list of chores or promises to be made in exchange for a cure or a quick fix. There was only one answer to all my what-ifs. My father was dying, and there was nothing I could do to change it.

Looking back, I should have known something was wrong. Dad was always at home when I returned from school. He would claim he had left early or had taken some sick time to recover from the flu, but the truth was he had never left the house. My once active father, who normally spent his spare time hiking, fishing, and tinkering with his old pickup truck, had suddenly become a couch potato. I had never heard the television set in my house as much as in those last few weeks. When I think about it, there were changes in my mother that I hadn't picked up on as well. Mom's infectious smile, the one that greeted me each morning and whispered me good night, was rarely seen in those days. I would often hear her singing to herself while she cooked or cleaned the house, but her voice had been quiet for quite some time. My home, my family, had changed, and I had not noticed.

I remember lying in bed that night and thinking my world was falling apart. My father was dying physically while my mother was dying inside. And I had been so wrapped up in myself that I hadn't known it was happening. How had I not seen that my dad was tired all the time? My father was an athletic man, not large, but fit, so how could I have not noticed his clothes were suddenly too big? How had I missed the sad, red eyes Mom wore every day, or not caught the blank stares out the kitchen window while the kettle whistled and danced on the stove? But worst of all, I had not heard the silence between my parents, who were too afraid to speak for fear their voices would give away their dreaded secret. How had I not noticed? How had I been so ignorant? My parents loved me beyond words and had desperately tried to shield me from their sadness until it was no longer possible.

And I had been oblivious.

I laid there that night angry and ashamed. Angry that my parents had not trusted me to handle this news in the beginning, and angry with myself for being angry with them. I was even more angry that I had not known something was amiss in the first place. And then I was ashamed for having all of those feelings. I was ashamed that I had become that self-involved, conceited teenager who thinks the world revolves around her. That night I realized What If wasn't going to work with my parents. I could not bargain or make promises to them in exchange for my father's health or my mother's emotional well-being. It was time to put aside the childish game I played with my parents since I was old enough to speak in sentences. However, I was not about to give up the game altogether.

That night I learned to play What If with God.

2

I sit on the front porch watching my daughter, Lily, running through the water sprinkler that is desperately trying to revive my parched lawn. She lets out a squeal each time the cool water reaches her bare skin, as if each soaking is an unexpected delight. Our rescue pup, Sadie, follows her wherever she goes and seems to be enjoying the cool water almost as much as Lily. I remember the day we went to the animal shelter and picked Sadie from a litter of puppies that had recently been rescued from the city dump. Lily had begged and pleaded for weeks to get a puppy. She had a million and one reasons why she absolutely must have a puppy. The puppy would be her best friend; the puppy would keep her warm at night; the puppy would keep the monsters away; and on and on it went. And then she said it. Those two little words from my childhood that made my heart stop.

What if.

"What if I clean up the puppy's mess? What if I feed her every day? What if I walk her every morning before school?" she pleaded.

How could I say no to those deep brown eyes? Lily is my world, my every reason to get up and keep going day after day. I remember the day the What If game had come to an end for me and my father. I was devastated. I did not want Lily to feel what I felt back then. She was too young to stop playing the game. I did not want her to know the truth behind those words. Hence, we have Sadie.

She is a tan and white fluffy mutt with the sweetest black nose and the most lovable personality. She and Lily are best friends. They do everything together. At more than half Lily's size, Sadie has taken on the role of her protector. Lily thinks it is cute. But she is only seven and, thankfully, has no knowledge of how cruel and dangerous the world can be. She is young and innocent. Her world is filled with sunshine, butterflies, and puppies. And I will do everything in my power to keep it that way for as long as possible. Because I, on the other hand, know too well how evil lurks around every corner, waiting to catch you when you least expect it.

I know because I did not have Sadie, or someone like her, all those years ago when I needed a protector. I know because I fought my way through a nightmare and was lucky enough to come out the other side. Sometimes I wonder if I really was lucky. Even though my ordeal is over, it was never really finished. There was no closure, no finality to it. He is still out there. The monster that made my life a living hell still walks among us, and I live every day looking over my shoulder, watching and waiting for the other shoe to drop. Is that lucky? Is that living? But then I look into Lily's big brown eyes and hear her sweet laughter, and in that moment, I know I am the luckiest woman in the world.

"Mama! Mama! Can we have ice cream?" Lily yells from beneath the sprinkler.

"Lily, honey, it's almost bedtime," I reply, knowing full well she was not going to sleep any time soon.

"But Mama, it's so hot outside. What if I promise to go to sleep right after my bath?"

And there it is, the what-if. How can I say no?

"Okay, munchkin, but only one scoop!" I yell back.

"Yay! Can Sadie have a scoop, too? She's really hot, Mama."

"I guess so, but let's get the two of you dried off and inside before you get soggy!"

We go through the same routine as we do every other night before bed. We start with a bubble bath overflowing with lots of strawberry-scented bubbles. Lily plays while Sadie watches from the bath mat. I believe if I allowed it, Sadie would gladly take part in the bubble bath, but I draw the line here. Once bath time is over and Lily is set-tled into her pjs, she and Sadie have a bedtime snack. Tonight, instead of a bowl of fruit and a dog treat, it's vanilla ice cream—one scoop for Lily, and one scoop for Sadie. Oh, how my mother would have disap-proved. Two storybooks later and my off-key version of "You Are My Sunshine," and Lily and Sadie are tucked in for the night.

"Good night, Mama, I love you," Lily whispers, nearly asleep.

"Good night and sweet dreams, baby girl. I'll love you always," I reply. It is the same every night. No matter how tired or grumpy or anxious I am, I always make sure Lily knows she is loved. I know how lives can change in the blink of an eye, leaving us scared and confused, but the one thing I never want Lily to question is my love for her.

I tiptoe toward the door, but before I leave, I can't help but stop and stare at my daughter nestled under the soft pink covers. She is angelic, rambunctious, and so trusting of others. I am so blessed to have her in my life. She would not be here had it not been for him and my ordeal.

Ordeal?

I mull the word over in my head, like I have done so many times before. I am not sure that is the right word. What I went through, all that I endured, cannot really be labelled an ordeal. It was a nightmare—a nightmare from which I could not wake. Some might even call it a horror show. For me, it was reality. For three months, two weeks, and five days, it was my life. Yet here I am, watching my baby girl sleep by the glow of her Tinkerbell night light. I survived. I came out the other side, broken and forever changed, but alive. For three months, two weeks, and five days, I fought the devil with everything in me. He may have won in the beginning, but I came out on top in the end. Now I spend each day wondering when round two will begin.

What if he finds me? What if he finds Lily?

3

I don't remember much about the first week after my parents informed me of my dad's diagnosis and imminent death. I locked myself in my room every day after school and cried each night over the unfairness of it all. Why must I, at fourteen, have to say goodbye to my dad forever? My strong, loving, and supportive father could not be dying at forty-five. He had so much left to do, so many places to see, and so many people who depended on him. He was my mother's world—everything she did revolved around him. She loved me unconditionally, but with my father, it was different. He was her everything. I knew I was going to lose my father, but would I lose her, too? Would his death be too much for her? For me?

Then there was my grandma. The wonderful woman who loved to bake cookies with me as a child was now in a nursing home. Alzheimer's had claimed her years before, but her face still lit up when my father came to visit. Twice a week, we would stop by to visit with her, and each time she would smile and call him "Daddy." In her world, she was a little girl thrilled to see her father. Would she notice when he didn't come to visit anymore? Would she feel abandoned or neglected? I questioned it back then, but I am not sure she ever really noticed his absence. I always thought it weird how the mind could work like that—taking her back to another lifetime where the people and places of the present did not exist while, physically, she remained here with us, the people who loved her. I learned later that the mind can take you anywhere, especially when you need to protect yourself from the present and just escape reality.

And what about my dad's friends? His co-workers? The community? Dad had so many friends and co-workers who loved him. He was always involved with the community, helping with charities and social activities. Whenever someone was needed to take the lead or turn another's ideas into action, Dad was who they called. He could organize the biggest fundraisers and most entertaining events. He had this knack of getting as many people as possible involved and then making sure everyone had a job to do. He was a leader, but he always made it seem as though he was just a part of the team. Would they miss his voice, his larger-than-life personality, his leadership? Would they feel the void his death would bring?

And there was me.

How would I go on without my father? The man who helped me with my homework and taught me how to send an awesome serve in volleyball, the man who was supposed to watch me walk across the stage to receive my high school diploma and my college degree, the man I wanted to, someday, walk me down the aisle. How was I supposed to say goodbye to him and to all my plans for the future? When you're fourteen, you have all these hopes and dreams, visions of what your future should look like. For me, they all included my dad. I was Daddy's little girl. I had him wrapped around my little finger, and we both loved it. I did not want that to change. I could not let my father go.

That's when I started talking to God, or rather bargaining with Him. Each day as I sat in class, I racked my brain trying to find something worthy enough to bargain with the Almighty. What if I tried my best to get straight A's? What if I promised to befriend Allie Lockwood, the poorest kid in school who didn't have any friends? What if I committed to helping Mrs. Roberts with her Sunday school classes, even though I hated Sunday school? You name it, I came up with it. I tried everything I could think of to secure my father a cure. In the end, I had to settle for a possibility, an opportunity to try something new with no guarantee it would work.

Two weeks after I was informed of my father's illness, Dad entered a new clinical trial his doctor had recommended. He sold it as a last chance, a final opportunity to beat this thing that was killing him, rotting him from the inside out. He had nothing to lose and everything to gain. And for a while, we thought it was working. Dad seemed to be getting better. Little by little, he improved. His eyes were brighter, his smile was bigger, his appetite grew. I thought it was finally going to be okay, that my father was going to beat this thing. Whatever I had said to God, it must have worked! Now I just had to hold up my end of the bargain. The following week, I aced my mid-term exams, Allie Lockwood and I ate lunch together every day at school—I even shared my lunch with her most days—and I'd started helping Mrs. Roberts with her Sunday school class. I vowed I would do what I had promised in order to keep my father alive.

Just over two months into the trial, Dad contracted pneumonia. It was the worst possible situation for him. The cancer was in his lungs, and despite the advantages the treatment administered in the trial had given him, his lungs were just too weak to fight. Little by little, his lungs filled with fluid, and each day, each hour, he fought harder and harder just to breathe. Dad was slowly drowning in his own fluids, and just eight days later, we were told there was nothing more they could do, and it was time for us to start making plans.

Make plans? How do you make plans for someone you love to die? Do you set the date and time it should happen? Do you prepare a last meal, say prayers, reminisce about days gone by and all the good times we've shared? I was fourteen. I did not know how to say goodbye to the man who had held our family together. My mother was a mess. She cried all the time and begged my father to fight, even though a fool could see he had no fight left. I was fourteen. I needed my dad to get well and make everything right again, to take us back to the days when my biggest worry was if my team would win our next game, even though I knew those days were gone forever. I was fourteen. My father was going to die. My mother was losing herself in her grief. And I had suddenly become the adult in our family. At fourteen, I wasn't sure I could do it. I couldn't be the one to look after everyone else. I desperately needed my dad to get better, to live. I was not ready to give up on him or my mother. I could not give up on the life I so desperately wanted.

What if I didn't have to?

4

The day I escaped, it was warm and sunny outside. The sky was clear, and deep blue stretched as far as my eyes could see. The evening sun—or was it morning?—was blinding like rays of hope streaming down from heaven. It was the first time I had seen daylight in what felt like months. I could feel the heat penetrating my pale face and nearly naked body. It permeated my skin and warmed me to my core. It felt like a hot bubble bath or hot chocolate on a cold winter's day, but they were distant memories from a childhood long since passed. I wanted so much to just lie there on the grass and soak in the heat, to just let those wonderful memories come flooding back, but there was no time. He would be returning soon, and I needed to get far away from there.

I looked left, then right. Behind me sat a ramshackle building that appeared to be an old house, yet not really a house. Which way could I turn? I was in the middle of nowhere. I could not see any neighbours, I saw no shops or businesses, just blue sky as far as the eye could see over fields and fields of corn. It must have been nearing the middle of September. It was surely early fall, because the stalks were beginning to yellow and the corn looked ready for picking. My breath caught as I realized I had been there for months, that summer had passed by while I was held there in the bowels of hell. I shook off the overwhelming despair I felt that came with knowing how much I had endured. I forced myself to look for anything that would lead me to safety. I saw tire treads in the dirt, no doubt from the van he used to transport me there and then for his return visits. They all turned right at the end of the driveway, so I followed them, slowly, placing one foot in front of the other, pain searing through each sole with every laboured step.

Walking barefoot down the red, dirt road, I tried to remember what day it was, what month. I was sure fall was approaching, which meant I had been held captive for three months, maybe more. I wanted to lie down and cry with the realization, but I had just escaped. I had just emerged from a dark, fetid basement, with windows and bars as black as night, where I had spent the last months simultaneously fighting for my life and praying to die. I had lost track of time. I had no idea what time of day it was. I did not know what day of the week it was or even what month. It was frightening to imagine how much time I had lost to this monster.

And to contemplate how much more I would let him take.

I did not know why, but I stepped off the road and into the cornfields. I suddenly felt the urge to conceal myself, to hide. The tall stalks reached just above my head and provided perfect cover should he return. I had to keep moving. The ground beneath me was baked hard from the sun, and the dried weeds and stalks cut into my bare feet. They grew sticky with blood, but I did not care. I had decided I was never going back to that place. Not ever. I would rather die than return to that hell. If that meant my final days would be spent somewhere in the middle of nowhere, deep in that cornfield, then so be it. There was no hell worse than the one I had just escaped.

It had taken me weeks to pry loose the only rusty nail I could find. I found it protruding ever so slightly from the floorboards in the far corner. For days afterward, I used the nail to scrape and pry around the largest window in the room. There were two windows, and both had been painted black from the outside. I traced my hands around the edges to determine their size, and I knew if I could only loosen the windowpane, I might finally see a way out. I spent hour after hour digging and gouging around it, scraping away layers of caulking and paint and listening for his return. I gathered every particle of wood and aging paint that fell to the floor and brushed them under the dingy mattress in the opposite corner. I could not risk him discovering what I had been up to. Thankfully, he didn't allow enough light in the room to find the evidence. The day I finally moved the windowpane enough to see a sliver of daylight on the other side, I knew I had found a way out. An escape.

The only thing holding me back were the rusted iron bars criss-crossing from side to side and top to bottom, like a sheet of paper readied for a game of tic-tac-toe. With enough force, I hoped to pry them away, but I wasn't sure I had the strength. So I dug some more, and I gouged and I scratched until my fingers bled and my wrists were sore. The old wood was rotten and chipped away piece by jagged piece, and eventually I was able to move the last barrier holding me back, if ever so slightly. Gradually, the bars became looser and looser, and the question of whether I could move them became a question of when I would take the chance. I just had to stay alive long enough for the right time to arrive.

He did not spend every moment in the basement with me or even in the house above. He would come for a while, have his fun, and when his thirst for torture had been sated, he would leave again. Sometimes he stayed away for days, other times only hours. It had been a while since his last visit, so I knew he might return at any moment. I promised myself the last time he left, it would be the last time he ever touched me. At least while I was alive.

I worked non-stop after he left until I could get the window open far enough that I could nearly squeeze through. I was almost there, but no matter how much I dug with the rusty nail or how hard I shook the windowpane, it would not open any wider. It just sat there teasing me with a view to freedom that was just out of reach. The bars had released their grip after only a few hard pulls, yet there I was staring at the opening and fighting back tears, not tears of defeat, but tears of anger. How could I have come so far only to allow fate to laugh in my face? I slammed the window down, shutting out the sunshine that had been a beacon of hope, and in a split second my fist pounded through the glass and I was climbing to freedom.

I looked at my hands as I moved through the cornfields, at their tattered nails and fingertips. There were fresh cuts, inflicted when I crashed my fist through the blackened glass, which were still oozing blood. They were black and purple with bruises both old and new and partially hidden in the blood crusting on my skin. I was afraid to look at the rest of my body. After being battered and beaten for so long, the picture was surely not pretty. I was sure my nose was broken. Was it crooked now? I knew there were bite marks on my breast because I had felt the pain of his teeth penetrating my skin, leaving them too tender to touch. I felt the bruises on my legs where he pried them open again and again with his large, calloused hands. The burning between them, where he forced himself inside me so violently, made it hurt to walk. I looked away from my hands and kept moving forward.

If I stopped to process everything that had happened, I was not sure I would find the strength to continue. A mirror would reveal the harsh reality of my personal horror show, but had there been one available to me, I was not sure I could look. Would you? Could you stand naked in front of a mirror and inspect every bruise, bite mark, and broken bone? Could you stare at your damaged body, ripe with infection, and relive each and every time he abused you? Violated you? Tortured you just because he could? I do not know how long I stood here staring at my hands, but thankfully, I found the strength to keep moving. I had escaped the basement, but I was not yet safe. I wiped away a loose tear, one I did not know was left in me, and moved forward, a little faster than before and with a little more determination. I was not ready to give up. I had come so far, I had to keep going. I was going to find help.

Or die trying.

5

Nighttime is always hard for me. Once Lily is asleep and Sadie has settled for the night, the demons come calling. I have tried to forget, to move on, but the darkness outside will not let the demons rest. I tune the television set to some random channel, just to fill the silence. I sleep with the lights on and a baseball bat beneath my bed. Yet each night I wake in a cold sweat, fighting just to breathe. I have moments, even days, when I think the memories, the nightmares, are finally over, that I have pushed them down so far inside of me they will never resurface to torment me again, but just as I am getting comfortable in this new life I have created with Lily, the monster returns to remind me that I have not beaten him yet, that somewhere out there in the darkness he is waiting for me.

It has been nearly eight years. You would think eight years would have been enough time to put the past behind me, enough time to forget the hell I endured for three months, two weeks, and five days. Yet there are times when I lie awake at night fighting for my last breath, when the memories and the fear are so vivid, so real, it feels like it was only yesterday when I awoke in a pitch-black room, cold and terrified, and wishing my father were still alive to come save me.

I am sure there are many details I have forgotten or have not allowed myself to relive. Some, maybe, were not important enough to remember, while some were so horrific I cannot bear to remember them. The one memory that never changes is the fear. To you, fear is a racing heart, maybe goosebumps on your skin, or a sharp intake of breath. Be thankful you do not really know what fear is. Until you have been unfortunate enough to be held powerless by circumstance or animal, either human or otherwise, you will never truly understand what fear really is.

Fear is not a feeling or an emotion you experience. Fear is an all-consuming, all-encompassing being. Once fear enters you, it takes over. No longer are you able to control its effects on you. You cannot decide what to do with it or where to put it. Fear makes your heart pound so hard you believe it will break your chest; fear sends the blood pumping through your veins so fast it deafens you; fear makes you lose your voice. Your mouth may open and close, but no sound emerges. It barely allows the air to pass to fill your lungs, and sometimes it is so bad, no air will pass at all and you feel the weight of the world sitting on your chest, squeezing away your last breath. Fear will make you lose control of your bodily functions, leaving you soiled and ashamed; fear will bring you to your knees, pleading and praying for mercy and, sometimes, begging for death. Imagine feeling all of these at once.

Most of you do not know what fear is. I hope you never will.

I get out of bed and recheck each window and door for the third time tonight. I know they are locked, but it never hurts to check, just to reassure myself. I have become obsessive about checking and rechecking the locks, but I can't help it. It's not just me I have to worry about. I have Lily, and I will do everything in my power to protect her.

I hear the soft beep of my cellphone left charging on the nightstand. I know who it is without checking. No one else has this number. I do not have friends anymore. It was so hard when I first returned home. Everyone wanted to help me recover and move beyond the memories and constant fear. It was hard for me to pretend everything was getting better when I was constantly on edge, waiting for him to find me, to force me back into that hellhole. I couldn't sleep because he haunted my dreams. I didn't go outside for fear he would be watching. It became awkward for my friends to be around me, and I them. Not knowing what to say or what not to say, not knowing how to act, or react, when in each other's company. I could feel the apprehension each time one of them held my hand. I heard the pity with each soothing word spoken. It put such a strain on our relationships. Gradually, they stopped coming by, and soon they stopped phoning to check up on me. There were those who persisted, some well-meaning friends who truly wanted me to feel better, to feel normal, but I did my best to alienate them. I did not have the time or the energy for relationships. I needed all the strength I had just to wake up each day, to put one foot in front of the other and keep moving forward in a world that was now foreign to me.

Eventually, I was all alone in my own little world, built around fear and the need to survive. As days turned into weeks, the need to survive was replaced by a need for revenge, a need for closure. And that's when I allowed myself my one and only friend. David Campbell is the only person I trust enough to give my cell number. He has been in my life for nearly eight years. He has only known the me I am now. He knows my story—he understands my life today, such as it is. Our relationship, although professional, has been for the most part easy. He knows what I went through and understands that I cannot forget. There are no awkward moments of silence between us. It is a comfortable balance between two people who know monsters really do exist. I trust him with my life, with Lily's life. Today, I live each day waiting for the other shoe to drop, and when it does, I know this time David will be there to help me.

You see, the monster, *my* monster, has not been caught. He is out there somewhere, watching and waiting for the right moment to make his move. I know he will come. I do not know when or how he will make his appearance, but the day when round two begins is inevitable. You see, I am the one who got away, the girl who survived his reign of terror, and he will never forget, just as I cannot ever forget him. We are bound together forever in pain, in unbearable sorrow and unthinkable madness. I am as much a part of him as he is a part of me. And we are forever joined through Lily, my beautiful, innocent little girl who was created in the middle of a nightmare, not a product of love, but a ray of light in the darkness, a seed of hope and survival. I know he will come for me and for her, but I will be ready for him. At least this is what I tell myself each time I kiss Lily good morning or tuck her in at night. But what if I am never ready?

What if I do not see him coming?

6

It was a Thursday when the doctor told us to make end-of-life plans for my father. Five days later, on a cold, wet April morning, he was gone. Just like that, it was over. The suffering, the pain, the desire to live, and the waiting to die, all over. Here one minute and gone the next. I felt numb at first. Numb and empty. I had cried so much during his fight with cancer and with God, my tears had dried up. I had bargained everything I could think of, but nothing had worked. My dad was gone. A body lay on the hospital bed next to us, battered and defeated by this terrible disease, but it was not my father. Dad was a vibrant, happy, charismatic man, and I decided as I stood by his bed I would always remember him this way, not as this rotting heap of flesh my mother clung to in desperation.

When I close my eyes, I can still hear the droll whine of the monitor telling us it was over. I can smell the scent of his long, drawn-out suffering melding with the fragrances of hospital cleaners and bleach, and my stomach churns. For a long time afterward, I believed these were the smells of death. I learned later death has many facets. There was a lone chair sitting in the corner, so I sat. My mother was screaming in agony, begging my father to come back, to fight just a little longer, and still, I remained numb. I felt cold, not because the room was chilly, but because I felt nothing at all. Was I thankful his suffering was over? Was I in shock? Was I happy we could finally move on with our lives?

The first days after Dad passed, Mom lay in bed, unable to bring herself to face the day. Had it not been for a few of her close friends and our minister, my father would likely have been buried in the city plot, unmarked and forgotten. The day we laid him to rest, it was still cold and wet. It was as if the sun had refused to shine on such a sombre occasion, for fear it might bring just an ounce of happiness to those of us left behind to grieve. At the end of the service, my mother was carried away from the freshly dug grave by two ladies I didn't know. Rain splashed on her face as she was led from the plot, washing away her tears and streaks of black mascara. I knew in that moment she would never recover from this loss.

She will always be my mother and I her daughter, but from that day onward, our roles in life had been reversed. At fourteen, I had become my mother's keeper. A lonely child with no idea what to do with my feelings or where to put them had just become responsible for her mother. Mom was shattered by the loss of my father, broken into a million pieces. How was I even to begin the process of piecing her back together?

Days passed, then weeks turned into months, yet Mom remained the same. Every morning I coaxed her from the bed before leaving for school just to make sure she ate. I washed her face, combed her hair, and dressed her like a mother would her child, before I shut the door behind me and left for school. I sat through class praying she would be okay until I returned. I gave up volleyball and hanging out with friends. I stopped going to church each Sunday to help Mrs. Roberts with her Sunday school classes. It was not something I missed, to be truthful. It was just another thing I had to give up in order to care for my mother, another thing to resent. My life after my father's death became a blend of attending school and caring for my mother.

And Allie.

Allie, the girl who ate lunch alone until a few months ago, when I sat with her just to hold up my end of a bargain with God. She came to school dressed in tattered clothes that were either two sizes too big or two sizes too small. She was not always fresh, and more often than not, her ripeness and less-than-desirable appearance were the subject of one too many snickers and slurs. God had not held up His end of our deal. No longer did I have to pretend to befriend this poor girl who had next to nothing. Yet Allie was the girl who understood everything I was feeling. She stood by me through it all. She became the one bright spot in my miserable life—until I pushed her away.

I learned Allie's dad was killed in a horrible car crash a year before she moved to our school. Her family did not have insurance, and it was impossible for her mom to provide for their family on her own. For a while she tried the best she could, but when it became apparent her best was not good enough, she gave up entirely, and Allie was the one paying the price.

In the beginning, Allie offered me her ear, a place to rage and to cry without the intense feelings of guilt that usually followed. Gradually, we began to talk more of our struggles, our hopes for the future, and of our dreams. Our unlikely friendship started to grow, and Allie soon became my best friend. We were an odd pair, like a mismatched pair of socks or shoes that would never fit the same feet. Yet it worked. We were each other's saving grace, someone we could be our true selves with without fear of judgment. For the next four years of high school, we became inseparable. Then came graduation.

My family was not poor. Dad had provided very well for us. He had planned for every possibility, including his death. He had insurances, a pension, and education funds. I would have the opportunity to go to college if I were so inclined. I had always wanted to go, to become something, someone my father could be proud of, but that desire had evaporated. That possibility vanished the day my father died. It was just a pipe dream now. How could I leave my mother? Who would care for her if I left? What would become of her?

The day I received a university acceptance letter in the mail, I was dumbfounded. And I was angry. Who? How? When? Why? I asked all the questions, but I had none of the answers. Who would take it upon themselves to apply on my behalf? Why would someone want to do this when it was like a slap in the face, knowing I could never accept? I was certain it must have been Allie, but the expression on her face told me I was wrong. Her eyes could not hide the disappointment she felt at the prospect of my leaving. For a moment I was sure I saw a flash of anger dance across her face.

I learned that night, as I combed my mother's hair, it was she who had filled out the application. She said I had spent enough of my life caring for her and it was time for me to go out into the world and make a life for myself. We argued that night. It was the first time we had argued since Dad died. I argued that I did not want to go, that I was happy at home with her, but she saw straight through me. My mother, who had lived her life in a fog ever sense we laid my father to rest on that cold, rainy day in April, had known all along what I wanted out of life. What I needed.

We talked that night, really talked for the first time since Dad had died. She swore she was feeling better. She even promised to see someone, to seek help for her depression. And for a while it was great. The mother I once knew slowly began to emerge from the darkness. Throughout that summer, before school started, we spent all our time catching up. We talked into the wee hours of the night; we took long walks along the lake; we worked in our overgrown, neglected garden, bringing life back into it and our relationship. She was doing so well. I thought, I believed, I might really get the chance to live my dreams.

The day I left on the bus for university, eight hours away, I had the strongest feelings of apprehension. I questioned everything I had only just begun to believe. Was Mom really doing better? Did I want this so badly that I had invented her recovery as the grounds for my leaving? Was it the excuse for my way out? I did not know if leaving her was the right thing to do or even if she would be okay without me. I remember thinking as the bus rolled away from the station, *What if she still needs me?* Yet I kept going. In the back of my mind, I knew I needed to go. I needed to find *me*, the person I lost the day I learned my beautiful dad was dying. The niggling in the back of my mind and the knots twisting inside my stomach were not enough to keep me from leaving. The guilt I felt back then is nothing compared to the guilt I carry today. I will always wonder if things could have turned out differently.

What if I had stayed?

7

I had been wandering through cornfields for so long it felt like days. Night had come and gone, yet I was no closer to freedom than when I first crawled through the blackened, broken window. My tattered, bare feet were swollen and unrecognizable and barely able to hold my weight. I was hungry, I think. I should have been hungry, but I had done without nourishment for such long periods of time, I was unsure of the feeling. Hunger was another of the cruelties I had to learn to accept and adapt to in order to survive. Even though food was scarce, he made sure he left water, warm and dank as it was—it was life-saving, and I drank it. Now all I could think about was how thirsty I was. Even to wet my cracked lips would be a blessing. But there I was, lost in a maze of cornstalks, blue sky, and parched earth.

I had no idea how much ground I had covered since my late afternoon escape the day before. Had I walked for miles? Was I close to civilization and freedom? I feared I had been walking around in circles and would end up where I started, exhausted and defeated. My flesh was sunburnt, my lips split and bleeding, and my feet, my poor feet, were in shreds. I wondered how much longer I could keep going. I tried to force myself to put one foot in front of the other and move forward. My will to live, my hope and determination, were all gone. Lost to a monster who, in the end, I feared would win. He might not have had the satisfaction of killing me with his bare hands, but he was the reason I was lying there in the red dirt at death's door.

I do not know how I ended up on the ground. Maybe I fell, maybe I just gave up. I watched the ravens circling above me, calling their friends as they waited for their next meal, and I thought they would leave hungry because there was not much of me left to satisfy their appetites. And then I cried—tearless, gut-wrenching sobs. I cried for the life I didn't get to live. I cried for my parents, whom I missed dearly, yet I was thankful they would never know the fate of their only child. I cried for the young women who might endure this same fate as I was not able to stop him. I cried, long and hard I cried, until I fell blissfully asleep.

It was not a fitful sleep filled with nightmares and fear. It was peaceful. I had finally made peace with my circumstance. I had accepted my failure to escape, and I was ready to welcome death with open arms. I had lost the will to live and the desire to fight. I was tired. Physically, my body could endure no more; mentally, I was exhausted; and emotionally, I was numb. My death would be a welcome blessing. After three months, two weeks, and five days, I had given up, and the ravens were welcome to my beleaguered carcass.

I lay there on the baked earth, staring into the pure, blue sky surrounded by walls of cornstalks, and dreamt of happier times, times before my father became sick and my mother fell to pieces. I remembered the days when Dad and I practised my volleyball serve while Mom watched from her rose garden. I dreamt of afternoons at the beach when we ate ice cream and built sandcastles, just the three of us, together and happily oblivious to what was to come. I remembered my grandmother and winter days baking cookies together in her warm, cozy kitchen, with shower caps on our heads and homemade aprons tied around our waists. I could even hear the timer telling us our cookies were ready.

Beep. Beep. Beep.

But it was not the timer.

The beeping grew louder and more persistent. The noise pulled me from the comfort of my dreams. I thought I smelled the sweet scent of chocolate wafting from the oven, but I forced my eyes to open, and the memories vanished like ghosts from my past. The sunshine burned into my retinas like piercing hot pokers. The pain shot deep into my fragile brain, and for a moment I believed it was a cruel dream meant to pull me from my reverie. But then my eyes adjusted to the glaring sun and I began to focus. I realized the soft hum of machinery and the repetitive *beep, beep* that followed was not a figment of my imagination after all. They were not the distant sounds of a faraway dream but rather the sounds of approaching freedom.

A truck, maybe?

A tractor?

Whatever the case, it meant a human being was somewhere nearby working in the cornfields. I was afraid to believe my journey was over. I could not allow hope to seep in through the walls I had built around myself, yet somewhere deep inside me there was a tingle, just the slightest glimmer of hope, that I might have finally escaped the dark, musty basement and him. It took every ounce of strength I had to bring myself to my feet. My body screamed in protest, but this was my last chance at survival, and I somehow had to summon the will to live in order to claim one last shot at a life on the other side of this nightmare.

I took a moment to steady my legs and focus my thoughts. I heard it—the soft hum of machinery and the occasional *beep, beep* as it moved about the field. Maybe a farmer harvesting his crop? If so, where was he? In front of me? To my right? My left? I stood there frozen with panic. My brain screamed at me to choose a direction and move, but I could not decide. The hope of rescue and the fear of it slipping away had me transfixed. I had spun around so many times, frantically trying to determine which way to go, that now I was dizzy, and the anguish once again threatened to explode from my chest. My heart pounded in a frenzied crescendo until I could no longer contain it, and I screamed in frustration at my indecision. While I stood there with my feet firmly planted in the red dirt, the machinery moved farther away, and my heart sank.

From somewhere inside me, from a place I did not know still existed, I summoned the will to keep fighting. I was certain this was my last chance at survival, my last shot at a life beyond this horror. So, I moved. I did not know if I was heading in the right direction, but I could not stand in this spot any longer. The walls of cornstalks were closing in on me, and if I did not keep going, I would be consumed by them.

Thud. Thud. Thud.

The sound of my tattered feet pounding into the baked earth vibrated in my head, growing louder with each quickening step. I kept going as the thumping of my feet began to meld with the pounding in my chest.

Thud. Thud. Thump. Thump.

It resonated like a war dance playing in my head before I went into battle. The rhythm of the music consumed me. I felt it from the tips of my fingers all the way down to the tips of my toes. It was in my head, it was in my heart, it flowed through my blood.

Thud. Thud. Thump. Thump.

It grew faster and faster, louder and louder. And I ran. I ran like I had never run before, screaming and crashing through cornstalks like a wild boar. And the rhythm continued. Pounding and dancing like a beating drum. "Hurry, hurry," it cried with each resounding beat, "you must hurry!" It reached a crescendo, then ceased just as I burst through the wall of cornstalks and onto an open field that stretched for miles and miles and I fell to my knees. The final rush of adrenaline was spent, and my legs were giving in to exhaustion and pain. I listened for a sign the harvester remained nearby, but the only sounds were the pounding of my heart inside my chest and my laboured breathing. Yet there was hope.

For the first time in a while, I had hope. I had finally found my way beyond the cornfields. There was a new horizon before me, one with a pretty white farmhouse and an old, weathered barn, but were they too far away and possibly out of reach in my current state? Right now I was sitting precariously on the fence between life and death. I wanted to run to the farmhouse and beg for someone to help me, but I was not sure I had the strength or the will. I wondered if someone was waiting there on the other side, waiting to rescue me, to bring me home. But what if this vision was just that, a vision? A cruel dream meant to tease and torture? Or the figment of a mind that had been fractured and broken beyond repair?

What if I was more lost now than I was before?

8

How r u?

The message flashes bright green on the phone screen, then disappears. Before I get the chance to type in a reply, it beeps and flashes a second time.

I have news. I need to see u.

My hand hesitates as I reach for the phone. I feel the panic rising in my throat, and it becomes difficult to breathe. The messages are unsettling and ominous. David has news, but what news must it be that it requires him to tell me face to face? If it were good news, he wouldn't waste time with text messages. He would have already been outside knocking on my door, which means the news is not good. My mind races through all the possibilities. Has new evidence been discovered? Do they know where he is? Has he taken another helpless girl? Before I have time to conjure up more questions and scenarios, my cell beeps again.

R u there?

This time I grab the phone and press CALL. David answers on the first ring, but I don't give him the chance to say hello.

"Is he back? Do you know where he is? Is he here?"

I fire one question after the other until my voice cracks and threatens to reveal my biggest fears. As much as I have tried to put on a tough face and go on with my life with Lily, I am still afraid—

afraid that he will come back, afraid that he will find me and my daughter, afraid this time he will finish what he started. But most of all, I am afraid I will not get the chance to finish this once and for all. I have known since the day I escaped through the broken basement window that he would come for me. I do not know when he will reveal himself, or even how he will find us, but he is coming. I am certain of it. Could he be here? Is the day I have been both longing for and dreading finally here?

On the other end of the line, I hear David's deep, calming voice. "Don't panic, Helena. Stop conjuring up every possibility and scenario imaginable," he soothes.

"I can't help it, David!" My voice is shrill with panic and anger. "It's not just about me this time. I have to think of Lily now. If he ever discovers the truth, I know he will come for us, for her. I cannot let that happen. Not ever!"

"I know, Helena. Believe me, I know. I have been by your side now for nearly eight years, remember? I will not let anything happen to you or to Lily," he insists. "You know you can count on me. I am not going anywhere."

"I know you believe that, David, but you don't know him. He's a monster, capable of such cruelty. I don't know if anyone can stop him."

"I will. We will, Helena. Together we will stop him. I know it's late, but I'm coming over. We need to talk."

"I would have insisted you come now, anyway. It's not like you can just tell me you have news and then think I could wait until morning to learn what it is."

"I'll be there as soon as I can."

"I will be waiting," I reply, but he has already disconnected.

I stand there in the dark, imagining what David has discovered. Maybe it will be yet another false lead. There have been plenty, and with each discovery, my desire to find him grows stronger. I live in fear that one day he will come to finish what he started so long ago. But that fear has not crippled me—rather, it has led me on a mission to be the one to find him first. I will never give up trying to find my monster before he finds me, before he finds Lily.

I met David nearly eight years ago, the day I regained consciousness and found myself in a hospital bed. He was one of the Major Crimes officers assigned to my case. Everyone wanted a piece of the most sensational crime to occur in our area, or the country, for that matter. I was the girl held captive and tortured for three months, two weeks, and five days. I was a celebrity of sorts. I had somehow cheated death at the hands of a madman, and now everyone wanted the answers to all the questions I was still asking myself. David thought he was one of the luckiest cops around to land my case, but it turned out that I was the lucky one.

In the first hours and days after I awoke, I was very seldom left alone. I barely had time to gather my own thoughts, to even attempt to process what had just happened to me, before I was bombarded with questions from cops, profilers, psychiatrists—you name it, they came. Everyone wanted answers, they wanted information, they wanted clues. I just wanted to be left alone. Then came the bottom-feeders, as I have come to call them. Reporters and television personalities camped outside the hospital, yearning for the tiniest piece of information in time for the six o'clock news or that evening's prime-time program. Movie moguls, screenwriters, and true crime writers would call constantly, begging and pleading to speak to me, just to have the chance to get my first interview—an interview I have yet to give. For weeks they came like rats crawling out of the woodwork. They camped in front of the hospital as I recovered, they surrounded my home once I was released, and whenever I mustered up the courage to leave the safety of my home, I was followed. I felt like a celebrity trying to outrun a rabid paparazzi as they screamed, shouted, and pleaded for the tiniest of quotes, while I tried to shield myself from their cameras and iPhones. Everyone wanted a piece of the tortured girl, but I just wanted to be left alone.

I was approached by more than one eager writer, both amateur and professional, who came drooling at the chance to put my story in print. Movie executives and screenwriters alike begged for the opportunity to plaster my face all over television screens everywhere in return for very lucrative offers. I declined them all until, eventually, they accepted the fight was futile and I became old news. You're probably wondering why I would turn down the opportunity to make hundreds of thousands of dollars to secure my future or as some kind of retribution for the horror I endured. The answer is simple. How can I tell a story without an ending? It would be like reading a book with no conclusion or watching a movie that leaves you waiting for more. This ordeal is not over. I do not have closure. Nearly eight years later and there still has not been any sort of ending or finality to my plight. My life has become a long-drawn-out horror story that goes on and on with no end in sight.

Until now.

I am afraid to hope this time will be different, that this time I will find the ending I have been seeking for so long. I shiver with excitement, or dread, I am not sure which. Whichever it is, whatever this news David brings, I am ready. I have been ready for nearly eight years, since the day I awoke in the hospital bed and learned there was a life growing inside of me, a seed planted by a monster who tried to destroy me. I vowed then I would not let him have the last piece of me. I promised myself, and the little life in my belly, we would survive. In spite of him, we would survive. I—we—had come too far to give up.

My child, my Lily, will know love and devotion like no other. She will not know the monster who gave her life. At that moment, lying surrounded by machines and tubes, she became my reason for living and has been ever since. She is the reason I get up every morning and push through another day. She is the reason I torture myself with memories of him so I can keep him fresh in my mind. I try not to forget any of the horrid details for fear I may lose the memory that finally leads me to him. I am ready to do battle. I have been ready, or so I believe, for nearly eight years. I am not the young, naive girl he captured all those years ago jogging alone in the dark. I did not believe in monsters then. I thought monsters like him lived only in movies and books. I know the difference now, and I am ready.

But what if I am not?

What if I am only fooling myself?

9

The day I stepped off the bus, I stood staring at the expansive university campus before me and felt such immense relief. I should have been apprehensive, nervous, even a little scared at the unknown before me, but all I could feel was relief. And gratitude. I was so grateful my mother had forced me to take this next step, even if I was uneasy about leaving her alone. She wanted me to have a future, and even though I wondered about the depths of her feelings for me, she had loved me enough to push me away. And I grabbed the opportunity and ran, and I barely looked back. I squashed any doubts and feelings of hesitation that arose, and I got out of town as fast as I could, and for months I forgot about my life before. I was the new Helena Morris, and I tried desperately to leave the old me behind.

I made new friends from the dormitory and from my classes. I had a social life for the first time since my father died. I was invited to parties; I went out for coffee, which I didn't even like, and I dated. Classes were okay, but life at school was amazing. I felt young and vibrant again. I was thriving. I spoke to Mom nearly every night at the start of the semester. She was eager to hear about my classes, my new friends, and even the boys I was crushing on. It was like I had been transported back to a time when my life was perfect—before Dad died and Mom became lost in her grief.

Allie and I spoke often during the first few weeks I was away at school, but gradually our conversations became strained as our lives grew further and further apart. I had been able to move beyond our shared misery. I came to university and wiped the slate clean, so to speak. I pushed my sad situation and Allie, with her rotten family, into a tiny, dusty corner of my expanding world while she remained trapped in purgatory. She was stuck at home with her mother and with mine. She had promised to keep an eye on my mom and to help her out while I was away at school, and I had not protested. Her staying made it easier for me to leave, but it also put great strain on Allie and our relationship. I was out creating a fantastic life for myself that did not include her. She became a part of a past I was trying to forget, while I left her behind to pick up the pieces.

It was nearly the beginning of Christmas break when I got a call from Allie. It was the first time we had spoken in nearly two weeks when she phoned with the news that shattered my perfect new life. It was finally over. All the emotional pain and suffering my mother had endured since my father's death had come to an end. I felt like the rug had been pulled out from under me. I could not understand how Mom had gone from the attentive, engaging mother I spoke to over the phone several times a week to a woman so overwhelmed with grief and loss that she had taken her own life. I was shocked, angry, confused, and hurt all at the same time. I was an alphabet soup of emotions. It was like waking in a fog so thick I had no idea which way to turn or what to do next. But I had Allie.

Allie met me at the bus stop that day when I stepped through the door and landed back in time. Everything looked and felt the same as the day I left. My childhood had been lost in this town. My father was buried here. And now my mother had taken her own life here. I nearly stepped back on the bus and left again, run away for a second time. If not for Allie's hand on my arm, I think I might have done it. I looked at her as a single tear trickled down her cheek. I hadn't felt so inadequate in all my life. I had failed our friendship greatly, but more importantly, I had failed my mother. I had left her even though it had felt so wrong. I did not put her first. I had not put Allie first. I was that selfish teenager all over again, putting my own needs and wants before anyone else's, and because of it, my mother was dead, taken from my life forever by a handful of pills and bottle of booze. I sank to my knees and cried for the first time since Allie had made that fateful call. And once again she was there to pick me up. I had treated her horribly, yet she remained my rock in this ocean of sadness and regret.

We had a small, private funeral for Mom. Many of her friends had drifted away and moved on. She was an only child, and I her only daughter. Her parents had passed away long before I was born, so it was just Allie and me. She held my hand through the entire service and propped me up when my knees threatened to buckle as they lowered her into the ground. I learned from Allie that she had fooled us both into thinking she was doing well. She was as surprised by my mother's suicide as I was. Allie told me of long walks she had taken on the beach with Mom. She spoke of nights when they sat in the garden, watching the fireflies and talking into the late hours of the night, and of rainy days watching the birds at the feeder. I was happy they had found some joy in each other. To be honest, I was jealous I had not had those experiences with my mother, yet I could not help but question how attentive Allie had really been. After all, she was the one here caring for and engaging with Mom. But who was I to have these thoughts? I was the one who had left both my mother and my best friend behind in search of a new and improved life that barely included either of them.

I stayed for a few days after the funeral. I had to decide what to do with my parents' home. It was my home as well, but it had not felt like a home to me in a very long time. The decision to list it was an easy one. I spent hours going through my mother's things and rummaging through my own keepsakes and teenage treasures. In the end, all I kept were a few family photos. I told my agent to do whatever he thought best to get the house sold. It was to be placed on the market at the beginning of the new year. I had made my choice, but I did not have the heart to inform Allie of my intentions. I am not sure I could handle her hurt and disappointment. She was happy I was home, and I knew she expected I would stay, and that everything could go back to the way things were, but nothing was the same. Not our friendship, not this town, and most certainly not me.

There was nothing here for me anymore. I had no family and no friends aside from Allie, and our friendship was something I needed to let go. It was a union born of a bargain I had made with God as a young, emotional teenager. Our friendship grew on our shared misery and a need to escape our situations at home. My home was empty now, and all that remained was a heartache full of memories and regrets I would just as soon forget. When I finally found the courage to tell her I was going back to university, I could see the hurt and the anger in her eyes. She did not speak to me any more until the day I was scheduled to leave. She met me at the bus stop and wished me well. It felt like I was finally severing the last tie of a life of sadness and disappointment. We promised to keep in touch, knowing this would likely be the last time we spoke. That day, I stepped on the bus with the intention never to look back. I made arrangements with the university to allow me to spend Christmas break in my dorm room and spent my time getting acquainted with my winter courses and just losing myself in a sea of memories and regrets.

I had so many unanswered questions. What if I hadn't left home? Would my mother still be here? Did I miss the signs she was regressing? Or did I just not want to see them? Why didn't Allie notice something was off? In the end, it was no one's fault. Mom had suffered greatly with the death of the one person who had given her a purpose, a reason to live. She had loved me enough to send me away in search of a better life when she knew that she could not give me what I needed. She just had not loved me enough to stay. I will always wonder if things would have turned out differently had I not left to attend school. I will always ask myself what I could have done differently.

What if I had stayed?

10

I found my running shoes and secured my earbuds in preparation for an evening run. It was an activity I had picked up since returning to university. At one point, I was so lost inside my head with the memories, questions, and regrets, I was afraid I was becoming my mother. So, I laced up my running shoes and hit the pavement in search of an outlet for all my tangled emotions. I was finally free of a sad and lonely past, yet I could not bring myself to move on. I needed to sort out my thoughts and emotions. I wanted to wrap them up in a box and tuck them neatly away in some faraway corner of my mind, but it was not as easy as that. So, I ran. There were days I ran for miles, and there were days I barely made it down the street, but I kept going. Eventually, running was the part of my day that was most important to me. Without it, I found myself drifting off to the dark recesses of my mind to find that box. Now that I had been able to close the lid on it, I was afraid to lift the flaps again, not even for a peek, for fear I would end up falling down a rabbit hole. So, I ran. Every day, without exception, I ran.

That night, there was a damp fog rolling in from the sea. The mist cooled my face and wets my hair as I ran the trail along the shore. Soft waves were rolling in, and the gravelly beach was protesting the disturbance. I had not lived near the ocean until I went there for school, and I had discovered an immense love and respect for it. I had seen it calm and soothing as an orange sun sets on the horizon, and I had witnessed intense anger as it crashed and pounded the weary shore. I felt the ocean, like me, was a living being filled with emotions and regrets, and that night I thought it was sad and lonely. The fog thickened as I travelled farther along the trail. My clothes were getting damp, and there was a slight chill. Maybe I would cut my run short and go home to cuddle up on the sofa with a blanket and a hot chocolate, but the sea wasn't the only one who was sad and lonely tonight, so I kept going.

In the distance, the lighthouse beacon beckoned me forward. The foghorn blasts came at even intervals, warning sailors of dangers nearby. It could be an eerie sound when running alone on a darkening trail, but for me it was a welcome distraction. Tomorrow was the anniversary of my father's death and the first time I couldn't share it with my mother.

The fog grew thicker and surrounded me in a thick blanket like a beast swallowing me whole. The atmosphere changed, and suddenly a cold wind wrapped around my feet, and I shivered. I was almost at the end of the trail, so I kept running forward. There was a clearing up ahead that allowed vehicles to approach with supplies meant for occasional repairs and upkeep. The lighthouse had been automated in recent years, and caretakers only came by a few times a year. The neglected, narrow dirt road leading into the area had become overgrown with brush and littered with potholes. No one used it anymore, hence the lighthouse had become the point on the trail where users turned around and went back the same way from which they came. It was my intention to do the same. It was a path I had taken almost nightly since I discovered the trail along the shoreline. However, that night was anything but routine.

When I reached the clearing, the wind began to whistle, and I was certain it was calling my name. I was puzzled at first, then uneasy, as I realized it was not actually the wind that was calling but rather an actual person, a man. Someone was there by the light-house. Waiting for me? Was it someone I knew, even though I did not recognize the voice? I stopped and looked around, but I could not see anyone in the dusk and encroaching fog. His voice grew taunting, and a chill crept down the length of my spine. This was not a chance meeting between friends. Someone was waiting for me, and I feared his intentions were not good.

I turned quickly and ran. I was certain I was running for my life. I heard his footsteps pounding the earth behind me, and each step grew louder as he closed the gap between us. Then his hands were on my back, and he was pushing me to the ground. I felt his weight upon me as we struggled. His breath was foul, and he reeked of body odour. But he was strong, stronger than me, and soon our struggle was over. He had a knife to my throat, and I could see a roll of duct tape in his hands. If I screamed, no one would hear me on this lonely trail. If I fought, he might slice my throat and I would bleed to death there alone. So, I laid there on the wet, muddy earth and allowed him to bind my hands and seal my lips. I was not giv-ing up as easily as he thought I was, rather I was biding my time in hopes the situation would change and I could take my chance later.

He pulled me to my feet so easily I felt like a rag doll being jerked around. "Let's go," he said, and he dragged me toward the brush. I wanted to scream and fight, but instead I allowed him to lead me to a rusty old van hidden in the undergrowth along the dirt road. I feared if I ended up in the vehicle I wouldn't be seen or heard from again. I had to make a move now or I wouldn't get another chance. Before I could think about what I was about to do, I lifted my foot and stomped it into his so hard he yelled out in pain. He let go of my arm, and I ran. Into the brush I went, tripping and crashing through tangled alders and raspberry bushes. Thorns tore at my hands and exposed arms while the dead wood dug into my thighs and calves. I did not get far in this tightly woven web. My hands were still bound behind my back with duct tape, and without them to break my way through the brush, my efforts were futile. I felt like a rabbit trapped in a fox's den with no way out.

"Helena," he called. His voice was so calm, but I could detect frustration and a hint of anger seething underneath his cool exterior. "There's no way out, Helena. Come, let me take you away from here."

Tears quietly trickled down my cheeks as I realized I had nowhere to go. I was trapped by this man I did not know, yet he seemed to think he knew me well. I searched my brain for some hint of recognition. Did I know him? Had I met him before? Why had he chosen me? It did not matter. I was certain I did not know this person, tearing through the brush, hunting for me. It was just more bad luck in my life, more tragedy. As if I hadn't had enough to last a lifetime. Grandma used to say, "God doesn't give us more than we can handle, child." That moment, I thought Grandma was full of shit and God must be a hateful, vindictive being.

I staggered my way deeper into the brush, moving only inches with each laboured step. Blood and tears trickled down my cheeks as more thorns and twigs scraped across my skin and tore at my clothes. The heavy mist had turned to rain, and in the distance I heard the rumblings of an angry thunderstorm threatening to explode. He was getting closer. I could hear him muttering curses under his breath. He was angry with me—for what, I was not sure. Running from him? Forcing him into the brush? Or just for being alive? Whatever the reason, I was going to pay for escaping. I just knew it wasn't going to be good. I pushed harder into the tangled web before me, but my efforts were pointless.

"You can stop now, Helena," he said, only inches away from me now. So close, in fact, I could feel his warm breath on the back of my neck. "You are wasting your time, and mine."

He had a large, calloused hand on my arm once again, only this time his grip was more forceful, and his fingers dug into my flesh, making me flinch. He spun me around to face him, and I found myself staring into soulless, black eyes filled with hatred and loathing. He dragged me back into the open, stumbling, crying, and unable to scream. This time when we approached the van, he was more cautious and forced me to walk beside him. He opened the side door and motioned for me to climb in. I shook my head in protest, and he just smiled back at me, then shoved me inside and slammed shut the door.

In that moment, I was certain I would not live to see the sun rise in the morning. My biggest fear was of what I would have to endure in the hours between now and then. I had no idea how I would cope. I did not imagine that that night was just the first of many horrific and torturous nights to come. I wondered, what if I had gone running in the park instead? Or what if I had not gone running at all?

What if I had fought harder?

11

David arrives twenty minutes later. It seems like hours since his phone call. I watched the hands on the clock ticking off each long-drawn-out minute, and I could swear there was more than sixty seconds between each movement. I am waiting in the entrance for him and open the front door before he has a chance to knock. I am dying to know what he has learned. Is it something new? Is it the missing piece of information we were hoping for? It is possible, of course, the information he carries will fall into the pile of many other false leads that sent us off chasing our tails in futility. I pray this will not turn into another wild goose chase, but if it does, so be it. It is the only way we can find him. Someday, the chase will be real, and my monster will be revealed.

"How are you, Helena? And Lily?" David asks as I close the door behind him and begin the process of locking the collection of bolts and chains that I had him install years ago to keep us safe in our home.

"We're fine, but I don't want to make small talk, David. That's not why you're here. I need to know what you have learned. Have you found him?"

I am in no mood to chat about anything other than the reason he is here. I know I sound abrupt, but David has come to know me well in the last eight years. He knows there is nothing more important to me than finding the monster who held me captive for three months, two weeks, and five days. He tortured me beyond comprehension and—perversely—gave me the greatest gift I have ever received. I live in fear he will return to destroy my life again. David understands I must find him before he finds us.

"Okay, I know you're anxious. Let's sit down first."

We sit on the sofa in front of the fireplace. It is far from cold outside, but for some reason I am feeling a slight chill. I look at him, waiting for him to speak. I can see he is hesitant and cannot help but wonder why. Is the news that bad?

"Enough, already, spit it out! What have you found out?"

"Last week, a girl was found in a drainage ditch by a farmer inspecting his fields. She had been dead for a couple of days and was unrecognizable. With the temperatures during the day and the animals at night, there wasn't much left. Luckily, the coroner was able to identify her through dental records. Her name is Melody Scott. Does that ring any bells with you?"

"I don't think so. Should it? Why do you think I might know her?"

"Helena, Melody Scott is from Deer Lake. That's your home-town, is it not?"

"Yes, you know it is, but I don't recognize her name. How old was she? I have been gone from Deer Lake for over eight years."

"She was only eighteen years old, soon to be nineteen. She had just left home for college. She doesn't have any family, but her foster family had not heard from her in nearly a week and started to get worried. It turns out Melody made it to school in time to register and settle into her dorm room, but she never did make it to class. She had been gone for five days before they filed a missing persons report."

"So, she was found a few weeks later in the drainage ditch? Murdered?"

"Helena, she went missing last September. Her body was dis-covered last week."

"You're telling me she was held captive for over a year?"

I am dumbfounded by this news. It immediately brings me back to the dark, dingy basement, and days and nights of physical torture and mental anguish.

"Do you think it was him?" I ask, almost afraid to hear the answer.

"I don't think it is a coincidence she is from the same town as you. Do you?"

"It is eerily similar to my experience . . . young girl away at college . . . but maybe it is just a coincidence."

"Helena, there is more," David says grimly. "The coroner was able to retrieve viable DNA from her body. It was sent to the lab, and the results came back today. It's the reason I am here tonight."

He hesitates.

"Well, don't stop now, David. What did you find out? Do you know who he is? Do I know him?"

"Helena, his name is not in our database. However, his DNA is. When it came back as a match to a previously known offender, I was notified immediately. It's him, Helena. The DNA retrieved from Melody Scott's body is a one hundred per cent match to the DNA doctors obtained when you were brought in nearly eight years ago."

"So, what you're saying is the monster who kidnapped me and tortured me for all that time is the same monster who snatched Melody Scott and held her captive for over a year. Oh my God, that poor girl! Was she tortured as well, David? Did she live through that terror for nearly a year?"

David pauses.

I cannot bear to think of the horrors she must have endured during all that time in captivity. After three months, two weeks, and five days, I did not think I could have survived another moment in that basement. What she must have gone through is unimaginable.

"So, what is the next step? What are we going to do now to find him?" I ask.

"We aren't going to do anything. I will find him, Helena, and when I do, you will be the first to know. This guy is dangerous. You need to stay here with Lily, where it's safe."

"If you think I am going to sit here on my hands and wait for you to find this guy, you are sadly mistaken! You think I don't know this creep is a monster? I know first-hand what he is capable of, and I am not taking any chances that he will find me or Lily while we idly wait for you to make it safe." My voice grows louder and more anxious with each word. I know David cares about Lily and me, but this isn't about him. This is my story, and I must be the one to end it. Lily is my daughter, and I am the one responsible for keeping her safe and far away from this monster. "So, what is our next step?"

"You are not going to let this go, are you?" he asks in exasperation.

"David, you know I can't. If I had stopped him all those years ago, we wouldn't even be having this conversation right now. Melody Scott would be enjoying her days at college, and I wouldn't be living each day in fear, waiting for his return."

"I was expecting this, but I had to try. I want to keep you two safe, Helena. This is about more than putting him away. I want you to finally be able to move on from this, to have a life without living in fear all the time. I want you to be able to go to bed at night without feeling the need to recheck every window and re-lock the six deadbolts on your front door. I'm afraid if I let you help me, something might happen to erase all the progress you have made. And I'm afraid that if I don't, you will never forgive me."

"David, I know you care, but I have to do this. I have to be a part of whatever comes next. It is the only way for me to find closure. I can't help but wonder if Melody Scott would still be alive if I had done more to find him earlier. It has been almost eight years.

Surely I could have done something before now to find him. I can't stand by while someone else tries to stop him. If I do, someone else may suffer while I sit at home waiting. I couldn't live with myself if that were to happen."

I can see his demeanour changing as I speak. I know he understands my position, and his reluctance is coming from a good place.

"Okay, then. We have to figure out the best place to start. We know he attacked you while you were attending university, and he grabbed Melody when she left to attend college. You were found in the cornfields, and Melody was discovered in a drainage ditch by a farmer, only a few kilometres away from where you escaped. So, I think he is familiar with the area. He knows the farmlands, so it is possible he is a farmer in the area or maybe works on the fields."

"I was held in the abandoned house on the outskirts of town. He must know the area, or he wouldn't have chosen that place to keep me. He would not have known about it had he come from somewhere else."

"I agree with you." David nods his head as he speaks. "He must have some connection to this area. We just have to find out what it is. And there is one more very important piece of the puzzle."

I look at him for further explanation, and then it dons on me.

"Both Melody and I came from Deer Lake. Is it possible he followed us from there? We might not have been random girls he forced into a nightmare, but rather known targets of his delusional mind."

"That is exactly what I've been thinking. It could be a coincidence, but you and Melody have a connection with Deer Lake," he confirms. "You know what this means."

"It means he may have known exactly who we were. It means I may know him, but I honestly do not believe that I do. I spent all that time with him, and I would remember if he were someone I knew," I say with certainty, yet I can't help but wonder if I am forgetting something important.

"It also means something else, something that might not be easy for you," he suggests, a little apprehensive.

"It means I have to go back to Deer Lake," I answer, while a knot starts to form in the pit of my stomach.

I have not been to my hometown in ten years, not since the day I said goodbye to Allie and stepped on that bus for the last time. I said goodbye to my friend and a life of heartache and vowed I would never go back. Until now. Now, I have no choice. If I want to find out once and for all who he is and stop him before he gets the chance to terrorize another girl, or worse, kill her like he did Melody Scott, then I must go back to the beginning. Deer Lake is the common denominator between Melody and me, and now I have to discover how we connect to him. This is the most promising lead we have had in this eight-year search. What if it's another false lead, and more false hope? What if this trip home leads me nowhere but back to a past I'd rather forget?

What if it leads me straight to him?

12

The first semester after my mother killed herself, I walked around in a daze half the time. My grades were not great, and my budding social life had become non-existent. One day, I went to class in a huge lecture hall and discovered my psychology professor had arranged for a guest speaker to come speak before his class. I was about to get up and sneak out through the back door when a couple of students came and sat down in the empty seats beside me, essentially blocking my chance for a quiet escape. And so I stayed. It turned out to be the best thing that could have happened to me at the time.

The speaker was a well-dressed, middle-aged woman who, on first appearances, seemed to be another educator or professional telling us how to behave and what to think. As it turned out, she was neither. In fact, she was so far from what I had assumed that I could not take my eyes off her. I soaked in every word she spoke that day like it was the gospel. Her story was one of tragedy and heartache. She spoke of the healing that comes when we learn to cope and accept the things we cannot change. I felt she was speaking directly to me, touching me in ways no one had in the months since my mother's suicide. That day, her words spoke to me and moved me toward the process of accepting the deaths of my parents and toward healing. That day, I laced up my running shoes for the first time. I ran only a mile or two, but it was exhilarating. Running became an outlet to work out my feelings for a while.

Eventually, my grades started to improve. I called up former friends and rekindled those relationships. I started living again. By the time the first-year anniversary of Mom's death came, I was doing well. I had my moments, of course, but on those days, I'd run a little harder or go a little farther. I was coping. I was healing. I was living. I was doing well.

It was a Monday night when my friends decided to take me out for coffee to take my mind off the first anniversary of my mother's death, the next day. I had confided in them bits and pieces of my former life; yet not one of them knew my entire story or how close I came to sinking into depression like my mother. I liked to keep some parts of me private. We were laughing and joking around over hot coffees and doughnuts when she walked into the café. She looked at me right away, and I knew it wasn't a coincidence that she was here. She had come looking for me, and I wondered how she knew to find me here.

Allie looked much the same since the last time I saw her about a year ago. She was still as skinny and her clothes just as ill-fitting as they had always been. I could tell by the sad look on her face that life had not changed much for her, and I wondered why she continued to stay in Deer Lake. I told my friends I must go and excused myself from the table. Allie motioned me outside to the lit outdoor patio, and we took a seat in a far corner, tucked away from the other patrons.

"Hi, Allie," I said. "I am surprised to see you here. How've you been?"

"You don't think I fit in a world like this," she replied harshly. "You think I don't belong here in your world?"

"I did not say that. I am just surprised to see you. I had no idea you were here," I said, a little on the defensive.

I was not sure why Allie was here, but I did not have a good feeling about it. We had not spoken since Mom's funeral. We both knew when the door closed and the bus pulled away that our friendship was over. It had been a friendship built on sadness and centred around heartache. I had to let it go for fear I would drown in the misery. I was sure Allie understood that. If she were here now for me, she must need something.

"I came because, even though you left and didn't look back, I thought you might need me. You do know what tomorrow is, right? Or have you forgotten that, too?"

"Of course I know what day tomorrow is. How could I forget? You might be angry with me for leaving, but don't you dare suggest that I would forget that day," I answered, getting a little angry myself, even though I was not sure what this conversation was about or why she was even there.

"I didn't mean that. I know you remember. But I remember, too, Helena. Your mother and I grew close after you left for school. I miss her, too. I thought you might like to be together tomorrow."

"I'm sorry. I know you loved her, too, Allie. It's hard remembering her. I try to think about the good times when my father was alive, but they seem to be overshadowed by all the hurt that came later. I loved my mother, but I am finding it hard to forgive her for giving up on herself, for giving up on me. I still needed her. I still do."

"You had me. I would have been there for you, but you left me behind," she said. The hurt in her voice was unmistakable.

"I am sorry, Allie, but I had to go. I had to move on, or I would have died there, too. I thought you understood."

"I know tomorrow is the first anniversary of her death. I can't stop thinking about her or you, and I thought you might feel the same," she replied, changing the subject.

"I will never forget my mother or the day she died. Her actions that day changed my life forever. How could they not?"

"I was thinking you and I might go back together tomorrow.

You know, visit her grave, bring flowers, that sort of thing. We could spend the day in her garden, remembering her."

"What do you mean, spend the day in her garden? I sold the house, Allie, about a month after she died. I cannot go back there now."

"Yes, I know. Had you bothered to keep in touch, you would have known that we live there now. Your house was bought by the Newfoundland and Labrador Housing Corporation for a low-income family. Turns out that family was us. I live there now with my mom. I have been tending to the garden ever since we moved in. We kept your room the same, if you ever want to come back," she replied.

The look on her face as she spoke was strange. I got a weird feeling, but I couldn't pinpoint exactly why.

"Are you for real right now?" I asked, confused. "Are you really living in my old house? With our things?"

"Yes. Turns out our house was too far gone to fix. The social worker, Mr. Blackstock, said it was going to be condemned and we would have to find somewhere else to live. I couldn't think of a better place than your house. After all, you had abandoned it, too. I thought someone should look after the place and pretend it was a happy home. So, I suggested it to the social worker, and he made it happen.

"If you come home with me tomorrow, you can see for yourself. It really does look the same. You sold the house as is, so most of your old furniture is still there. Even the walls look the same. It would be like going back in time," she added, and I was speechless.

"Allie, I am not going back to Deer Lake with you tomorrow. I am not going back there again. That house is not my home, and there is nothing and no one in that town that I want to see again. I am sorry you came all this way, but I think it is time you left," I told her, maybe a little more harshly than I intended.

"You know, Helena, I only wanted what was best for you. I

know you don't think that we are meant to be together, but we are more than best friends. We have a special bond that even time apart cannot change. We will forever be a part of each other's lives whether you like it or not. When you realize that, you know where to find me.

"Despite what you may think right now, I care about you. I know you. I know how you think, and I know how you feel. I know the things you desire, and I know your hopes and your dreams. Me and you, we are the same. I just chose to stay, while you chose to run away. But you cannot run from yourself, or me, forever. Someday, you will realize everything I have told you is true, and like a true friend, I will be waiting with open arms to welcome you back home. Home to Deer Lake and home to me."

I watched her as she walked away from our table and through the exit. I was baffled by what she had said and how she had said it, and I wondered how we had ever been friends in the first place. I was glad she had left. Relieved, actually. Her appearance here was unusual and the conversation disconcerting. I was troubled by what had just transpired and could not help replaying bits and pieces of the conversation in my head. I understood she may have cared for my mother and would want to remember her on the anniversary, but I could not fathom why Allie would want to live in my former home, unchanged and kept as a shrine to its previous owners. It was weird. It felt creepy. I had just entered the twilight zone, a reality where things were the same yet vastly different.

I wondered if my leaving had changed her in a way that I could not possibly understand, and was not sure I even wanted to. What if my former friend had lost herself in that town? Maybe, if I had taken her with me, she would not be stuck in the past, stuck trying to create a life from the pieces I had left behind. I thought she had somehow become trapped in a weird reality of her own making. What if she never escaped?

What if she came back for me?

13

I woke on a disgusting mattress in a cold, musty room. It was nearly pitch black, and were it not for a faint ray of light trickling in from beneath the door, I would not have known it was there. I looked around, searching—for what, I was not sure. Was it morning? Was it afternoon? I had no way of knowing. Somehow, I managed to stand and fumble around the perimeter of the room, inspecting the walls as I went. I discovered two blackened windows and a second door that led to a toilet and sink. I was hopeful for a moment the tap would produce water, but neither of them was in working order. As expected, the door to the outside world was locked tight. I continued my laborious inspection of the room by walking back and forth from wall to wall. I stumbled over uneven floorboards but found the room completely empty, aside from the smelly, damp mattress in the corner.

I found myself at the door with the faint ray of light creeping beneath and started pounding with all my strength. I screamed at the top of my lungs for someone to set me free until my voice was so hoarse I could barely speak. And nothing. Not a sound: no one yelling for me to be quiet; no one laughing at my futility from the other side of the door; no one stomping around in another room, angry with my frantic behaviour. There was nothing but a long, eerie silence that completely engulfed the dark, musty room and threatened to suck all the air from my lungs.

I was alone, utterly and completely alone. Would anyone find me there, wherever there was? I had no idea where he had taken me. The last thing I remembered was being forced inside his beat-up van, and then, waking up in that room. Was I still in town? Had he taken me beyond the city limits, outside the province? I did not have any of the answers, and I had no way to find them. Despite my fear, I was relieved to wake up alone. However, I would die there in that room if he did not come back.

I suddenly felt so alone and scared. I was not ready to face my own mortality. I had no water, no food, and no way out. I felt like all the progress I had made over the last couple of years had been for nothing. What difference did it make if I had found ways to cope with my anger and my grief? Who cared that I was doing well in school, that I was going to become someone? In a matter of days, maybe weeks, I would be dead in this dungeon. How long did it take for a human to die of thirst? I could not tell you exactly how many hours and days. The only answer I had was that it would be far too long. I could not accept this fate. How could a family be wiped off the face of this earth so tragically? Cancer, suicide, and now murder? It just wasn't fair. I could not accept this was how my family would end. I was the only one left, and I was not going to die there in that hellhole.

As suddenly as the anger appeared, it vanished when I heard footsteps above me. I must have been in a basement. The steps grew closer, and I heard keys rattling like someone was grappling with them in his or her pocket. I heard a click, then another, and the light under the door grew to a beam streaming inside and illuminated the room in a dusky glow. There was a small, low window beyond the room that had not been blackened, and sunlight was struggling to break through the glass. I saw blades of grass obscuring the window. It was confirmation I was being held in a basement. As quick as the light filled the room, it was hidden once again by a tall, masculine figure who filled the doorway. There was just enough light for me to see the smirk on his acne-ridden face, and I shivered at the thought of what came next.

"Hello, Helena. How'd ya sleep?" he asked, as if I were a guest in his home.

His voice was familiar in that it was the same voice I heard calling my name at the lighthouse. I had no idea who this man was or why he had brought me there. I just stared at him, afraid to speak and not sure I could find my voice if I tried. The door was still open, and a faint light illuminated the room. I glanced around only to confirm what I had already discovered. The only way out was the open door before me. The problem was the man standing between me and freedom.

"Cat got ya tongue this morning?" I thought he believed we were old friends or at least familiar. "C'mon, girl, speak," he demanded, and I feared he was getting angry with me.

"Who are you? Why have you brought me here?" I asked.

My voice was barely audible, but I knew he had heard me. I felt he was young, even though his look was hard and ragged.

"I asked ya a question!"

His voice grew a little louder, and I could sense his anger was seething just beneath the surface. I was afraid to answer, and I was afraid not to.

"I am cold down here. It was hard to sleep," I lied.

Whatever he did to me or gave me in order to get me here had knocked me out completely. I had slept. I had no idea for how long, but I was sure I had slept. I knew if I was forced to stay there any longer, I would need something to keep me warm, so I tried again.

"Maybe I can go upstairs where it's warmer?" I asked, but he did not reply.

"S'pose ya feel like breakfast, now, do ya?" he asked instead.

I was starving. I had not eaten since lunch the day before, and my stomach grumbled at the thought of food.

"I'm not hungry," I said, and I regretted it as soon as the words were said. If I was going to survive, I would need food to keep me going.

"I need to pee. Can I go upstairs? The bathroom down here doesn't work," I asked, and once again, he ignored me.

He was not interested in anything I had to say. He was asking questions, but he clearly did not want to engage in a conversation.

"Why did you bring me here? What do you want with me?" I cried. I had found my voice, and I was trying desperately not to yell at him. I saw the anger flash across his pockmarked face and felt like I was poking a stick at a beast.

"Stop talkin', girl," he yelled. "I'll be the one askin' the questions, not you. Ya got that?"

"Please," I begged. "Please let me go. You don't really want to do this. Please let me go home."

I rushed toward him. I am not sure if I thought I could get past him and through the open door, or if I was going to fall on my knees before him and beg. Either way, I didn't get the chance. The moment I stepped close to him, I felt the back of his hand strike my jaw, and the force sent me flying across the room. I stumbled as pain shot into my brain, and I swore I could see stars twinkling throughout the blackened room. I hit the wall and crumpled to the floor, just as he left the room and slammed the door shut behind him. I heard the keys fumbling in the lock and his footsteps moving farther away until they were once again above me. Then silence. Deafening silence.

And I cried. Heavy sobs that took my breath away. I cried with the pain in my jaw, and I cried because I was hopeless. I remembered my mother and how she could not cope with the loss of my father, and I remembered my father and how he fought like a warrior to beat the cancer. I decided to be like him. I was strong like him, I told myself, and I was going to find a way out. When the tears stopped flowing, I heard footsteps once again. He was returning. I heard the keys in the lock for the second time, and then the door opened just a crack. This time he did not enter the room. I heard something land on the floor and the sound of something being pushed across the floorboards. Then he was gone. The room fell into darkness, the locks were turned, and he walked away.

I felt my way toward the door in search of whatever it was he had left behind. The first thing I stumbled on was a blanket. It smelled of mothballs and dust, but it would keep me warm. I picked it up and held it close. I found a tray and on it a single bottle of water and a peanut butter sandwich. It wasn't much, but at that moment it smelled like a gourmet meal. I wolfed down the sandwich and half the water, saving the remainder just in case. I had no idea how long I would be down there, and I had nothing but the blanket and half a bottle of water to sustain me. I felt a lump forming in my throat and tears filled my eyes, but I refused to think I had just eaten my last meal. I was not giving up that easily.

So, I searched. And I searched again. And again. I scraped the floorboards with my fingers in search of loose boards until my fingers bled. I tried with all my might to jimmy the windows, but they had been painted shut and were completely black. Even if I were able to move them, rusted bars would have prevented me from leaving. I was trapped. I felt like an animal in a cage with nowhere to go. I wanted to cry. I wanted to scream.

Instead, I stood in what I thought was the middle of the room and talked to God. You might think talking to God is a common reaction, and you would be right, but for me, talking to God was difficult. I had not spoken to Him since the day my father succumbed to his cancer. I believed I had kept up my end of the bargain with God. It was God who had failed. When Dad died, I was furious, and I put the blame solely on God's refusal to save him. I could not accept it was the disease that ravaged his body until he could take no more. No, it was God's fault. I had done everything I had promised, but he died anyway.

Standing there now in that darkened prison, I found myself

once again bargaining with God. What if I promised to forgive Him for failing me the first time we had this conversation? What if I promised to finish school and go on to help others?

What if I promised to be a good friend and reach out to Allie?

14

I show up in David's driveway at dawn the next morning. I have been up all night packing and planning our next move. I have rehearsed in the mirror a dozen times the conversation I know is coming. He is not expecting me, or at least I don't think he is, but here I am, staring at his front door and praying he doesn't make this difficult. I am going to be a part of this investigation whether David likes it or not. I am just hoping I can convince him that he needs me with him. I would rather do this together than on my own. But if that's how it is, then that's how it will be. This horror story started with me, and I am going to be the one to end it, for my sake and for Lily's.

She is sleeping in the back seat of my car, still in her pink pyjamas from the night before. Sadie is curled up next to her, at ease but attentive to the goings-on. I can tell she knows something has changed. Dogs are amazing creatures, and she senses when I am uneasy. I have no family with whom I can leave Lily and no friends I trust enough to keep her safe. I will take her with me if I have to, but I know this is not a reasonable option, nor a safe one. David has been a police officer for years. He has contacts I do not have and resources I can only dream of. I am banking on his agreeing to work with me and find a secure place for my daughter while we hunt down a monster. I know I am expecting too much, but I have no choice. It has to be this way or Lily and I may never be free of him.

The front door opens just as I step out of the car, and David stops. He doesn't look too surprised to see me, so I am hoping this is a good sign. He turns to check the lock and continues down the steps before speaking. I can feel the tension in the air. I do not want to argue with this man who has been by my side for the last eight years, who has witnessed me at my worst and has helped me pick up the pieces of my shattered life. I love him in my own way. I am not sure if I am capable of romantic love after what I have been through, but however you choose to define our relationship, it is one I do not want to lose. He is my protector, my confidant, my friend, and the only human being I will ever trust with my life and Lily's.

"Helena, you know you can't be here," he starts.

His voice is not angry, so I am hoping he is at least willing to listen.

"Just hear me out, David. You know I have to be here. I have to stop him before it's too late!" I plead.

"Helena, it's my job to stop him. I am trained to do what needs to be done in order to end this. I am very good at what I do. I will find him this time."

"I know you will, and I know you are good at your job. Why do you think I've trusted you all these years? This man, this monster—" I throw my hands in the air in frustration. "—he's my monster, and because I haven't been able to stop him, he's now Melody Scott's monster. I cannot let him hurt anyone else! And you need me to help find him."

"The safest place for you and Lily is at home. I'll have patrol keep an eye on your place. He doesn't know where you live or where to find you. It's best to keep it that way."

"David, I don't want to argue with you, but I am going back to Deer Lake whether you like it or not. I have to at least try. I cannot sit at home any longer, worrying and waiting. I deserve better. Lily deserves better. I need to put this part of my life behind me. I need to put him behind me. He's all I think about every morning when I wake up after a fitful night's sleep, and he is all I think about when the sun goes down and I am surrounded by darkness.

"I want to go to bed at night and sleep until morning. I want to be able to take Lily to the park without constantly looking over my shoulder to see if we're being followed. I want to go to the mall, or a fair, or an amusement park without feeling like every man I see might be him. I want a life, David, for me and Lily. I need to be a part of this. Please don't make me go it alone."

I know I am baring more of my soul than I have allowed anyone to see since my father died, but I will do whatever it takes to be involved in the hunt.

"What about Lily? We can't take her with us. If things go as we hope, it will be too dangerous," he says, essentially agreeing to take me with him.

"I don't have anyone I can leave her with. You know my family are all dead, and I haven't exactly made a lot of friends over the last eight years. I was hoping you would have a solution," I reply, relieved the argument is over but still worried about Lily.

"I can ask my parents to take her for a while. They live on the coast. It's beautiful this time of year. Lily will love fishing with my dad, and I'm sure Mom will keep her busy. And they have a dog as well, so Sadie will be happy, too."

"Are you sure they won't mind? Will she be safe with them?" I ask, unsure of leaving Lily with complete strangers, even though I know it is what I have to do.

"I am a third-generation RCMP officer. Dad is a retired RCMP sergeant. He will keep Lily safe. He may be retired, but believe me, that man is in nearly as good a shape as I am. He won't let anything happen to her," he assures me.

"Okay, then, now to explain to Lily why her mama is leaving her in a strange town with strangers," I lament. I have a knot in my stomach, but I know it is what I have to do.

It was daunting having to convince David to take me with him on his investigation, but I did it. This next task will be daunting and heartbreaking at the same time. How do I convince Lily that everything is fine when I am leaving her alone with strangers? How do I let her go when I know we may be heading down a path that leads us straight into danger? I do not have a choice. These words I've said to David about wanting a life, they are true. I want this part of my life to be over. I want to move on, and the only way I can do that is to close the chapter on this part of my story once and for all.

It takes a while to convince Lily she will enjoy this adventure without me. I try to tell her she is a big girl and she will have the most amazing vacation with David's parents. I finally win the argument when I tell her they have a dog. Who would have thought a parent could be trumped by a dog?

"What kind of dog is she?" Lily asks when David joins us by my car.

"He is a border collie," David answers enthusiastically. "He loves to be outside and loves to play."

"What's his name? What colour is he? Can he do any tricks? Sadie does tricks, you know," she continues.

"Well, his name is Thunder, and he's black and white and really fluffy. He loves to play fetch, and he can catch a Frisbee, too. I think you'll like him a lot, Lily."

"What about Sadie? Will she like him? He's a boy, and I don't like boys very much, so maybe Sadie won't like Thunder," she says, and David tries not to laugh at her questions.

"Yeah, I know boys can be a bit of trouble, but I think Sadie and Thunder will be fine."

"I don't think boys are trouble," she informs us. "I think boys are just gross. They are always going around the playground at school seeing who can belch the loudest, and they smell each other's farts just to see who has the stinkiest. I think that's just gross, don't you?"

I turn my head so she doesn't see me holding back the laughter. I imagine David is trying his hardest to keep a straight face.

"You are right, Lily, that is so gross," David agrees with her. "What do you say we get going so you and Sadie can meet Thunder and see for yourself how great he is?"

"Okay, but Sadie will still be my favourite even if I do like to play with Thunder," she states as she climbs into the back seat with Sadie.

"Well, that was quite the interrogation!" David laughs as I close the car door and Lily buckles herself in.

"Ha ha, you haven't seen anything yet!" I say. "Just you wait until you have kids of your own someday, and you'll know just what I'm talking about."

"Maybe someday," he says. "It's hard with this job. So, do you want me to drive in your car, or would you rather follow me up the highway?"

"I'll follow you," I reply. "I don't want to risk Lily picking up on what we are planning to do. The less she knows, the better. Right now she thinks I am sending her on a great adventure, and I'd like to keep it that way."

"Okay, then, let's get going. We have a lot to do and plans to make before we head back to Deer Lake. You sure you're ready for this?"

"As ready as I'll ever be. There has to be an end to all of this."

But what if there is no ending? What if we are chasing a ghost and I don't get the closure I so desperately want and need? What if we are heading into the lion's den? What if we are embarking on yet another wild goose chase? What if we find him? Will this part of my story finally be over? What if it never ends?

What if I am never able to move on?

15

It was the day before my nineteenth birthday. My last year as a teen, although I had not felt like a teenager since the night my parents told me my father was dying from lung cancer. I had not told my friends of my birthday. They would insist on a party, and there would be cake and cards and laughter. All the things I had not enjoyed since I was fourteen years old. After my father passed, my mother was broken. She was lost in her own world of sadness and grief, and my birthday became just another day of the week we would have to survive—another day to care for my mother and pray we made it through.

I do not think she remembered my birthday again until my first semester away at school, when I was trying to believe everything was going to be okay and my mother was once again my mother. I didn't know it was all an act, and she was really drifting further away from me than she had ever been. It was three weeks after my eighteenth birthday when she took her life, when she washed down a handful of sleeping pills with a bottle of booze and called it quits.

I remember that birthday now with mixed emotions. I was surprised to receive a card in the mail from Mom. I thought it must have been Allie's doing, since Mom had not remembered my birthday in years, but that afternoon I returned from class to find a bouquet of flowers and a bunch of balloons in my dorm room.

I cried at the sight of it all. I wasn't overjoyed she had finally remembered or angry about all the missed birthdays and failed celebrations. I cried because seeing the flowers and those balloons sitting there on my desk made me realize how much I had resented my mother for her mental illness and the years it took from us. It wasn't her fault she couldn't cope without Dad. I had stepped in to keep us both from drowning, but I had resented having to do that at fourteen, and that resentment had been festering in my heart and my mind for the past four years. It was the reason I could not wait to get away from home. I was so ready to leave it—and her—behind in Deer Lake, and start over here at school that I forgot how much she truly meant to me.

Mom called that evening to wish me a happy birthday. I was so glad to hear her voice. It wasn't the same flat, emotionless voice I had grown used to. In fact, even though Mom had been feeling much better over the past few months, that day she was my mom—the mom I had been missing since I was fourteen. We talked for hours that night. We reminisced over happier days when there was the three of us, and we cried over losing Dad and how unfair it was. I hung up the phone that night overjoyed and thankful my mother was really getting things together. I felt for the first time since Dad's funeral that Mom was going to be okay. We were going to be okay. Then, three weeks later, she was gone. And I had been angry and disillusioned ever since.

This year there would be no cards, no flowers or balloons, and no long conversations with my mother. This year my birthday would go back to what it was before, just another day to get through, another day to survive and then forget. I had no family to send well-wishes. It was just me in this world. I had friends here at university, but we were the kind of friends who helped each other with assignments, who chatted about boys and classes and that weekend's party. We did not share our feelings about life or bare our deepest, darkest secrets. The only friend who knew me that well was Allie, and we were not friends anymore.

Sometimes, I missed her and being able to share my inner-most feelings and desires with someone who understood everything I was experiencing. I thought back to a few weeks earlier and her surprise visit. It was the first time we had spoken since I left home that very last time. Allie and I had shared so much. We experienced so much tragedy and sadness in our short lives that we lost our teenaged years to mental illness, poverty, and despair. I think our emotional burdens became too much for us, and at some point we lost the connection that held us together. For me, Allie was a reminder of all I had lost and all I had left behind. She was a symbol of all I was trying to escape. She was still in Deer Lake, pushing through every day. I do not know how she could do it. I felt like a hamster spinning around and around in a wheel and going nowhere. I had to leave for my own sanity, and I had to put everything and everyone from that time in my life behind me, including Allie.

There was a soft knock at my dorm room door. I was not expecting anyone. It was probably one of the girls from a nearby room who needed to borrow something, or one of my friends looking for a distraction from schoolwork. Before I got a chance to open the door, an envelope slid in from underneath. It must have been our dorm leader distributing the mail. I checked the clock. It was nearly six. Mail was seldom delivered that late in the day. She must have gotten busy with something else, I assumed. I picked it up, and my name was written in black marker across the middle of the envelope. There was no address and no stamp, so I immediately realized it had not arrived in the mail. Maybe one of my friends had discovered the next day was my birthday. I had not shared this information with anyone, but what other explanation could there be?

I used a fingernail to rip open the top. It was indeed a card, and I wondered who had learned of my birthday. I was not excited to open a card with joyful birthday reminders. The last such card

I had opened was from my mother a year ago tomorrow. It was one of the most special cards I had ever received from her, and the last. I was so angry when I returned to school after burying my mother, I tore the card to shreds and burned it in the garbage can. I did not want any reminders of how Mom had fooled me. With that card, she had made me believe we would survive to put the past behind us and move forward as mother and daughter for the first time in four years. Then, three weeks later, she had yanked the rug out from under my feet and left me alone to figure it out all on my own.

I pulled the card from the envelope. On the front was a picture of a bouquet of flowers and, beside it, a bunch of bright and shiny birthday balloons. I immediately flashed back to the scene waiting on my desk a year ago. It was just artwork on a greeting card, but there was meaning in that picture, I could feel it. I was nervous to open the card. I didn't know why. It didn't make any sense. After all, it was just a greeting card, wasn't it? I opened it cautiously, afraid to unveil what was waiting inside. What did it say? Who was it from? I was both anxious and curious. No one knew it was my birthday. No one except for Allie. My stomach did a flip-flop when I saw her name scrawled across the bottom of the card.

I had not seen or heard from her since our last awkward, and somewhat hostile, encounter nearly three weeks before. I hadn't expected to hear from her now—or ever—after our last conversation. The card did not have a pre-written verse. It was one of those blank cards that allowed the sender to express how he or she was feeling and/or send their own well-wishes. She had used the same black marker on the inside of the card as she had to write my name on the outside. Allie had been angry when she left that day, maybe even a little unhinged, and I was almost afraid to read what she had written. The knot in my stomach tightened with each haunting word.

For Helena,
Circumstance brought us together,
Two hearts badly broken.
Time has healed our wounds and our souls have become one.
You are a part of me, and I a part of you,
You can run from me forever, yet we will never part.
I know your hopes, your dreams, and all your secret desires,
I am waiting, I am watching.
The distance between us is closing.
I will be here with open arms, and soon you will see,
I am where you belong.

She had signed the card with her name enclosed in a red heart. I didn't know what to make of it. Her attempt at poetry was strange. I knew Allie hated English when we were in school. Her choice of words was unsettling, even creepy. I was nervous about what it all meant. Was she really watching me? Then it donned on me that there was no address on the envelope, just my name, which meant someone who knew me had to slip it under my door. No one there knew Allie. Could she have asked another student to deliver her card? Could she have done it herself? That thought was a little scary. I did not want to believe she was there, just moments ago, outside my dorm room. What if her words meant she really was becoming unhinged? What if she was watching me, stalking me?

What if I was in danger?

16

The first three days in the basement were long and frustrating. I was alone for the most part and tired of waiting for something to happen. I needed to know what he wanted from me, what he was expecting. At first I was scared to wonder about his plans. I didn't know if I would be dead before sunset or live to see another sunrise. But each day he returned to bring me food and make small talk. I quickly learned not to ask too many questions, or he would become angry. I was expected to answer every mundane question he posed, like, "Did you sleep well?" or, "Are you cold?" He didn't offer any clues as to why I had been forced into that basement in the first place, and when I insisted he answer my questions about why I was still there and what he wanted from me, the conversation ended with his hands around my neck or a fist to the face.

I was pretty certain I had bruises around my neck where his hard, calloused hands had squeezed until I could barely breathe. It was easy to see the anger that simmered beneath the surface. His eyes were cold, and I was certain it was impossible for him to feel anything—not love, not hate, not remorse. I could feel how close he came to losing control and just squeezing a little too hard, for a little too long. I felt him shake with frustration before he left and slammed the door behind him. He was big and much stronger than I was, yet I felt mentally he had not yet grown into the large body he possessed. It was hard to determine his features there in the dark basement, but his acne-ridden face and hot temper told me he was a young man not yet in control of his emotions and desires. And now I had become the outlet for all his anger.

My right eye was swollen shut from the blow the night before. He had come to bring me dinner, a cold and sticky KD cup with an overboiled wiener cut up on top. It was far from gourmet, but I ate it greedily. The conversation consisted of the same mundane questions he asked each time he came. I was angry, fed up, and desperate to get out of the basement, and I expressed those feelings relentlessly until he had had enough, and my eye bore the brunt of his frustration. It was tender to touch, and I could feel the dried blood crusted around a split in the skin covering my brow.

I knew it was not wise to poke an angry bull, but I had no other means to fight. I had no way out of the basement. He owned all the power and had all the control. I had nothing but my tongue. So, when he returned today—I had come to expect him now—I would use the only weapon I had and bombard him with questions and demands. Maybe I would sustain another blow or be choked into unconsciousness, but either way, I will have tried.

I thought it was well past morning. The beam of light seeping in beneath the door was getting dimmer, a sign the sun was moving higher in the sky and above the house, leaving the basement window on the other side of the door with light that was filtered and barely reached my prison cell. I was a little worried that I might have pushed him too far. He had not yet returned that day to bring me food. It was always peanut butter sandwiches in the morning with a bottle of water. My stomach growled just to remind me I had not eaten yet today, and the hours were creeping by. I paced back and forth the room, feeling anxious, scared, and alone.

Then came the sound I had been waiting for, even hoping for—footsteps above my head. He had returned. I hated him for bringing me here. I hated that he hurt me and would not give me reasons for his actions, but I was thankful he was back. I depended on him for my survival. He would likely be the reason for my death, but for as long as I was alive, I depended on him to return to bring me food and water and, above all, hope. Without him, I had no hope of survival, no hope of ever getting out of the basement prison again.

Yet something felt different tonight. He was pacing back and forth the floor above me. I heard him speaking, but I couldn't make out the words. I believed he was talking to himself. I didn't hear any footsteps or voices other than his. He was frustrated, I thought. I heard him shouting, "No, no, no!" I believed he was struggling with something, but I had no idea what it might be. I'd had a constant knot in my stomach since I first woke up in the basement, but now, at that moment, I was afraid. Something was changing. I could feel it. Tears rolled silently down my cheeks, and I prayed he would make it quick and painless.

He paced and yelled for what seemed like hours. I found myself scouring the room for the hundredth time, desperately searching for an escape I knew in my heart was not there. Suddenly, the pacing stopped. The room was silent. And I prayed he had left, but my hopes were dashed when I heard him descending the stairs. The keys fumbled in the locks, and the door opened slowly. I could feel the tension as I waited for him to speak. I had come to hate the boring conversation of the past three days, but now I longed to hear his litany of stupid questions. He was sweating. I could smell him before he had even entered the room. It was the putrid smell of an animal on the hunt, and I knew what he had planned next was going to be horrific and unbearable.

"Please," I begged, "please let me out of here. You don't have to do this." Tears were flowing profusely, and my voice caught with the lump in my throat.

"I don't have a choice, Helena," he replied. "I have to. Maybe ya will enjoy it."

The grin on his face made my skin crawl. His rotten teeth and fetid breath made my stomach churn, and my body froze with the realization of what was coming next. He walked toward me, and I retreated to the corner of the room that was farthest away from the dingy mattress lying on the floor. I curled into a ball, hoping he would walk away, even though I knew there was no stopping him. He was excited now, like a child at a birthday party. His eyes were wild, and he was ready to jump out of his skin. I wondered if he had taken something to ready himself. I had to fight him in whatever he chose to do to me, but engaging with an individual hopped up on drugs is as scary as trying to fight off a monster. In this case, they were one and the same.

He pulled me by the hair and yanked me to my feet. He dragged me across the room to the filthy mattress, and I knew what he was planning.

"Please," I cried, "please don't do this." I was crying uncontrollably. "Please don't hurt me!"

I tried to fight him, but he had me by the hair, and I cried out as he pulled tighter. He pulled even harder just as I tried to free myself from his grip, and I felt a clump of hair ripping from my scalp. It gave way, and I was free for just a moment. He had a handful of my hair, and I could feel the blood trickling down the side of my face while my head burned fiery hot. I didn't have time to think about the pain before he was by my side again. This time he grabbed my arm and squeezed so hard I feared the bones would break. He forced me to the mattress and was on top of me before I could react.

"Stop fightin', Helena," he demanded. "Ya can't get away from me. Don't worry, I will make sure ya enjoy it."

He was laughing now, and I cried so hard I could barely catch my breath. I tried to move my body beneath him, but he was much bigger and stronger than I, and my actions were futile. He tried to kiss me, so I spat in his face, and the moment I did, I instantly regretted it. His hand rose above me, and I prepared myself for the blow I knew was coming. Instead, he grabbed my face between his thumb and forefinger and forced me to look at him. He was angry now. He forced my lips on his, and I choked on the vomit that was rising in my throat. I felt my skin break with the force of his mouth on mine, and I tasted the blood on my tongue. I was so scared I was afraid I might pass out.

He was unzipping his pants and preparing himself for the main event. He pulled at my jeans, but I refused to help him. He popped the button and pulled apart the zipper, then used his free hand to pull them roughly from my body. I was naked from the waist down, and he was fumbling to do his thing. I held my legs together with every ounce of strength I had while his harsh fingers dug into my thighs and tried to pry them apart. He lowered himself and forced himself inside me. I closed my eyes and tried to block out his grunting with each thrust. He was too excited, and it was over quickly. I was relieved, but he was angry. He lifted himself up and quickly zipped his pants.

"I know we can do better next time, Helena," he said behind clenched teeth. "Try not to fight so hard and ya might enjoy it."

He abruptly left the room, slamming the door behind him. I heard the keys turning in the locks, and I curled into a ball and cried. I cried because of what had just happened, and I cried because I knew this was just the beginning. I used the blanket he gave me on that very first day to try and wipe the scent of him from my body, but the action was futile. I searched the edge of the mattress and found the water bottle I had stashed there the day before. It was almost empty. I so desperately wanted to use the meagre amount that remained to scrub my body, but I couldn't waste the little I had left, so I drank the last of the water and washed away the taste of blood and vomit stuck in the back of my throat.

I listened for the silence that told me he had left the house and I was all alone. I hoped he stayed away forever. I decided I would rather die there alone than ever have to live through that again. But I knew I was dreaming and resting my hope on wishful thinking. He hadn't left the house this time. He was upstairs once again, pacing back and forth, back and forth. I knew he was coming back soon. Our game had only just begun. Would I survive the next time, or the time after, or the time after that? How long would this go on? Would it get easier each time? Would I lose a little of myself with each passing day, alone there with that monster until there was nothing left of me? What if he was angrier the next time? What if he couldn't control himself?

What if I couldn't survive?

17

We are getting close to Deer Lake. I can tell by the familiar landscape. I have not been back here in ten years, yet nothing has changed. The highway still leads down the hill to the end of the lake, the sandy beach still stretches from the power plant to the park at the other side of the lake, and boaters are still out on the water trying to catch the last of the few remaining warm days of fall. When I was a child, my parents took me to the beach on hot, sunny days and we would swim and splash in the rolling waves. I can still feel the sand between my toes and hear my father's laughter as he splashed us with the cold water. Deer Lake is an idyllic place to grow up with its hot summers and snow-filled winters. There are more than enough activities to keep even the most restless child, or adult, busy. It was perfect for us, too, once upon a time. I often wonder how things would have been had my father not gotten sick. Would I have been one of those people out enjoying the last blast of summer? Maybe I would have left, anyway. There's no way to know.

"Are you nervous about being back?" David asks, jolting me back to the present.

"I'm not sure how I feel," I reply. "I have a lot of good memories of growing up here, but it's hard to think of them without remembering all the bad that came later."

"This is the first time I've stopped here," he offers. "It looks like a great place."

"It was. I guess it still is for most. Too much has happened here for me. It makes it hard to remember the good times. They seem so far away, almost as if they weren't even real," I reply. My attention drifts back to looking out the window again, my mind fading back to happy times at the beach.

"So, what do you plan to do?" David asks.

I don't answer right away. What are my plans? I don't have family to visit. I sold my home years ago. I have no friends here. There's Allie, but I'm not sure if I want to see her or not.

"I'm not sure," I answer, uncertain. I knew I had to come here, but for what, exactly, I wasn't too sure. "Maybe I'll tag along with you."

"That can't happen, Helena. You know you cannot be a part of this investigation, not officially, anyway. You are a civilian. You're lucky to even be here to begin with. I have a lot riding on how this turns out. My CO was very reluctant to allow you to come at all. It took a lot of convincing on my part, and we cannot do anything to screw it up," he says sternly as if he is talking to a child.

In his own subtle way, he is warning me to stay out of his way and to behave myself. I have no intention of causing him any trouble. Our goal is the same—to stop a monster. He is bound to follow the law to the letter. I am not. I am fully prepared to do whatever it takes to get the answers we need. I want this over, really over. My daughter is safely tucked away, for now. I need to close this chapter quickly, finish it once and for all, before he finds out where I am and, God forbid, that he is Lily's father. It's past time we all go back to living normal lives, whatever that is.

"David, I'm not going to get in your way or cause you any trouble," I answer a little petulantly. "I figured I could show you around first. Doesn't look like things have changed much since I left."

"I have to stop at the police station first, introduce myself, and tell them why I'm going to be in town asking questions. It's just a courtesy, but necessary."

"I can take you to the depot. I can reacquaint myself with the rest of Deer Lake while you are there. You can text when you're done, and we can meet. We'll take it from there. Sound good?"

"Fine with me. Just remember what I said, Helena, don't do anything stupid to mess this up. We don't want to tip him off if he's here, and I don't want you in any danger," he warns, but once again I am staring out the window, my mind flooded with memories from long ago. This trip home is going to be difficult. It is hard to keep the memories at bay when they come popping up at every corner.

Ten minutes later, I leave David at the police station and pull out of the parking lot, not sure if I should turn left or right. Right will take me back to the house where it all began. Left will take me past the graveyard where my parents are buried and on to the school, where I was both a precocious preteen and a lonely teenager trying to keep her head above water. I turn left, I am not ready to go back home.

The school looms ahead. The red brick is as dingy as ever with black mildew staining the walls beneath the window ledges. The old windows are the same drafty windows from a decade ago. I remember thinking back when I was freezing my ass off in history class that these windows must have been old enough to be represented in our textbook somewhere or other. I guess some things never change for the better. I pull into the parking lot. It is nearly empty now. The kids have all been sent home for the day, except for a few stragglers who have stuck around for after-school activities. Once upon a time, that was me staying for volleyball practice. Those days seem like a lifetime ago. I park the car and get out. I am not sure why, maybe just to stretch my legs, or maybe the pull from memories of the good days is stronger than I thought.

I walk the grounds around the school for a while, soaking in the memories and the nostalgia. The basketball court is still in the same place; some kids are shooting hoops and laughing. They don't even notice me watching them, and I remember when I was that self-involved teenager. I notice the green space across from the schoolyard has been converted into a baseball field. I remember days cutting through that field to go to lunch with my friends. We'd barely have enough time to order our lunch and eat it before we were due back in class, but we did it every day, rain or shine, rather than stay in the school cafeteria with the other kids who weren't as cool as us.

"Can I help you?"

I turn suddenly, not expecting anyone to be nearby. The lady before me is older, a little past middle age, I think. She is a small woman dressed in a dowdy brown dress and wearing black-rimmed Coke-bottle glasses. Something seems familiar about her, but I can't pinpoint what it is.

"No, thanks. I'm just looking around. I used to go to this school years ago. It has been a long time since I left town. I was just reminiscing," I reply, slightly embarrassed for staying too long.

"Oh, that's nice," she says excitedly. "How long ago since you left? Did you graduate here?"

"Yes, I did, actually. I'm afraid it was ten years ago, though. I don't have any reason to come back anymore. My family is gone now, too."

"I see. Would you like to go inside? Maybe take a look around?" Nothing has changed much since I've been here, and from what I've been told, it's been even longer than that. "They just do the bare minimum to keep this place running. I swear it will fall down around them one day," she offers, and I feel like I know this woman from somewhere, I just can't remember where.

"May I ask you name? I feel like I know you. I'm sure that sounds weird, but I really do think we've met before. My parents were Holly and Samuel."

"Morris!" she exclaims before I get to finish. "My God, Helena Morris! What a surprise to see you here. How have you been after everything that's happened? I read all about you in the newspapers, such a tragedy what you went through. I don't know how you survived!"

"Mrs. Roberts?" I butt in, trying to distract her. I am certain I remember her voice giving lectures on the Ten Commandments and the Apostles' Creed to a group of bored Sunday school kids. Her hair is grey and she has it pulled into a bun, but the more I look, the more certain I am that it is her.

"Yes, it's me! It's so good to see you. You look wonderful for all that you've been through, child. You were all over the news every night. Didn't matter what channel I turned to, it was your face I saw, and I just felt terrible for all you experienced, especially after everything that had already happened with your family. Such a nightmare. I don't know how you didn't give up."

"Thanks for the offer to go inside, Mrs. Roberts," I interrupt before she can ask those inevitable awkward questions that I refuse to answer. "I am just here for a short while. Maybe next time I'm back in town," I say, even though I doubt there will be a next time.

"Okay, maybe next time, then," she replies, and I think she is disappointed I will not give her all the juicy details. If I did, she wouldn't set foot in a Sunday school classroom again wondering if God really did exist, or, if so, how He could have allowed such horror to happen in the first place.

"I have to get going. It was nice chatting with you again. Take care, Mrs. Roberts."

I turn and start walking back to David's car parked across the lot.

"Will you be stopping by to see Allie while you're home? I know how close you two were. I'm sure she would love to see you, especially now."

"I am not sure I will be here that long, actually," I lie. "You know Allie? Is she still here in town?"

"Oh, everyone at church knows Allie. Sure, I knew her when you two were friends back in high school, but she is quite involved in our church now. Helps out with all our fundraisers for the women's centre and the food bank. She is such a sweet girl. She has not had it easy, and now—well, now she is just heartbroken."

"Why is that?" I ask, and I immediately regret it. I am definitely not here to reconnect with Allie, and I have no intentions of visiting her in my home.

"Well, because of poor Melody, of course. Haven't you heard? She was found dead a few days ago, had only been at college a few weeks before she went missing. Allie took it really hard, and to find out she is gone, well, it's just heartbreaking, like losing a child."

"I'm sorry, I don't follow," I say, confused and a little nervous at the turn of the conversation. "Why would Allie be upset? I know Melody is from Deer Lake, but she was much younger than Allie and me."

"Why, Allie and Melody were very close, like mother and daughter, really," she answers, and I feel the knot in my stomach tightening. "Allie and her mother took her in when she had nowhere to go. It was rough at first, but they made it work. Melody turned things around, and she was heading down the right path. She was going to be a teacher, you know."

"I . . . I didn't know that," I stammer. "That's a sad story, for sure. It's been nice chatting with you, but I really have to get going. I have someone waiting for me."

I turn and nearly trip in a pothole as I hurry back to the car. What I have just heard is unbelievable. Allie knew Melody. According to Mrs. Roberts, they knew each other well. What did all this mean? What if the connection between Melody and me lies with Allie? What if there are more questions than answers now? And what if the answers are worse than the questions?

18

As the winter semester came to an end, I was once again faced with the dilemma of where to go. I had just sold my family home, not that I would have gone back to Deer Lake. I had no relatives with whom I could have stayed for a couple weeks. I had already decided I would continue into the spring semester. After all, what else do I have? School was the only positive thing in my life, the only thing keeping me sane. I begged the university administration to let me stay in my dorm room for the second time. After much deliberation, they finally gave me permission to stay but insisted it was the last time. When the spring semester ended, I was out, no more exceptions.

I had a month before that time arrived and I still had nowhere to go for the weeks in between. And no plan. I had the money from the sale of my parents' home. It sat in my bank account as a reminder of all I had lost. I had a scholarship for my education, thanks to my father, so the money was just sitting there. Sometimes I thought about giving it all away. I had no use for it, no reason to keep it other than it was mine. I wished I didn't have it. I would rather have had my parents, waiting for me to come home, but they were gone. My family was dead. My home had been sold. All that remained were the headstones marking their graves and this crazy sum of money in my bank account.

Other times, when I was a little more practical, and maybe a little more sane, I decided to keep the money. At times I believed there would come a day when I would look at it without anger and resentment. I was still angry—angry with God, with fate, with myself. I was pissed off at the world for taking my family and leaving me with nothing but old memories and a healthy bank account. However, as I sat in my dorm room staring at the figures on my computer screen, I wondered if maybe they were the solution to my dilemma.

What choice did I have? I had a month to find somewhere to live before the university locked the doors on the residence and forced me to sleep elsewhere. I hated that I had to use the money as much as I hated the reason I had it in the first place, but I had learned long ago that we cannot change the past. We live in the here and now, what's done is done. So, I set the wheels in motion, and two weeks later, I was the owner of a cozy little two-bedroom bungalow within walking distance of the university. My realtor handed over the keys on the same day the school residence closed at the end of the semester.

So there I stood on the front step to my new, two-bedroom home, and I was not the least bit excited. Buying a new home should be an achievement that is celebrated with pride, but I couldn't bring myself to cross the threshold. The house was empty. Furniture would be delivered in the afternoon, but for me, it would remain empty. I wasn't sure it would ever be a home. A house is a building with four walls and a roof, but it is devoid of all the qualities that make it a home. There would be no laughter in this house and no love from a happy family. The aroma of Grandma's famous chocolate chip cookies would never fill the rooms of this little bungalow. This house would be a roof over my head and a place to lie down at night, but I didn't believe it would ever be my home. I wasn't sure I would ever have a home again.

Over the next couple of weeks while I was on break, I set

about cleaning and organizing. Except for a few family pictures, there was nothing in the house that reminded me of the home I shared with my parents. When my mother decorated our home, before Dad got sick, she had filled it with bright colours and bold patterns of florals and plaids. It was filled with fluffy throw pillows, soft area rugs, and beautiful artwork. It was a representation of us, the happy, outgoing family.

This house was decorated in cool blues and lifeless greys. My walls were bare, and there were no knick-knacks adorning side tables and bookshelves. My shelves, rather, contained textbooks and binders filled with school material, but you would not find a favourite novel or sentimental ornament. It felt cold and distant. I had decided this house was a roof over my head and nothing more. I had not had any friends over for a housewarming party. I was certain I never would. They had all gone home to their families to spend time relaxing and catching up with loved ones and old friends while I had been there, alone. I had not shared my experiences and feelings with my new friends. Those were not that type of friendships. Those were friendships of place and convenience. When school ended, we would scatter in different directions to follow family, careers, and lovers, and all our so-called new friends would quickly be forgotten.

The backyard had a small flower garden along the length of the fence. It was becoming overgrown with weeds, and many plants had already come and gone for the season. Yet there was a bunch of orange lilies standing tall above the grass and weeds. It was a bright spot in this neglected garden and a blast from the past I was desperately trying to forget. My mother used to love her garden. She would spend hours pulling weeds, fertilizing the plants, and deadheading spent blooms. Then Dad got sick and her garden was left to die a slow, painful death much like my father. This garden reminded me of her, of how she had been so broken when my father died that she could not recover. She hadn't been the same after that, nor had the garden she had loved so much. And then, both she and her garden had died a slow, painless death filled with misery and neglect.

I walked over to the lilies, so bright and cheery, and I cut each one of them and brought them inside. I did not have a vase, so I put them in a water jug and placed them on the kitchen table. They looked so out of place there. They did not belong there in the house, and I wondered why I had cut them in the first place. They reminded me of my mother; that was the reason I had taken them from the garden. I thought bringing them inside might make the house feel a little more like a home, but it was a stupid thing to do. The house would never feel like home. I took the lilies from the jug and tossed them in the garbage can.

I spent the next day away from my new house. I couldn't stand to sit there any longer, staring at the blank walls and emotionless decor. Instead, I walked along the beach and spent hours lost in thought as the waves washed over the rocks, rolling in and out with the tides. Seagulls and ducks dotted the ocean as the sun sank lower on the horizon, emitting calls every so often to remind me they were still there. I saw the fog in the distance and knew that it would soon envelop the shore. It was time to go, but where? Home? I had a house, a roof over my head, but not a home. Regardless of how I felt, it was time to go back and make the best of it. Maybe I'd cook something. Maybe I'd bake chocolate chip cookies or banana bread like Mom used to make. I laughed out loud at these thoughts, because I realized I didn't have any of the utensils or ingredients needed to bake. I was lucky if there was enough food in the refrigerator to make dinner. Maybe I would go shopping the next day.

I hung my keys on a hook in the front porch, and I immediately felt something was not right. The lamp on a side table in the living room was lit, and I was certain it had been off when I left. I felt the hair rising on the back of my neck as I entered the house, even though I was trying to come up with reasons the lamp might have lighted on its own. I stopped in my tracks as soon as I caught sight of the kitchen table. The orange lilies I had picked the day before and then tossed in the trash can were sitting in the middle of the table. They were damaged and wilted, but someone had removed them from the garbage can, arranged them in the water jug, and placed them in the centre of the table.

There was a piece of paper on the table beside the jug. There was writing on it, but I was too far away to see what it said, and I was too scared to walk to the table to find out. I had no one to call and no intentions of calling 911. I didn't want to sound like a stupid girl who was afraid of someone who leaves her flowers, even if they were left inside a locked house. I summoned the courage to walk toward the note, and the moment I saw it, I knew who had been inside my house. The writing was the same, and the words were both contentious and troubling.

> *A year has passed since first you left,*
> *And cast us off like dirty clothes.*
> *You needed space to spread your wings,*
> *And we were in your way.*
> *Now she is dead, and I am alone,*
> *And you have erased us from your life.*
> *You can pretend we do not exist,*
> *But you will never forget.*
> *I will not be forgotten.*

The note was not signed, but she didn't need to sign it for me to know it was her. Allie had been inside my house. I had no idea how she had let herself in. I didn't understand how she even knew where to find me. I had not told anyone about the house. It was knowledge shared by no one but my realtor and me. I didn't think Allie would ever harm me, yet I didn't understand why she was so invested in my life. It was unsettling. She believed that I had moved on and forgotten her and everything that I lost in Deer Lake, when the exact opposite was true. I struggled every day with the memories, and try as I might, I couldn't ever forget. I just couldn't go back. I could not make Allie understand that I needed to let go, and so did she. We both needed to move on, just not together. What if Allie was never able to move on? What if I could never forget?

What if Allie would not allow it?

19

I was half-awake yet still half-asleep. I was standing in Grandma's kitchen with its bright sunflower wallpaper and red-and-white checkered curtains. We were making chocolate chip cookies, my favourite. I snuck a handful of the chips before they were added to the bowl, and Grandma scolded me. The smile on her weathered face and the twinkle in her faded blue eyes told me she wasn't really upset with me. It was the same routine we shared every time I baked with her. It was part of our fun. I helped her stir, and she let me lick the spatula when she was finished. Her kitchen was always warm and inviting to everyone who visited, but especially for me. I was her only grandchild, and she my only grandparent. Our relationship was special and unique.

I became more awake than I was asleep. The dream was fading quickly, and I longed to return to the comfort of her smile and her embrace. There were sounds dancing around me that I did not recognize. There were hushed voices, interrupted only by the soft hum of machines and an occasional beep of a monitor or instrument. I was afraid to open my eyes. I was not sure I wanted to know where I was or how I got there. I remembered the basement and the cornfields. I remembered being lost in the maze and afraid of dying there alone in the red dirt, and my heart raced with the possibility that I was once again trapped in the basement.

"She's waking up," I heard a voice say. It was the soft voice of a woman I did not recognize, yet I did not feel threatened. "Give her time," she ordered, and I realized I was in the hospital. How? I did not remember being transported there, and I did not bring myself. Was it necessary for me to be there? I tried to move, and the pain that shot through my damaged body told me I was where I needed to be. Yet I was still afraid to open my eyes. Opening my eyes meant having to view the horror he inflicted upon me, this time under the bright fluorescent lights of a hospital room. Opening my eyes meant having to endure everyone's stares while they tried to imagine what I went through and offer pointless apologies. But no one in the room could change what happened to me, nor could they imagine what I lived through each day locked in that basement, and I wouldn't want them to.

"Helena? Helena? You are in the hospital. You're safe here. Open your eyes, honey. We're here to keep you safe and to help you heal."

It was the same woman as before. Her voice was soothing, and I wanted to open my eyes and see her face. I imagined she was older than me, with beautiful brown eyes that would make me feel as if I have known her forever. I assumed she was my nurse, and I wanted to believe she was there because she was competent and could help me heal without the feelings of pity and disgust that I knew were coming, as soon as I opened my eyes and let everyone in the room know I was there. As long as I kept them closed, I could go back to the dream. I wanted to transport myself back to Grandma's kitchen, where the only worry was if the cookies were overcooked, and I wondered if I would have a place in my life that felt like Grandma's house ever again.

"She is awake." I heard the woman speak again. "Give her some time. She has been through hell and back. She will let us know when she is ready to acknowledge us," she continued to whomever else is in the room, and I was liking her more with each word.

She commanded the room, and no one wanted to be the person to oppose her orders. I heard shuffling and mumblings from other people around me, yet no one spoke to me or to her.

I decided I was not ready for their questions or my own. I did not want to offer explanations or provide details to strangers. I wanted to live in oblivion for just a little longer. I wanted to pretend I was with Grandma or practising my volleyball serve with my father. I wanted to be anywhere before my life began its slow, downward spiral to hell. I drifted off to sleep again, helped by the painkillers circulating in my blood, and landed on a white, sandy beach with my parents. We were happy. We had been swimming and were enjoying ice cream cones while we sat on our water-soaked towels and laughed at each other's jokes. I was not sure if this was a memory or a dream, but whatever it was, I was thankful to be there where I felt safe and loved.

In the dream, my parents started to fade into the sunset and I felt myself reaching out and calling for them to stay. I was begging them not to leave as tears streamed down my sunburnt cheeks, yet they kept going. They grew smaller and smaller and I could barely see them with the sun in my eyes, and my tears turned to heavy, heart-wrenching sobs as I realized they were not coming back.

"It's okay, Helena, you are safe now." It was the same woman as before. She was still there. I did not know how long I had been asleep since the last time I heard her voice, but it was comforting to know that she had stayed. I felt the wet tears on my face and realized I had been crying while I slept. I opened my eyes and looked at her before my brain decided I was not ready. She was not like I imagined. Her hair was grey and pulled high on her head into a neat and tidy bun. Her eyes were green like a cat's, and her face tan and wrinkled. I glanced around the room, and there were others standing by, waiting for me to speak, and watching my every move with anticipation and apprehension. I did not recognize anyone, and I wished I had not opened my eyes at all. I did not want to be the subject of their questions, assumptions, and imaginings. None of them would ever comprehend what I had endured, and I didn't have the energy to try and make them understand.

"Helena, you are in the hospital." It was the grey-haired lady again. "I am Dr. Banfield. I have been taking care of you since you were brought here. You have suffered a great trauma, but we are all here to help you and protect you," she continued as she motioned to the others sitting in the room, anxiously waiting for me to speak. "You are safe here."

She was not my nurse as I had first thought, but my doctor, which was why she was in complete control of the room. No one wanted to run the risk of being asked to leave, or be thrown out and miss the opportunity to hear first-hand what the bruised and battered girl in the bed had to say. I looked around again at all the expectant faces, and I felt like a birthday cake on display for eager children to pull apart and be left in pieces on the table. I closed my eyes again, wanting desperately to escape the room once more, but my throat was parched, and I needed water so badly I could not will myself back to sleep.

"Water," I said to the grey-haired lady by my bed. My voice did not sound like my own. It was barely audible and was gruff like that of a heavy smoker. "I need water," I tried again. My voice was a little louder this time, but just as foreign. The lady, Dr. Banfield, brought a red cup with a straw to my lips, and I drank greedily as half the cool water trickled down the side of my face and behind my neck. My throat ached as it flowed down my esophagus, but I could not stop. It was like biting the first chocolate chip cookie from Grandma's oven while they were still warm, like tasting a little piece of heaven. I wanted more, but I was coughing, and the doctor had removed the straw from my mouth and was wiping my face.

"Easy, Helena," she scolded softly. "You have a long road ahead of you, but we will get you there. I promise."

"How did . . . ?" I tried to ask, but my voice was still not ready.

"You get here?" she finished for me. "You fought your way to Mr. Jonas's farm, and he brought you here. Just in the nick of time, too. You are a fighter, Helena. Your body tells me you have endured unimaginable trauma and suffered a tremendous amount of pain, yet you are still here. It will be a long road, and not an easy one, at that, but you are safe with us now, and we will get you there."

"Who are . . . ?" I tried to ask another question as my eyes focused on the people waiting and watching my every move. They were perched on the edge of their seats, eagerly awaiting even the tiniest morsel of information, and for a moment my mind pictured a string of crows sitting on a fence, and I felt like a piece of meat that had been tossed out as bait.

"These people are here to help you. They want to protect you and find whoever is responsible for your pain. This young lady," she said, and pointed to a girl who looked to be no more than a teenager, "is Jessie. She is one of the nurses keeping an eye on you and making sure you are comfortable."

The girl looked my way but was unable to make eye contact. I decided I did not like her, even though I knew it must have been difficult for a young girl to witness the horrors humans can do to another. I had not, nor would I ever, forget my wounds and scars. They were evidence of the torture I endured, but they were also the proof I am a survivor. I looked toward the other people on the far side of the small room, and Dr. Banfield continued with her introductions.

"These two are from the Major Crimes Unit." She motioned toward the pair sitting farthest away from my hospital bed. "They are waiting to speak to you about what happened and who is responsible for putting you here. But only when you are ready, of course." She said that with the hint of a warning to the two police officers, and once again I admired how she controlled the people in this room.

"I am Sergeant David Campbell," the male officer introduced himself, "and this is Officer Cynthia Blouin. We know you have been through a lot, but we would like to ask you some questions about how you ended up here and who did this to you."

"When she is ready, Sergeant," Dr. Banfield interrupted firmly, and the officer nodded in compliance, afraid his conversation with me would end before it even got started. I was grateful for the reprieve. I did not know where to start with my story or if I ever wanted to.

"This lady here is Dr. Carpenter," Dr. Banfield continued. "She is a psychiatrist and is here to help you process what has happened to you. Talk to her, Helena. She can offer you more than any of us can at the moment. Your wounds will heal, I can make sure of that, but the mental scars from this trauma will take time, patience, and a lot of hard work. Dr. Carpenter is the one to help you down this road toward healing your soul. Listen to her and take her advice."

I looked toward Dr. Carpenter. I thought she was in her late forties or early fifties, judging by the wrinkles around her eyes and the grey roots peeking through her purple and blue hair. She was a beautiful woman, tall and slim, and I believed all eyes in the room would be on her had it not been for me, the main event at this circus. She looked me in the eye and smiled, and I felt it was genuine and not coming from a place of pity.

"Hello, Helena," she spoke, and her voice was deep and raspy, nothing at all like I expected. "I am here for you whenever you are ready to talk about what happened. You have gone through a great ordeal, and I can help you process that when you are ready."

"Helena, the gentleman outside your door is Constable Jenkins." Inspector Blouin looked at me as she spoke. "He is here to protect you. He and others who will take his place have been assigned to guard you until we know it is safe. You can rest knowing you are being protected."

I wanted to close my eyes and pretend they were not here. I did not want to talk to these people. I did not want to tell them how I allowed myself to be taken to a dark, dingy basement where I was beaten, raped, and tortured for weeks. I did not want to feel their pity or hear their false sentiments. They could not possibly understand what I went through, nor could they make my experiences go away. I survived, but I was not sure I could live. I was broken physically and mentally, and for the first time since my mother killed herself, I could understand how she must have felt when she swallowed those pills with a bottle of vodka to end her pain.

There was a commotion in the corridor, and the police were quick to their feet to see what was going on.

"Let me go! You can't keep me from seeing her!" a voice yelled from down the hall. I knew she was there for me. I knew that voice well. "They said she is awake! Let me see her!" She was getting frustrated and angry. I did not know what to do. Did I want to see her? Did I want her to see me like this?

"Allie." I said her name, but my voice was still strained and I could not form the rest of the sentence I wanted to speak. "Don't . . ."

"Helena, do you know this person who is trying to see you?" Dr. Banfield asked, and I nodded my head because it hurt my throat to speak. "Do you wish to see her? We haven't been able to identify any family members to be here with you. Is she someone you'd like to have by your side to help get you through this?"

"No, no." I forced the words from my mouth.

At the same time, the distress in my voice and on my face confirmed to Dr. Banfield that the person in the corridor was not someone I needed or wished to see, and just like that, it was taken care of and I heard her order Allie removed from the building. I was relieved, I think. What if she could not handle seeing me battered and bruised? What if I could not handle seeing the pity on her face when she did?

What if she left?

What if she stayed?

20

I find myself sitting on the beach staring out over the lake and trying to make sense of what I have just learned. Allie and Melody were close. Allie had taken her in when she had nowhere to go. It was both heartwarming and crazy. Allie had grown up poor, and for her to reach out to a young girl going through a similar situation, even though she struggled herself, was nothing short of admirable. She had been a wonderful and understanding friend to me until our relationship had grown too complicated. I needed a fresh start, and Allie could not accept that. I ended the friendship, and unfortunately, she did not take it well. Things grew weird between us and lasted for a while, until our last encounter, when she stormed away and I never looked back.

I have so many questions about her relationship with Melody. Were they friends? Were they confidantes like we were? Was Allie more of a mother figure than a friend? How long had Melody lived with Allie? I am getting nowhere sitting on the beach, and there is only one person I can think of who can answer all my questions. Am I ready to go back to my childhood home? The thought of it makes my heart sink and my stomach churn. It has been nearly ten years, but I am still not sure I am ready to face those memories, especially now. After all this time, I still cannot imagine Allie living in my house with all of our things, eating at our table and sleeping in our beds. It's unsettling.

My phone rings, interrupting my thoughts. I know it is David. I answer quickly, eager to find out what he has learned and to share my little bit of news as well.

"Hi, are you ready to be picked up?" I ask.

"Yes. Come on by. I'll be waiting out front."

"Have you learned anything?" I ask anxiously.

"Pick me up and we'll talk," he replies, and ends the call.

I brush the sand from my pants and head back to the car. By the tone of his voice, I know he has something to share, yet I am afraid to hope that we are finally heading down the right path to finding my abuser before he hurts someone else. I am used to days and months of nothing, when we have exhausted all of our leads and have no new clues to investigate. Everything we have tracked down over the last eight years has led to more dead ends than I care to remember. Yet this time feels different. This time we have Melody, and as much as it pains me to say, she may be the missing piece that finally brings closure to this nightmare. My nightmare. Is it possible the constant waiting and wondering can finally be over, that Lily and I can move on and live a normal life? I am afraid to hope.

I pick David up and we drive in silence to Joe Butt's Lookout. I decide that is as good a place as any for us to talk. We sit at a picnic table overlooking the lake. The sun is high and the weather unseasonably warm. There are a few stragglers on the beach trying to catch the last of the summer heat before fall settles in and the weather turns cool.

"This is where you grew up?" he asks, even though he knows the answer. "It is not like I thought it would be from what you've said."

"I think my perceptions of Deer Lake have been tarnished by everything that has happened here. I've been so angry with every-one, with the world, really, that I forgot how beautiful and tranquil it really is here. Someday, you might be able to see it in December, after a freshly fallen snow. It is breathtaking, like a picture-perfect Christmas card. But when all your experiences suddenly centre around sadness and anger, your perceptions change and your view becomes warped somehow. I forgot how beautiful Deer Lake can truly be. It's hard coming back here, but I am able to see the beauty again now. Yet pain and sadness will always be here with the memories of my parents," I reply, and my voice sounds far away while my mind is somewhere else. "So, enough about that. What have you learned? Are we headed in the right direction this time?"

David waits before he speaks, pondering just how much he is willing to tell me. I am impatient and in no mood to argue.

"David, you let me come here to help you. This has to work both ways or this partnership is pointless. You know what this means to me. I need for this to be over. So, what's it going to be? Am I doing this on my own or are we doing it together?"

I am demanding, and I know it, but I don't care. I am in no mood for bullshit.

He sighs. "Okay, I hear you."

"I don't want to have to fight with you every time you run off somewhere and have a private meeting and discover something new. It's a stupid waste of time."

"Okay, okay!" he says, and raises his hands in surrender, "I spoke with Sergeant Mackenzie at the detachment. He says that Melody left town to attend school, like I told you earlier. She was in the foster system, bit of a troublemaker for a while, but seemed to be turning her life around. Her father is in Millhaven Institution in Bath, Ontario, for the brutal murders of his wife, Melody's mother, and her lover. It happened in Trout River, which is—"

"About forty-five minutes up the peninsula from Deer Lake," I interrupt. "I've been there. How long ago?"

"It happened in July of 2013, which is about three years after you left, right?"

"July of 2013," I repeat. "I was in his basement then. I wouldn't have heard anything about it, even though I'm sure it was all over the news."

"That's right," he says, and looks away. "Melody was twelve when it happened. She was at a friend's house. The friend didn't know anything had happened until the next morning when the police showed up at her door with a social worker.

"Poor kid had her world turned upside down overnight. I know how that feels."

"She was in and out of foster homes for a few years and fell in with the wrong crowd. She was picked up a couple of times for drinking underage, got caught shoplifting several times, and the last time, she was arrested for beating another girl so badly she broke her arm. The judge threatened to send her to the detention centre in Whitbourne, but someone intervened on her behalf. A woman by the name of—"

"Allie Lockwood," I finish for him.

"How do you know that?" he asks, surprised.

"Allie and I became friends when my father got sick. She helped me through those months while Mom and I watched and waited for him to die, and she was there for all the years afterward, when my life was consumed with caring for my mother and trying to keep our heads above water. Allie didn't have it great growing up, either. Her father died in a car accident before she moved to Deer Lake. Her mother couldn't handle keeping the family afloat on her own, so they relied on social services for everything.

"Things changed for us after my mother's suicide and our friendship became something I couldn't maintain, so I ended my contact with her. Things happened between us that changed our relationship forever, and eventually we lost track of each other. That was until I escaped. Allie came back into my life to try and help me recover, but I refused to let her back in. That part of my life wasn't something I could share with her, or anyone, for that matter.

"I had just survived an unspeakable trauma, and then to find out I was pregnant with his child. It was too much. I didn't want to explain to Allie how I had ended up in this situation, and I didn't want to justify my decision to keep Lily. I couldn't even understand that myself. But that was a long time ago," I say, done with the explanation. "How did Allie even get custody of Melody? She was only just in her twenties herself, and they were on social services already."

"Well, according to Mackenzie, Allie is a bit of a success story in town. Girl had nothing growing up, as you know, but she managed to teach herself some computer skills, learned to type, and then somehow convinced the town manager to hire her to work in the office. She has been there ever since, he says, and everyone loves her. She volunteers with the church and is the first to jump in when something needs organizing.

"He said she turned up in court the day the judge was set to ship Melody off to Whitbourne. She had heard about Melody through the grapevine and thought she could help. She made a case as to why she would be a good fit as a guardian, and she was backed up by another older lady, a Mrs. Hilda Roberts. You know her?"

I nodded, and he continued.

"Well, she came to support Allie, and it was a done deal. Melody moved in with Allie three days later."

"It would be nice to speak to Melody's caseworker and get her thoughts on Melody and Allie's relationship. I saw Mrs. Roberts today, and she said they had a rough time of it for a while, but Melody had turned things around before she went off to college.

"I know Mrs. Roberts from years ago when I was helping her with Sunday school classes. It was the year my father got sick and the same year Allie and I became friends. I can't picture the Allie I knew volunteering with the church alongside Mrs. Roberts, but I guess things change when you have been gone as long as I have."

"Was it just Allie and her mom?"

"Yes, I think so. I seem to remember her mentioning a brother once, but he didn't live with them. She didn't talk about him and I didn't see him, ever, so I assumed he lived out of town and was probably older than we were."

"What about Allie? Did she ever marry? Any men in her life that you know of?"

"Like I told you, David, Allie and I have not spoken in almost eight years. A lot can change in that amount of time. I can't tell you anything about her other than she was a good friend for a lot of years until things changed between us. It was weird for a while, and I was starting to get a little scared of what she might do, but then I didn't hear from her anymore. There were no more unsettling incidents, and that was the way I wanted it.

"I didn't reach out to her in all that time. I have not seen or heard from her since our last encounter in the hospital, when I sent her away, and even though she persisted, I didn't agree to see her. Eventually she left and didn't come back."

"Do you think you're up for a visit with your old friend? I can go see her on my own, if you'd rather, but she might feel more comfortable talking if you were there with me," he suggests. I can tell by the tone of his voice that he understands how hard this is for me.

"I don't really have a choice. For whatever reason, fate has decided that Allie and I will have to share another tragedy. Melody and I are connected. How, I don't know, but I have to find out. If that means seeing Allie again, then so be it."

"Okay, I have her address here. Sergeant Mackenzie told me how to find her."

He tries to hand me a piece of paper with her address on it.

"That's okay," I sigh, "I know where Allie lives. She moved into my old house after I put it up for sale. I wonder if the place is still the same as it was when I lived there."

David looks at me, puzzled. "Are you serious? Your best friend moved into your family home after you sold it?"

"Oh, yes," I reply. "I sold it fully furnished, and the housing corporation bought if for a low-income family. Turns out Allie's was that family, and she informed me shortly after they moved in that my room was still the same if I ever wanted to visit. I couldn't believe what I was hearing when she told me."

"You are serious. I don't know what to say. It's just strange, don't you think?"

He is shocked by what I have just said to him.

"It feels like something out of a movie, I know, but I don't think Allie ever meant it like that. I believe, I hope, that she wanted what I had because she felt I had more than her, or because she wanted to feel close to me even though I had left."

Whatever her reason, saying it out loud to David and hearing my own words makes me feel a little uneasy. Maybe her actions weren't as innocent as I had wanted to believe. Yet it has been years since we have had contact. What if seeing her again stirs up all these old feelings of resentment or jealousy, whatever they were? What if walking into her home—my home—brings back all the anger and uncertainty I feel toward her?

What if going home is the worst idea possible?

What if going home uncovers the answers I need?

21

On the two-year anniversary of my mother's suicide, I tried not to remember, but the date was embedded in my brain. It was the day I became an orphan. When my father died, I thought my life had changed forever, and it had, yet I was able to adjust to the new normal of caring for Mom and trying to keep both of us from sinking into unrelenting despair and darkness. The day-to-day became a constant struggle to tend to her needs while trying to attend high school, put meals on the table, and keep our home reasonably clean. But however hard it was, it was a routine. It was my life. There was a purpose of sorts, a reason to keep going.

When I left for college, I was excited for this new chapter, for a new beginning. I wasn't saying goodbye to everyone and everything I was leaving behind. Rather, my world was expanding and I was reaching for a future I didn't think was possible. I was happy. My mother was getting better. I had a best friend who cared about me and my mother. I was excited to share my new experiences with both of them. Until it all came crashing down. Two years ago, my mother killed herself, and life as I knew it came to an end.

It was hard to keep going, to continue down this path we call living, when you have no one to share it with. I couldn't call my mom when I had a bad day. I couldn't tell her about the new boy who introduced himself to me in class. I would never hear words of encouragement or praise from the only person I had left who really mattered. I was alone in this world. An orphan. And two years later, I was still lost. I went to school. I hung out with school friends. I dated, sometimes. I was going through the motions of life, yet I was not living. I was stuck in the past with my terminally ill father and my mentally unstable mother. I couldn't move past the loss and the feelings of abandonment. I thought I was in my own personal purgatory.

I had Allie, but our relationship changed, or I had. I guess you could argue that I chose to be alone, because she would have stood by me after Mom's death. We could have grieved together. But I couldn't stay in Deer Lake, and she couldn't leave. I had the opportunity for a fresh start, away from the heartache and pain of my teen years, and I took it. Allie was a huge part of that period in my life. She experienced all the emotional ups and downs right alongside me. She held my hand, gave me a shoulder to cry on, and dried my tears. She was an outlet for my anger and the prop that kept me from falling. And now she was a constant reminder of all I was trying to forget.

I had not heard from her in many months, not since I moved into the little house and came home to find she had somehow let herself inside. I knew she had not forgotten today. She walked into my mother's house two years before, like she had every day since I'd left for school. Mom was lying in her bed, dressed in her favourite blue sweater. Her hair was done neatly in a long braid and her makeup applied to perfection. There was an empty bottle of sleeping pills on the floor beside her and a half-bottle of vodka on the nightstand. There was a piece of paper on her dresser, beside a portrait of my father and me taken after a volleyball game, and on it were two little worthless words, "I'm sorry." That was it. No explanation as to why she did what she did.

She didn't tell me she loved me or that she was proud of me. She said nothing but those two little meaningless words. How could she be sorry? If she were sorry, if she loved me at all, she would have fought harder. I knew that I should not feel this way, that I was wrong, but I couldn't help the way I felt. I hoped someday I could move past these feelings and accept that my mother killed herself because she had lost all hope and could not bear to fight any longer. But I was not there yet.

I didn't visit my mother's grave on the anniversary, or any other day, for that matter. Both my parents were buried in the graveyard next to our church in Deer Lake, but I had not been back since her funeral, and I had no intentions of ever going. But I remembered her on this day, the anniversary of her suicide. I remembered her with anger for leaving me here on this earth all alone. I remembered her with resentment for altering my teenaged years in ways that had changed me as a person. And as hard as it sometimes was, I remembered her with love. I remembered bedtime stories, days at the park and summer evenings on the beach, and I remembered staying up late to watch *Gone with the Wind,* her favourite movie, when it aired on CBC on New Year's Eve when I was twelve. Even though the bad times overshadowed most of my life, if I tried hard enough, I could sometimes feel the love I knew she felt for me. On the two-year anniversary, I tried really hard to remind myself of that.

I laced up my running shoes as I did most evenings after I was finished with school. Running was my reprieve from life. I was not sure where I would be without it. I started off slow, then picked up the pace. With each hard step on the pavement, I felt the stress of my emotions evaporating into the air. I needed the escape, especially that night. I took a left turn and started up the steep incline toward the beach. My chest was pounding, and with each breath, I could feel the anger subside.

I reached the beach trail twenty minutes later and slowed my pace in order to take in the scenes and smells of the ocean. I thought my mother would have loved the ocean and the way it changed colour with the mood of the sky, and the way it called to you with the soft swishing of its waves over the beach.

The ocean is an enigma. It is calming, yet powerful. It is both relaxing and mysterious. It gets inside your head and makes you forget the things that are bothering you. It is mesmerizing yet so unpredictable. I could spend hours looking out over the ocean. I had been drawn in by its allure often, and I had been lost in its infinity. That night, I hoped to gaze upon the ocean and forget.

I had been sitting on the same rock and staring at the blue-green water for over an hour. I had not forgotten the reason I was there that night, but the anger and resentment had disappeared, and I could remember the mother she had been before she became sick. It was getting dark and the sky was turning a fiery orange as the sun set below the horizon. It was time for me to head home. I called the little house I purchased a little over a year ago home, but after all that time, it remained just a roof over my head. It was not, nor did I think it would ever be, my home.

I unlocked the door, and the moment I entered I could feel something was not right. It was cold there. There was a draft coming from the bedroom, and I knew I hadn't left the window open. I was afraid to drop my key chain in the bowl by the front door and instead curled them in my palm with the keys poking through my fingers. It was not much of a weapon, but it was the only thing I had. I turned the lights on in each room as I went, but nothing seemed to be out of place. The kitchen was as I left it, with a single glass sitting near the sink and a tea towel hanging from the handle on the stove. The living room had a blanket bundled in the chair and textbooks littered the floor, but that was my mess, and everything was as it should be.

I looked down the short hallway to my bedroom, and I could see the navy blue curtains swaying with the breeze blowing in through the open window. Should I call 911? Should I run out the front door and seek safety with a neighbour? I should probably do both of these things, but instead, I turned and tiptoed down the hall to my bedroom, keys clenched tightly in my hand. I didn't know what I was expecting to find when I got there. I didn't know if an intruder was waiting there to attack me, or if my room had been ransacked by some pervert and my underwear was now littered all over the floor. Perhaps it was a burglar searching for money and trinkets to pawn. Whatever I imagined was waiting for me, it was not nearly as unsettling as what I found.

There was only one person in this whole world who could have been there and would have known to do this. I couldn't imagine why she was angry enough with me to do something so hurtful. I didn't understand what had motivated her to leave a bottle of sleeping pills and a flask of vodka on my nightstand. I didn't need those props to remind me of this unforgettable anniversary. That day was ingrained in my brain forever. I wanted to call her and tell her exactly how I felt. I wanted her to know how much leaving that there had hurt me, and how upset she had made me, but I thought the only purpose it would serve would be to give her the response she was aiming for.

I grabbed the pills and the booze and tossed them in the trash. I closed the window and checked the lock twice. It was not broken, so I assumed she had opened the window from the inside just to scare me. The front door was locked when I returned home, and I distinctly remembered checking to make sure it was secure before I left. I didn't know how she had entered my house for the second time. It was as if she were a ghost swooping in from beneath the door or passing through walls, but this was not a movie and she was not dead. The realization hit me when I finally released the keys from my hand and tossed them in the bowl. My parents were both dead. I had no siblings or other relatives who knew me well. She was the only person in this world who knew me and all my secrets.

My mind flashed back to a day years before, when I arrived home from school one day to find the front door was locked. Mom had been confused that morning when I left for school. While I was in class, she had for some unknown reason locked the front door, and when I got home, I couldn't get in. My father had always kept a spare key under the doormat in case of emergencies. I lifted the mat that day while Allie stood by and waited. And she had not forgotten.

I ran to the front door and out onto the step. I paused, afraid to lift the mat and find the key missing. It was there, right where I had left it, but beside it was a crumpled piece of paper left behind for me to find. I grabbed it and the key and went back inside, angry with myself for keeping a spare in such an obvious place, and with her for taking advantage of my trust. I stood at the kitchen counter and read the note, too angry and upset to sit. I was almost certain it was her handwriting, as I recalled similar loopy letters on the covers of her binders during high school. This note had the same unsettling message as the last note she had left me nearly a year ago.

> *Time keeps moving,*
> *People and places change.*
> *Our paths have splintered,*
> *But some remain the same.*
> *There is no escape,*
> *For two souls joined as one.*
> *You may have forgotten,*
> *But I never will.*
> *We are bound forever,*
> *You in me and I in you.*
> *You cannot hide forever,*
> *And time is running out.*

My hands trembled as I read the note for the second time. I dropped the paper on the kitchen counter; I didn't want to hold it any longer. I was angry with her for trying to scare me, and I was angry with myself for allowing her to succeed. What was she think-ing when she wrote these words? The message was ominous, and I couldn't understand her motivation for writing it, with the inten-tion of eliciting fear. What was her goal? Or even more poignant, what was her end game? And why was I the subject of her anger? What if she wasn't just trying to scare me? What if she meant to do more?

What if this was just the beginning?

22

I had been in the hospital for a week. It was another week of my life lost to that monster. My arm was broken and required surgery to repair it, and now I had a steel pin holding my bones together. Although I was not sure what was keeping the rest of me from falling apart. They told me I was malnourished and severely dehydrated when I was admitted. I had too many bruises and contusions to count, and my body now bore the evidence with white gauze and heavy bandages. An IV had been inserted into my left arm, and antibiotics slowly seeped into my vein and did battle with numerous infections. My doctor, Dr. Banfield, told me I could go home in a few days or at most a week. Home. I didn't remember what "home" was anymore. I knew I had a house waiting for me, but it was cold and empty. No one waited there for my return. I wasn't sure I could stay there alone—yet I wasn't sure I could stand to be in another's company.

Dr. Carpenter came by to see me every day. She told me things would get easier, but I didn't believe her. Our relationship was very contentious on my part, and our conversations were rather one-sided. She talked, while I pretended to listen. When I thought she was full of shit, I ignored her. I had turned my back to her more than once. I had even been so childish as to stick my fingers in both my ears—yet she didn't leave until our hour together was up. She was very determined. I would give her that. She said I should talk about what happened, but she didn't understand that I wasn't yet able to put into words the unspeakable trauma I had endured for three months, two weeks, and five days.

I was still trying to process that fact. I couldn't explain how it felt to wake up in a hospital and realize that you have had nearly four months of your life stolen. I knew I had experienced so many unspeakable horrors, but for now, they were tucked tightly away in a box in the far recesses of my mind. I wasn't sure I would ever be able to lift the lid off of that box and confront what was inside. Dr. Carpenter told me I couldn't move forward if I didn't look back, but I was afraid that if I looked back, I would get lost in the nightmare. I was afraid I would become weak like my mother and allow my pain to consume me. If I looked back, if I stayed there too long, I was afraid I would end up in bed with a bottle of pills and a flask of vodka. And the monster would win.

"Hello, Helena. How are you feeling today?"

It was Dr. Carpenter. I had been expecting her. I looked at her with her funky hair and gravelly voice, and I wondered how she had come to be a shrink. I wondered what had motivated her to want to reach inside my mind and unravel the thoughts and memories that had turned me into a damaged puzzle. Was it the lure of the unknown that motivated her? Was it the triumph of rebuilding my psyche and putting the puzzle back together that attracted her to me? Perhaps she enjoyed hearing about tragic events and unbearable pain, both physical and emotional. I had not shared anything with her. We barely conversed. She spoke, I listened. That was the extent of our relationship. In a couple of days, maybe a week, I would go home and wouldn't have to watch her pushing the purple and blue hair from her eyes again.

"We only have a couple of more opportunities to talk before you are discharged. Do you have a plan for when you go home?" she asked.

"I don't make plans," I replied. "Plans change. People change. That's life. Nothing stays the same."

"That is true. Plans, people, lives, they change all the time, but there are things we can do to control the amount of change that occurs and how we deal with it. Sometimes change is good, but oftentimes, like now, change is forced upon us and we have no choice but to adapt. If you let me, I can help you process all the change you have been forced to endure. There are ways you can deal with these changes that will enable you to move past what has happened and live a happy and fulfilled life," she continued.

It was the same jargon she had been preaching every day for the past week. She may have used different words or different analogies and comparisons, but her intentions remained the same. She wanted me to tell my story, and she was hoping that I would tell it to her. I had been in the hospital for weeks, but I had yet to tell it to anyone. I was not sure I could.

"Don't you get tired of spewing the same crap every day?" I asked, and my tone was unwarranted.

"No, actually, I don't. I'll tell you the same thing tomorrow, and the day after, if you will allow me. I will keep repeating these words to you until you believe what I am saying is true." She looked straight at me. "I only want to help you, Helena, if you would only let me."

"Why?" I asked harshly. "Why do you want me to talk to you? Do you want to hear all about how he pushed his dirty penis into me more times than I can count?" I screamed. "Do you want to know that when he couldn't get it up, he would become so angry he would use his fist instead? You want me to describe how he was so crazed that he didn't care how much I screamed in pain, because the more I cried, the more turned on he got, and could finally hold his erection long enough to force his thing in my mouth?"

I was angry at her, and I knew she didn't deserve it, but I couldn't stop.

"Do you really want to know what happened to me? Do you want to hear how I am carrying his spawn inside of me, and how I am afraid it is going to poison me from the inside out? Do you think you can handle hearing my story? I am not sure I can handle saying it out loud."

"Helena, you have experienced such unspeakable horrors. No human being should ever have to endure such pain and torture, but it happened. You experienced it. You endured it. Helena, you survived it. You are here. You are alive, and physically you are getting well. It is how you deal with the mental trauma that will determine how you move forward.

"I know how hard it is to trust someone after what you have gone through, but you can trust me. Everything you say to me stays within these four walls. I will not judge you, I promise," she said, hopeful she had finally made some headway. "Have you decided how you will deal with the pregnancy?"

"I don't think I can go home in a couple of days," I said to her as I looked toward the window and the grey skies outside. I was avoiding her question and she knew it, but I wasn't ready to talk about the baby, and I was unable to make eye contact.

"Can you tell me why you feel that way? Dr. Banfield has informed me that you will soon be ready to be discharged."

"Do you know I can't remember the last time I slept through the night without the help of the pills the nurses give me? Without them I wake screaming and terrified I am back in that basement. I am afraid that when I get home I will take a bottle of sleeping pills and down them with a bottle of vodka, just like my mother did."

"Is that something you think of often? Killing yourself?"

"No, it isn't. I am here because I fought like hell to get here, but now that I am, I don't know how to go back to my life before it happened. I feel like my life, such as it was, has ended and I am living in some reality in which I don't belong. If that makes any sense."

"It makes perfect sense. Your experience has changed you in

so many ways. You do not feel like the same person you once were, and really you are not the same, but that doesn't mean this new version of you can't somehow find a way to fit into the same world as the old Helena. You are still the same person. You just have to find a way to reconcile the old you with the new."

"How in the hell am I supposed to do that?" I asked, and the disbelief in my voice was cutting.

"We can do it together, Helena. If you let me," she replied, and I was beginning to like her in spite of myself.

"How are we supposed to do that when they are sending me home in a few days?"

"Maybe there is a way for you to stay here for a little while longer, but you will have to agree and commit to the healing process."

"What do you have in mind?" I asked, skeptical of what she was about to suggest.

"I can admit you upstairs on the fifth floor for further treatment. We can spend more time together there, and I can help. There is just one catch."

"What's that?" I asked with even more skepticism.

"The fifth floor is the psych ward. If you let me transfer you upstairs, you are consenting to thirty days of in-hospital treatment. You cannot change your mind, which means you cannot leave until the thirty-day period has ended."

I looked her in the eye, but I didn't reply. I didn't know what to say. Could I stay there for another thirty days? If I didn't, could I go home? I had no idea how to make this decision. I had too many decisions to make, and this was only adding to my stress. I wished I were back in Grandma's kitchen, where everything was simple and carefree. Life was easy then, before everything got complicated and my life went to hell.

"Take some time to think about it, Helena. I'll see you tomorrow, after Dr. Banfield checks in on you. We can talk some more then."

I nodded in agreement, and she rose and turned to leave the room. She stopped before she opened the door.

"Helena, is there anyone who can help you get through this? Someone who can help you make this decision?"

"I have no one. My parents are both dead. It's just me."

"I remember the day you woke up, there was a young woman causing a commotion out in the hallway and insisting she see you. Is she someone you can call on now? A relative or friend?"

"She is not my friend. At least not anymore."

"She seemed to think that you were. She was very adamant that you needed her."

"Allie is not someone I wish to have in my life. She knows the deepest and darkest secrets from my life before everything changed. She was there when I tried to make a new start, and she was there when it came crashing down. I don't want her here with me now. She is a part of my past, and whether she likes it or not, it is the way it has to be," I replied sternly.

"Do you know that she is still here at the hospital? She comes every day and sits in the waiting room, hoping you will ask for her. Are you sure she is not someone you can lean on now when you can use all the support you can get?"

"I am sure. Allie is not someone I want or need in my life. It's complicated. She and I have been through a lot together. Not all of it has been good. Actually, I think there has been more pain throughout our relationship than anything else. I'm sorry, Doctor, but Allie is a conversation for another day. Just know that she is not the person she pretends to be, and having her around would only cause me more stress."

"Okay, I'll trust your judgment. But Helena, if there is anyone you can reach out to, right now would be the time to do it. It is going to be harder to go down this road alone," she said, and walked out of the room.

Do I stay? Do I remain for another thirty days? Thirty days

would mean I had lost five months of my life to him. Did I even have the courage to leave? I wasn't sure if life beyond these walls was even possible. I thought about what Dr. Carpenter had said about reaching out to someone, but there was no one in my life I could trust to help piece me back together. I was completely alone, except for the baby growing in my belly, and I had not yet decided if he or she was the spawn of Satan or a seed of hope.

Then there was Allie. Could I trust her? What would happen if I reached out to her? Could I let her back into my life after everything that had been said and done? Could I trust her with my secrets? After everything I'd been through, I couldn't allow myself to be sucked back into our old routine of sadness and misery. I'd had enough of that to deal with without adding more drama to my life. What if I allowed her back in only to have her pull me back down?

What if I couldn't stop myself from drowning?

What if I lost myself forever by letting her back in?

23

Somehow, I have found myself standing outside the gates of the cemetery where my parents are buried. It is a serene place, with lush green grass and tall, majestic trees. It sits on the outskirts of town, close enough to feel like a part of the community, yet far enough away to escape the noise and attention of people and traffic. I have not been here since the day my mother's body was lowered into the damp, red earth. I promised myself I would never return, but here I am, almost ten years later, frozen beside the path outside the gate. I want to go inside to find my parents and just sit with them, but so much time has passed and so many things have changed. My brain is telling me to keep going, to do what I came here to do, but for some reason my feet refuse to move.

I tell myself there is nothing to fear—they are gone, and I am only here to see two chunks of granite engraved with their names and dates. They will not know I am here, nor will they hear what I came to say, but it is so much easier to tell myself this than it is to actually believe it. I think I feel guilty that it has taken so long for me to return, and truthfully, I have not come here solely to see them. I am not sure I would be standing outside these gates had it not been for the horrible circumstances that have brought me back to Deer Lake. I take a deep breath and push myself to open the gate and walk inside.

The grounds are well cared for, and colourful flowers and other remembrances litter the headstones and gravesites. I know where my parents are located. It is a place I won't forget, a place I had visited often, but not after my mother died. Their plots are situated in the far right corner of the cemetery, close to the huge stand of birch trees. I notice the number of graves beyond their headstones has grown considerably since I was last here. A lot can change in ten years.

I am surprised to see that someone has taken the time to maintain the graves in the years I had purposely neglected them. I expected to find that weathered grass and weeds had overtaken the plots, but the grass is neatly trimmed, and fresh flowers lay on the ground beside them. A lantern has been placed between them with a solar lamp to brighten the area at night. A verse is written across the side, "Forever in My Heart," and I am puzzled as to how and why it is here. I am an only child. Both my parents have no other family who would have reason to place something such as this on their graves. It gives me an uneasy feeling, like I should not be here after all.

"Hello," says a soft, feminine voice from behind me.

I start and turn to see who has spoken, not recognizing the voice. "Hello," I reply. "Can I help you?"

"Oh my, it is you, Helena!" she says, and I am still unsure of her identity. "You don't remember me, do you?"

"I'm sorry, no. Should I?"

She is of medium height and build, and her dark grey hair rests on her shoulders. She is older than I am, and the wrinkles around her eyes and forehead tell me she's on the downward side of middle age. Her smile is friendly, and I feel like I should know her, but I have no recollection of her from my past.

"My name is Susanna. I was a friend of—"

"My mom," I finish for her. "I kind of remember you. Your hair was long and red back when you guys used to get together, if I remember correctly."

"Yes, that's me! Time has turned my red locks to grey now, and I have no desire to fight my age with hair dye," she says nonchalantly.

"My, you look so much like your mother. You are the last person I expected to see here today. What brings you back after all this time?"

"I have some things to take care of here in town. Is this your doing?" I ask, pointing to the flowers and lantern on my parents' graves.

"No, this isn't me. This is your friend's doing. I believe she comes by at least once a week," she replies, and my heart skips a beat, knowing which friend to whom she is referring.

"My friend?" I ask coyly. "Who do you mean?"

"Well, Allie, of course! You two were joined at the hip ever since your father got sick. Who else did you think I was speaking of? You are still friends, are you not?" she asks, a little confused.

"I thought you were referring to Allie," I reply, "but I'm just not sure why she would do this. We haven't spoken in many years."

"You mean she hasn't been tending to your parents' graves at your request? I always assumed that was the reason she cared for them the way that she has," she says, even more confused.

"She may think she is doing me a favour," I say, not wanting her to sense my unease. I have yet to see Allie, and I don't want to do so after possibly starting a bunch of rumours around town.

"So, you haven't kept in touch through the years?" she asks, and I sense she wants to say or ask me something more.

"Allie and I lost touch many years ago," I answer. "Do you come here often?" I ask, wanting to change the subject.

"I come here once a week to visit my mother. My father lives in a long-term care facility. He has dementia and can't come here himself. He used to bring Mom flowers every week, so now I bring them for him. I stop by your mother's grave while I'm here. Some people find a graveyard to be creepy or unnerving, but I find it peaceful here. I like to come here and sit with my mother, sometimes with yours, and just chat about whatever—the weather, my kids, anything at all, really."

"I thought you two lost touch after she got sick."

"Yes, we did. It was a very difficult time for her, I know. It was easier for me and the rest of our group of friends to keep away rather than stay and help her fight. She made it very difficult—you of all people know that—but we, or I, shouldn't have given up on her. You won't ever know how much I regret that, but I was hoping to have the chance to make it up to her."

"How were you planning on doing that?" I ask.

"I'm not sure, but when your mother reached out to me, about a month before she died, I was so happy. Happy to have my friend back and have the chance to redeem myself. I wouldn't have thought that four weeks later it would end."

"She would kill herself," I say sadly, knowing exactly how she felt.

"It was a complete shock to me, as I'm sure it was to you. She told me that you two were talking often. She felt badly for all you missed out on, and all the sacrifices you made for her while she was sick. She wanted nothing more than to make it up to you."

"I don't understand how she could say that and then swallow all those pills. It doesn't make any sense to me."

"I know. It's hard to understand. It just felt like she was doing so well, like she was finally getting back to her old self."

"I guess she fooled us all," I say, my mind wandering back to the past with all its anger and hurt.

"Maybe, but . . . never mind. It was nice running into you today, Helena. I hope to see you here again sometime," she says, and turns to go.

"What were you going to say?" I ask Susanna.

I have an uneasy feeling that she is leaving something out, something important. She is a virtual stranger to me, yet at this moment, I need to hear what she has to say.

"Oh, I shouldn't have said anything. It's not right for me to put things in your head over something that happened so long ago," she says, trying to deflect.

"If you have questions about my mother, I'd like to know. Please," I say, "I have questions, too. She never did tell me why she did what she did. If you have the answer to that, I need to know."

"Helena, honey, I can't answer that for you. All I know is that your mother was doing so well. She was excited about the future and making things right with you. Allie was there with her all the time. Maybe she can tell you what you want to know."

"I'm not sure I can ask Allie that question or trust the answer she might give me."

I regret it the moment the words have left my tongue. I have said too much, and I can see by the look on Susanna's face that I have piqued her interest.

"How much do you know about your mom's relationship with Allie?" she asks, and I feel a change in her tone and her demeanour.

"Not much, really. I asked Allie to look in on Mom while I was away at college and to help her out. Mom didn't say much about her when we spoke, so I assumed the relationship wasn't that important. Yet to hear Allie tell it, they grew very close while I was away. It's odd, really. Why do you ask?"

"I'm not sure I should be saying this, but I've always wondered about Allie's intentions when it came to her relationship with your mother. Yes, she helped her out around the house and with errands, but there was always something more going on, yet I couldn't put my finger on it. Or at least that's the impression I always felt when I visited and Allie was there, which seemed to be most of the time. I almost asked your mother about it once, but I couldn't get up the courage. It wasn't my business, really. She had just reached out to rekindle our friendship, a friendship which I had failed miserably, and I didn't want to make her question herself or her surroundings. Maybe I should have."

"Do you think it would have made a difference had you asked? Do you think Allie's being there contributed in any way to my mother's decision to kill herself?" I ask, nervous as to where this conversation was heading.

"God forgive me for thinking this, and even more so for voicing these thoughts out loud, but don't you find it odd that your mother was doing so well and finally getting her life back, when all of a sudden she decides that it isn't worth it anymore? I just couldn't accept the image of her happy and excited with life one day and then gone by her own hand the next. It doesn't make any sense to me. I think something was going on. I just don't know what that was."

"I've always had trouble reconciling those thoughts as well. Our relationship had its struggles. It was very difficult for us after Dad died, but we were getting there. We were falling back into our old roles as mother and daughter. It was such a relief to hear her talk about rebuilding her life that I forgot she was still depressed. It felt as if I finally had my mother back, after all those years keeping things together. I don't understand how she could just take her own life like that, but how else can you explain it?"

"What if your mother didn't die by her own hand?" she asks, and she covers her mouth as soon as the words are out, as if she can catch them and put them back.

The words shock me. Not once, in all the years since it happened, did I think that Mom didn't kill herself.

"Are you asking if it's possible Mom did not take her own life? I don't understand. She took a bottle of pills and washed them down with vodka! Her note said she was sorry. What is there to dispute?"

"Helena, your mother hated vodka! She said it tasted like rubbing alcohol. I can't see her chugging it down like they said she did. She was happy. She was excited to make it up to you. And she told me she had stopped taking the sleeping pills, that she didn't need them anymore. It just doesn't make sense. The only thing that does make sense is she didn't take those pills or swallow that vodka of her own free will. There. I've said it. I've wanted to say that for nearly ten years, but I was afraid no one would listen, or they'd think I was crazy or trying to cause trouble. Now I've told you, the one person who knew your mother as well as I did. Now you tell me, do you really think she killed herself?"

"My God, Susanna. You're saying my mother didn't commit suicide. That you think she may have been murdered?"

I'm in shock. I can't believe she has come to this conclusion, but at the same time, I can't discount her reasoning.

"I can't think right now!"

"I am asking, do you think it's possible, Helena?"

"I . . . I . . . I don't know what to think," I stutter. "I haven't spoken to you since I was a young girl. I have no idea if I should believe you or pass you off as the town kook. I feel like I'm in the middle of a bad dream. Why are you even telling me this? What do you expect me to do with this theory of yours? It's been nearly ten years! Surely there is nothing to be done about it after all this time."

"I've said what I have wanted to say since the day I learned what happened. It's up to you now. You decide what to do with it. But let me ask you this. Don't you think it's odd that only a few months after Allie discovers your mother's dead body in her bed, Allie and her mother move into that same house? Your home? I'd want nothing to do with anything that reminded me of something so terrible, yet she lives with the memory every day, literally," she says, and turns and walks away toward the gate, leaving me standing there, shaking, while my thoughts swirl around me.

She doesn't look back as she heads for the parking lot, and I let her go. There is nothing more to say. All the air has been sucked out of my lungs, depriving my brain of oxygen and preventing me from forming a single logical thought. Allie was in my home because I asked her to be. She was with my mother as a favour to me. What does it say about me if the person I chose to be my best friend, and to care for my mother, is the same person who is responsible for her death? What if she is the reason my mother died that night? What if I sealed my mother's fate by asking Allie to look after her?

What if it's my fault that my mother is dead?

24

The first time it happened, I was too scared to fight back. I lay there as he rammed into me until, thankfully, it was over. He left angry, and I knew this was just the beginning. I had only gotten a taste of what was to come. Sometimes he came to the house only to have his fun. Sometimes he came to leave food and water on the floor and to throw a bucket of water into the filthy toilet. Sometimes he came because he had nowhere else to go. He was connected to me as much as I was to him—him in ways I would never understand, and me in ways I couldn't explain.

I had not showered in weeks. I stank of sweat, bodily waste, and sex. I tried to use a little of the water he brought me to clean myself, but there was so little, and it was far more valuable to me as drinking water. My hair was slick with grease and matted together in clumps. My head itched with discomfort and what I was afraid to admit might be bugs. I couldn't see them in the dark. Sometimes, I felt them crawling around my scalp, and I had swatted more than one as they crawled down my cheek.

I had cuts and scrapes that were ripe with infection. I could feel them oozing with pus and smell the stringent odour they emitted. At night I heard the rats scurrying around the room. They were waiting for me to die. I was their next meal. If I slept too soundly, they would sneak up for a nibble of rotting flesh, and I woke screaming and trembling with fear. If I didn't escape soon, I would die of sepsis and the rats would have what was left of me.

I heard him upstairs pacing back and forth. I thought he was in a mood. I was scared of his moods. When he was angry and couldn't get an erection, I paid the price for his dysfunction. The first time it happened, I was thankful for the reprieve, but what followed was far worse than the rape I escaped. He beat me so violently I thought I saw my dead father beckoning for me to follow him. I wanted to go so badly, but something held my hands tightly and I couldn't move. I realized later he had bound my hands with a piece of weathered rope with stiff fibres that pierced my flesh and left burns on my skin. He had many plans for me, but dying wasn't one of them.

When my hands were secured, he tied the end of the rope to the door handle so I couldn't move. And then he raped me with his fist. I screamed so loud I thought my eardrums would burst. The pain was excruciating as his hand tore my skin with the force of his thrusts and I felt the blood running down my legs. I tried to force them shut, to kick him away, but he was so much stronger than me. He drove his fingers into the flesh on my thigh and forced me to stop fighting or endure even more pain. I prayed I would die that night. I just wanted to be with my father, where it was warm and peaceful, but death eluded me, and I lived to experience the same trauma again and again.

He was not always angry, though. Sometimes he came just to visit. Those times I was almost glad to see him. It didn't make any sense, I knew, but I spent so much time alone. Human contact, even from him, was sometimes better than all the loneliness and time spent in my own head. Those are the times he brought me more food than normal, or an extra bottle of water. Once he gave me new underwear and a sweater that felt soft and warm. One time, he even brought a teddy bear. It was so big and fluffy and comforting, until I misspoke one night and he tore it limb from limb, then filled my mouth with the stuffing as punishment.

Sometimes I thought he felt remorse for what he did to me, but he told me he had no choice. He came to talk when he was in those moods. I had to sit and listen. I learned early on in my captivity that he was not interested in anything I had to say. I was his sounding board as well as his punching bag. My job was to sit there and act interested in everything he had to say while I kept my mouth shut and my opinions to myself. Or suffer the consequences. Sometimes I thought he was pure evil, yet there were times when I thought he was mentally unstable and not able to control what he did to me.

I was alone in the dark there. Most of the conversations I had were with myself. Sometimes I thought the solitude alone would drive me crazy. I imagined myself dying in that basement and no one would miss me. I was alone in this world, except for him. I hated him more than I ever thought possible to hate someone, yet I was scared to death he would not come back. He was my only link to the world beyond those four walls, and without him I would die. He came to hurt me, and inflicted such horrific pain upon me, I was not sure I would survive, but without him I did not have a chance. Without him I would die of thirst or starvation.

He was coming down the stairs. I heard the stairs creaking with each heavy step, and I tensed, wondering which version of the monster I would see that night. The door opened, and his large frame filled the doorway. There was a light in the hallway beyond my room, but it was still too dark for me to read his mood. I didn't ask him to let me go anymore. I didn't beg for my life. He would do whatever he was planning, and there was nothing I could say or do to stop him. I had learned this the hard way. What was meant to happen would happen. It didn't matter what I said or did. I had learned that keeping quiet and submitting to his desires would make it hurt less and end faster. I thought I was becoming numb to it and to him. I was afraid I was losing the will to fight.

"Hello, Helena," he said. I could tell by his voice that he was in a mood, but I was not sure what it meant.

"Did you bring food?" I asked. I had not eaten since last night, and the bottle of water he had left was empty.

"Sit down with me and we'll have dinner," he answered, and I obeyed. We sat on the dirty, bloodstained mattress, and he opened a paper bag that I hadn't noticed. He took out a candle and lit it, setting the room in a yellow glow, and for the first time since he locked me in there, I could see all four walls at once. He put his hand back in the bag and pulled out two wineglasses and a cheap bottle of wine, and I felt like I was about to vomit. There were sandwiches in the bag, a chunk of cheese, and slices of apple. My mouth watered at the sight, and I noticed the sandwich was made with turkey or chicken, not the usual peanut butter and jelly. He set everything out and offered me a sandwich.

"Here ya go, eat up. I know ya must be hungry," he said, as if we were on a date.

I ate the sandwich quickly, afraid he might change his mind. I couldn't take my eyes off of the chunk of cheese and couldn't resist the urge to reach in and break off a piece, but before I got the chance, he grabbed my arm. He squeezed so tightly, I winced with the pain. He could snap my bones if he wanted to. I knew it was my fault—I had overstepped.

"Did I give ya permission to have some of that?" he asked, and I knew better than to not answer.

"I'm sorry. I should not have done that."

"Don't let it happen again," he said sternly, then reached over and broke off more than half the cheese, and ate it slowly, while I was forced to watch as he laughed heartily at the tortured look on my face.

"Here, ya can have what's left."

He tossed me the remainder of the cheese. It was soft and sticky from being held in his hands while he bit away bits and pieces with his mouth. I could feel his spittle on the morsel, but I didn't care. I was still hungry, and it might be days before I saw food again. I bit into the cheese and devoured what was left in three bites, spittle and all. I washed it down with the wine he had poured, and it burned my throat as it went down. The liquid was warm in my belly, and I could feel its effects soon after. I was eyeing the apple slices that were still sitting on the plate. They were starting to turn brown from the exposure, but I couldn't take my eyes off of them. I swore I could taste the juicy sweetness without even taking a bite. He watched me as I stared at them, and he laughed knowingly.

"Ya want some, eh?" He laughed, and I nodded. "Well, what do I get in return if I decide to let ya have 'em?"

I remained silent, but my eyes didn't move from the apple slices. I had no suggestions for him. I didn't want to give him anything more than he had already taken, but the apple slices looked so good, and my mouth was watering just thinking about how good they would taste. I could almost feel the crisp flesh on my tongue, and I felt like a dog waiting for permission to eat. He watched me intently, then took a slice and rubbed it across my cracked lips. I could smell its sweetness, and I thought it must be a Pink Lady or Golden Delicious. It took every bit of willpower I had not to bite down on both the fruit and his fingers. He pulled it back and laughed loud and hard at his joke, and I wished I had the power to wipe that smile off of his ugly, pimple-lined face.

"Here," he said, "ya can have a bite," and he leaned in and held the apple to my mouth. I opened my lips and moved to take a bite, and again he pulled it away and laughed. I felt the tears welling up in my eyes, and I fought to push them back down. I didn't want to give him the satisfaction of seeing me cry. Not in a million years would I have thought that at twenty years old I'd be crying over a piece of apple like a child, but this was what he had reduced me to.

"I'm sorry," he laughed, "but ya should see ya face. Ya look like ya about to cry! Here, I won't tease ya this time."

He reached his hand toward me. I didn't want to give him the satisfaction of being tricked a third time, but I had no choice. I had learned very quickly to do whatever it was he asked of me. If that meant we had to play this game all night, then that was what we would do. Thankfully, he was done with his childish play, and he let me take the apple from him and eat. It was sweet and juicy, and I wanted to devour every slice sitting on the plate, but I had to wait for permission.

As I sat there and waited, I wondered why he had come tonight. He had not been talkative, nor had he been angry or physically cruel. He just sat there on the edge of the mattress and sipped his wine and watched my every move. I felt like a mannequin on display. I couldn't look away, and I had no way to hide from the eyes that followed me. I wanted to ask him what it was he wanted from me or why he was there, but questions were not allowed, and if I disobeyed, there would be consequences. So instead, we sat, like an old married couple pretending to enjoy each other's company, comfortable with the silence and hating each other's guts.

"What was ya life like before we met?" he asked out of the blue.

"What do you mean?" I asked, afraid my answer would not suffice.

"Were ya happy? Did ya have a lot of friends? Do ya have a boyfriend who's pining away while he waits for ya to come home?"

"I was neither happy nor sad. I was existing. I have friends, but none of them close. I have had boyfriends, but none who will notice my absence. My family will notice I am missing, and they will send people out to look for me," I lied.

"Don't lie to me. Ya family is dead!" he shouted, and I flinched as he raised his hand above me, but for some reason he did not strike.

"I am sorry," I said, wondering how he knew so much about me. "The only people who will notice my absence are my professors and maybe my classmates. I had perfect attendance before now."

"Nah, they just think ya quit and went home. No one cares about ya, Helena. You're a nobody with no family, no friends, and no life. I'm all ya have." He laughed as he said this, and it hurt because I knew it was the truth. "I decide if ya live or die. I decide if ya eat tonight or if ya starve. I decide when ya speak. Hell, I even decide what ya say when I let ya speak."

"Please." I couldn't keep the emotion from my voice. "Please just let me go home."

"Home? Ya don't have a home. This is ya home now. Ya have to stay here. It's ya own fault, Helena. Don't ya know?" He looked at me with anticipation, but I didn't have the answer.

"I don't know what you want me to say," I cried, and my voice caught.

"No one gets to leave, Helena, especially not you. No one ever gets to leave."

"I don't understand. What do you want from me? I can't do this forever."

"It's just the way it has to be, Helena. We don't have a choice. Ya have to stay, and it's my job to keep ya here," he answered, then stood and stared at me for a moment before he left the room.

I was angry and frustrated, but thankful the night had passed without him inflicting physical pain. Physically, I had escaped the night in no worse shape than I had been in before he arrived. Mentally? Emotionally? I was at my breaking point. I had the nail tucked securely in the mattress, hidden safely away from him. I resumed scraping the layers of paint away from the old windowpane. I had to get out of the basement, and it had to be soon. The window was the only way, and he had made it very clear that I had no future outside. So, I scraped and I dug with bloodied fingertips. It was the only choice I had, when the other option was to become dinner for the rats. What if I scraped and dug forever and never found a way out? What if it wasn't enough?

What if I died there, alone?

Or worse, what if I spent the rest of my life there in the basement with a monster?

25

Dr. Carpenter discharged me from the hospital a month before, and every day since, I wished I could go back. Before the basement, I was used to spending time alone. I liked the solitude my house offered from the busy university campus and the loud, boisterous students. I liked the quiet for studying and the tiny garden in the backyard as it reminded me of life before things changed for my family. Now everything was different. Now I hated the solitude, but I also didn't want the company of others. The stillness in my house at night brought me back to the dark basement where I laid awake praying for freedom. So, I slept with the lights on and the doors locked when I slept at all. I needed to put the past behind me and try to forget, but the house made it difficult to move on, and I knew with certainty I would never forget.

The first week after I returned home, the press camped outside my door day and night. After two days, I pulled the phone from the wall after hundreds of phone calls. From the small-town eager reporters begging for just the tiniest tidbit of information, to the big-time network news anchors, to wannabe authors and moviemakers, they all came. They called. They knocked on my door and left notes with contact numbers and promises of large sums of money. They were vultures swooping in for a piece of a new carcass, only I was the carcass. I was the piece of meat everyone wanted to taste, and they were relentless in their pursuit of the biggest story to descend on this province in years, if not decades.

Sergeant Campbell came by every day. His partner, Corporal Blouin, accompanied him sometimes, but as time went on and the details produced no leads, her visits dwindled. I thought she might be getting bored with me or with the case. I got the feeling she was ambitious and wasn't interested in a case that appeared couldn't be solved. I thought she believed I was withholding vital details, but I had told them all I could. Sergeant Campbell told me she was being transferred next month and I wouldn't hear from her again. He hadn't stopped checking up on me. I had a feeling he never would.

At first, they came with questions or requests for clarification of some detail or another. I had told them everything I could recall, but my story came in bits and pieces and in no particular order. When you endure trauma like I had, time has no meaning. The days and the experiences do not flow in chronological order. They do not come in a detailed list of least to worst. They can't be weighed from smallest to biggest. The details are random.

They came when I least expected them. They arrived when I thought I was finally able to put the whole ordeal behind me. They came when someone touched my leg and I freaked out because it had just triggered the memory of him raping me with an empty water bottle he found on the floor. They snuck up on me when I fell asleep after hours of fighting it, only to wake screaming and fighting for air because I was certain he was choking me. And some were buried so deep I might never remember them at all.

Sergeant Campbell had been very patient with me, and I am not sure where I would be if not for Dr. Carpenter. They told me this behaviour was normal for someone who had experienced a trauma such as I had. I didn't think anything about this situation or me was normal. It was not normal for another human being to torture someone physically and mentally for three months, two weeks, and five days. It was not normal for a human being to be raped, beaten, starved, and tormented. That was not normal. I was not normal and wouldn't be ever again.

Dr. Carpenter offered me sleeping pills to help me sleep at night, but I refused to take them. She told me I was not my mother, that I was a fighter or I would not be here, but I was afraid if I accepted them, I would follow in my mother's footsteps. She did not push me. Mostly, she listened to my fractured memories and failed excuses. She didn't accept that I was responsible in any way for my trauma, but I had not told her how I hoped he would return each day. She didn't know how I allowed him to ease the hours of loneliness by sitting on the mattress and listening to his useless banter and cruel jokes. I had not revealed to her how I allowed him to violently abuse me yet hated for him to leave for fear he would never return. I wasn't sure I could ever say those words out loud to her or anyone else. It was my secret and my burden to bear. She told me it would get better in time, but it was her job to say that, and I wasn't sure I believed her.

After time, the vultures camped outside my door dwindled away. I don't know why. Maybe a new, bigger story came along, or perhaps they just got bored waiting for me to offer up a comment or two. Whatever the case, I was relieved they were gone, yet sometimes I missed their presence. In a weird, messed-up way, it was comforting to know they were so close. Now I was truly alone and not sure how to deal with it.

My belly was showing a little bump where the baby grew inside me. I didn't know how I would care for him or her when it arrived, but I had decided I would keep the baby. I wasn't sure why I had decided this. I often wondered if he or she would look like the monster who gave them life. I was afraid I would hold the baby in my arms for the first time and look into his or her eyes and see the cold, vacant eyes of its father. But it was a risk I was willing to take. I had no family left in this world, and I was afraid to be alone for the rest of my life. I had decided this creature inside me was also a part of me, to share with me the kindness of my father and my grandmother's goodness. He or she was all the family I had, and I was willing to take the chance it had my family's genes. I didn't want to be alone. I knew it was selfish of me, but so be it.

I walked to campus one day, not to attend class, but to see if it were a place where I could feel like I belonged. I saw school friends going to and from classes. Some stopped to offer an awkward hello and to ask how I was doing. Others caught sight of me just in time to turn their heads away and pretend they hadn't noticed me. I understood how they felt because I felt the same way. I realized I didn't wish to see them, either. I didn't want to witness their pitied looks or answer their well-meaning questions. I couldn't pretend to be myself for these people any more than I could fake belonging at school. My entire life had changed. It was altered in ways I had yet to realize. All I knew for certain was I was not the same girl who had gone to school looking for a new start. I didn't belong there. I wasn't sure where I belonged anymore. If not with my friends, if not at school or in my own home, where?

I needed to start over somewhere where no one knew me— away from this place where everyone knew my name and thought they knew my story. I was tired of trying to explain how I felt to people who didn't matter to me. I was sick of the sideways glances and the hushed voices that were just loud enough for me to hear. I'd had enough of the pity and the fake empathy. I had decided it was time for me to go. Soon, my growing belly would be too large to hide, and the town gossips would have me front and centre once again. I didn't want to be the hot topic of conversation. I had played that role for far too long. I walked back to my house and called the realtor. My decision was made.

Dr. Carpenter said she understood my desire to leave, but she cautioned me to stay close enough to continue our weekly visits. I was aware of how much she had helped me. Without her I would be living in the past, still trapped in the basement. Sergeant Campbell, or David, as he had asked me to call him, begged me to stay so he could continue to investigate my case, but I had not made him any promises. I had yet to discover where I would go. It would depend on how far I had to go to find a community where no one knew my face or my name. Maybe I would have to make changes in order to find the anonymity I craved.

It didn't take long to sell my house. It was situated close enough to the college to make it a highly sought-after location. I wasn't sad to leave. It hadn't ever felt like home. When I took out the last box, I stopped to look around at the same four walls I stared at the day I first moved in. I had no attachment to this place. It was only a stopover on my way to somewhere better. I hoped the place where I ended up would bring me some much-needed peace and happiness, but I was afraid to hope for too much. Things had not gone well for me over the years, and I was not sure I trusted what fate had planned for me next. One thing I knew was it couldn't possibly get worse.

I had loaded the last box in the back seat of my car and walked around to the driver's side door. I noticed a piece of paper pinned beneath the windshield wipers. It must have been an advertisement or flyer of some kind, since parking tickets were not handed out in driveways. I pulled it free and went to crumple it to toss in the garbage, but something about it caught my eye and I unfolded it instead.

I knew the minute I saw the handwriting that it wasn't a random piece of paper. This was a note, maybe a warning, meant just for me. I was sick of her harassment, but I wouldn't give her the satisfaction of a reply. I wouldn't give her the very thing she wanted, which was to speak to me. I read the note for the second time and couldn't understand why she chose to communicate with poetry, and bad poetry at that. The note read like something from a B-grade horror movie:

You cast me aside
when you needed me the most,
Like a piece of gum on the bottom of your shoe.
I know your heart
And I know your soul
I know how to make you hurt
And I can take the pain away.
You are leaving once again
Running off to places unknown
But I will find you, wherever you go.
You should know by now
No one gets to leave.

The note was unsettling, and after the ordeal I had just been through, it should have been scary, but it was Allie. She might be a little off balance, but she was not crazy. She would never hurt me. At least, this was what I told myself. I tossed the note in the garbage can sitting by the curb and drove away. Allie Lockwood would have to wait for another day. That day, I was leaving town. I was about to start over for the second time in my life. This time I would use my mother's maiden name. Helena Douglas had a nice ring to it, I thought. Some brown hair dye to change my blonde locks and I would be a new person with a new start. If only I could make the memories disappear, but that was an unreachable goal.

I drove away from the house almost happy to finally have a plan, a goal that seemed attainable. I wondered as I navigated the side streets leading to the highway if Allie was nearby watching me leave. I glanced in the rear-view mirror, but I was alone on the street. What if she saw me go? What if she followed me as I left? I never thought I would be trying to escape my one-time best friend, but there I was, hoping to never see or hear from her again. But what if she found me?

What if I was never entirely rid of her?

26

It is mid-afternoon when David finally calls. He has been gone most of the afternoon conducting "police business," but we both know he doesn't want me around for fear we will learn something he doesn't want me to hear. He is afraid that I will get some wild idea in my head that I can find this monster and bring him down all on my own. He is partly right. I want to be the one to stop him, but I don't want to do this on my own. I have spent most of my life doing things on my own, and so far that hasn't worked out too well for me. When I told him we were in this together, I meant it. I just wish he trusted me enough to let me be a part of whatever he has been up to.

He tells me to pick him up in front of the Community Health building, so at least I know where he has been, and I can guess why. Melody Scott was in the foster system. Allie was the one fostering her, which meant she had a social worker assigned to her, someone responsible for her well-being and for finding her a good home. I can't imagine what kind of caseworker would think placing Melody with Allie would be a good idea. I'd actually like to meet this person myself. I'm sure I could come up with more than a few interesting questions. First and foremost would be, Why did Allie want to take Melody into her care in the first place? Hopefully David was able to find out the story behind this whole mess.

I am eager to talk with him about my encounter with Susanna in the cemetery. I am still trying to process what she said. I have no idea if what she implied was the truth or her version of it, but she was successful at casting doubt on Allie's sincerity. It seems the more I study my friendship with Allie, the more I wonder if I ever really knew her.

"How was your afternoon?" David asks as he climbs in the front seat of the car.

"Um, I'm not sure," I reply, wanting to gather my jumbled thoughts first. "Why don't you go first? What did you learn from the social worker?"

"Well, mostly she reiterated what we already knew. Melody's father killed her mother and her boyfriend and is now rotting in Millhaven. She was in and out of foster homes, and trouble, until Allie reached out and agreed to take her in," he recaps. "What we didn't know was that Melody complained more than once that her new home was abusive. She claimed that Allie would punish her for hanging out with friends by locking her in her room and taking her phone. She withheld meals if Melody kicked up a stink about all the weird rules. She once said that Allie made her take cold showers for a week after she caught her sneaking out at night."

"And what did the caseworker find? They did investigate, right?"

"Well, the caseworker is a lady by the name of Emily Roberts. She said she knew Allie from their church and didn't think any of the accusations had merit, but she did ask Allie about them. Mrs. Roberts said that Allie had punished Melody for hanging out with a bad group of kids and that she had taken her cellphone to prevent her from talking to them. She said that meals were always prepared and available to Melody, but it was her choice if she ate them or not. She said she was a picky eater, if you believe that. When I asked her about the cold shower incident, Mrs. Roberts said that Allie denied ever doing that and she had no reason to doubt her."

"Emily Roberts? I'd bet she is some relation to another Mrs. Roberts I know. Remember the lady I helped with Sunday school classes? She had nothing but good things to say about Allie. It may be that she influenced your Mrs. Roberts to take Allie's side or to discount Melody's claims. Although that sounds like a lot of accusations, don't you think?"

"Yes, but Melody was a troubled kid. It's easier to believe the foster family when the kid is a troublemaker, and Melody Scott was out of control for a while. After living with Allie, she got back on track and even left to start college. I'm not sure she would be able to do that if she were in an abusive home."

"Unless you are too afraid not to do as you're told," I add. "When it becomes a matter of survival, you can and will do anything."

"I guess I haven't had to go through something like that, but you're right."

"Is it possible Melody toed the line just to please Allie, while she worked toward what she believed was the only way for her to get out of town? I've been there, David. College was the ultimate escape from my life in Deer Lake. It was my one-way ticket out, and I had no plans to ever look back. It may be the one thing that Melody and I have in common."

"You both wanted to get out of town," David suggests.

"We were both looking to escape and not have to go back," I add.

"But how does that connect you both to the man who kidnapped you?"

"Because someone didn't want us to leave," I say. To hear the words out loud makes the idea real.

"Okay, but who?"

"That's what I'm hoping we'll find out. It might be the answer we've been searching for all along."

"Where do you want to go from here?" David asks.

"I need to see Allie," I state, and finally I tell him about my conversation with Susanna.

"So, Susanna thinks Allie may have helped your mother to commit suicide," he says in disbelief. "This is just getting crazier."

"Or forced her to take those pills and swallow the vodka," I suggest, "and yes, everything is messed up."

"Helena, what you're suggesting is murder. You're saying it's possible Allie may have murdered your mother all those years ago. But why? What reason would she have?" David asks, not entirely believing my theory.

"I have no idea, but I have to find out," I reply.

"And how do you propose to do that? It was ten years ago!"

"I don't know, but I'm going to start by talking to Allie."

"You can't just go up to someone, especially if you think she is capable of murder, and ask, 'Hey, did you murder my mother?' You'll spook her if it's true, and if it isn't, she'll throw us out and we won't get to question her about Melody. Don't forget she is the real reason we are here. I know this is important to you—and yes, it's worth exploring—but you have to remember the reason we came in the first place. We have to find the connection between you and Melody, and if Allie has some of these answers, we need to hear them," he argues.

I know he is right, but I have questions, too. I need to look Allie in the eye and ask her. I need to see the look on her face when I do, then I'll have the answer.

"So, you expect me to walk up to *my* house and have a casual chat with the woman who may or may not have killed my mother and not say a word about it? I don't know if I can do that, David."

"I know you have incredible strength inside you, Helena. You're going to have to draw on that now if you really and truly want to stop this monster once and for all."

"You know I do." I sigh, knowing he's right. "Is Allie our only lead?"

"No, but she is the most important one right now."

"What else do you know that I don't?" I ask.

"Nothing right now, but I have an idea where to look," he replies, and I motion for him to continue. "I just spoke to Melody Scott's social worker about her situation and her relationship with Allie, and while I was there, I remembered something you said about Allie."

"Which was?"

"You told me once that Allie's family was receiving social assistance, right?"

I nod in agreement.

"Well, that means her family was also assigned a caseworker. I'm curious to know what kind of background she came from, and after what you've just told me, I wouldn't be a very good detective if I didn't check her out thoroughly."

"Okay, that makes sense, but how will you do that? It was so long ago."

"I already asked Emily to check the records. She said the caseworker who looked after the Lockwoods retired a few years ago, but he still lives here in town. I have his address, but she didn't have a phone number. I was thinking I would stop by this evening around six. Most people are home watching the news then or eating supper."

"Okay, but I'm coming with you this time," I state. "Please don't argue with me. I have spent enough time wandering around Deer Lake reminiscing about the good ol' days. I can't handle running into someone else I used to know who can't wait to impart some more juicy gossip or add another tidbit of information to the mix."

"What's wrong, Helena? Not getting the homecoming you'd hoped for?" he joked, trying to lighten my mood.

I smile at his attempt to make light of the situation, but the things I've heard today are just too unsettling. Melody being fostered by Allie is one thing, but the possibility that she may have helped my mother commit suicide—or worse—is just too much. And we are only just beginning. I wonder just how far these questions are going to take us, take me. Do I really want to dig deeper? What if it all becomes too much? What if I am my mother's daughter and cannot handle the things I learn? What if the things I learn lead to even more questions?

But what if they lead me to the answers I've been seeking?

And what if the answers are better left unknown?

27

The first time I sat with Allie in the school cafeteria, she was sitting alone at a table in the back corner of the room. It was her usual spot, tucked away from the hungry mob of teenagers with their relentless snickers and sideways glances. Allie was the school joke, the poor kid who came to school in dirty, ill-fitting rags and smelled like old french fry fat and tobacco. When I sat down in the chair across from her, half the cafeteria kids stared at us. Most of them were waiting for me to say or do something that would light up the room with laughter and send Allie running for the door, but I just sat there and ate my turkey sandwich in silence. I offered her the other half, and she stared at me with hard, uncertain eyes. She didn't say anything, nor did she accept the lunch.

The next day, I returned to her table and sat in the same chair across from her. Many of the other kids out for lunch stared at us, but with less interest and anticipation as the day before. Again, I offered her a portion of my lunch, and once again she remained silent. No words were spoken during those first days. We kept up this routine for the entire week, until finally on the last day she found her voice and, in not so many words, told me to fuck off. I listened to her speak, then stayed until the bell rang, both of us sitting in silence while I ate, as she stared at my food.

Monday came again, only this time her seat was empty. Allie

was not in school. Tuesday came and went, yet she was still absent. I was about to give up on the bargain I had made with God to befriend this girl when, on Wednesday, she returned to the table in the corner. I pulled out the chair across from her and once again sat down to eat my lunch in silence. Right away I could tell she was in a foul mood. Her face was drawn up in a scowl, and her eyes were ablaze with anger. I was not sure who her anger was directed at, but I took a chance it wasn't at me and opened my lunch box to eat.

"What do you want from me?" she asked defensively.

"I don't want anything from you. I am trying to be your friend, but you are being such a bitch about it," I replied, thinking maybe today wasn't the best day to try and win this girl over.

"No one asked you to be my friend. I don't need a prissy little brat like you to make me your charity case," she fumed. "Why don't you go on over to your own table so you can all have a big laugh at how ugly and messed up I am?"

"That wasn't what I was doing, but if that's the way you want it. No wonder you have no friends," I fired back, wondering what the hell I was trying to prove in the first place.

"Screw you. You have no idea what it means to be me. You have everything you need and more. Prissy friends, boys who want to be around you, a star on the volleyball team, and a nice little family to go home to. Don't you think I don't know why someone like you wants to be around me? You're here because I'm the butt of some big joke between you and your shitty friends, or because you think you can somehow make my life better just by being around you. Whatever your reason, you can pat yourself on the back for giving it a try and then leave me the hell alone. I don't need you or whatever this is."

"You think you're the only one with a crappy life? Well, think again. It may look like I have it all, but everything I have is crumbling around me. I don't know why I'm here at your table. I'm beginning to think it was a big mistake, but I'm not sure where else I should go. Nothing about my life makes sense anymore."

"Oh, boo-fucking-hoo. What's wrong? They kick you off the volleyball team? You don't have a date for the school dance next week? No, wait, I know what the problem is. You can't find the right outfit to show off all those curves you think you've got. Well, too bad for you. I've got bigger things to worry about, and I sure as hell don't need to listen to your drivel along with it. So, I think it's time you leave me the fuck alone."

"You think you are so intimidating standing here telling me off, but let me tell you something, Allie Lockwood. You don't scare me one bit. And I understand that everything isn't sunshine and rainbows in your world, but don't you think for one minute that everything is perfect in mine. My father is dying. He has cancer and looks like a sack of bones lying in the bed. My mother is so distraught she doesn't know I even exist anymore. And supper, well, if I don't pick up the groceries and prepare the meals, we wouldn't eat. I'm here because I thought you could use a friend, but also because I thought you might be the only person who would understand how it feels to have your life turn to crap. Guess I was wrong, because you seem to like your shitty life just the way it is."

"Fine," she says after a pause, "pass me half of that sandwich if you're not going to eat it." And that was it. The ice was broken, and each day going forward, I sat in the chair across from Allie and shared my lunch with her. For the next four years, we were together every day. She became my rock, and I hers.

We didn't speak much the first few days, but as we grew more comfortable with each other, the conversations grew as well. She listened while I spoke about my father's illness and our search for a cure, and over the weeks that followed, she spent hours online with me researching new treatments. When Dad was selected for the drug trial, Allie was the one who celebrated with me. When he died, she was the one who gave me comfort when my mother was unable. I would have been lost without her. She understood my need to care for my mother when she could barely bring herself to get out of bed, and she helped me to not forget about my own needs and desires. Without Allie by my side, I am not sure I could have made it through the four years to graduation.

At the time, I thought we were the crutches that held each other up, but looking back at our relationship, I realize it was very much one-sided. Allie was my crutch. She was my confidante and the only one who offered me the encouragement I needed to keep moving forward. I thought I did the same for her, yet all these years later, I still cannot tell you who Allie Lockwood really is. I know her father died in a car crash and her mother struggled to keep the family going. I think she mentioned a brother, but I don't know his name, nor have I ever met him.

I have been to Allie's house once in all the years of our friendship. It was a dilapidated bungalow with peeling shingles and faded cedar shakes. The yard was unkempt, and the weed-filled lawn was littered with dead, yellow circles left by dog urine. I waited outside by the broken fence while the dog barked at me from its chain by the doghouse in the front yard. She claimed her mother did not like visitors, but I guessed that Allie was too embarrassed to invite me in. She had very little of her own, and judging by the condition of the clothes she wore, I assumed her home would be similar, with old, worn-out furniture and the mingling odours of cigarette smoke and fried foods. She barely spoke of her mother and offered few details of her life at home. And I was so caught up in my own drama, I didn't realize that I was the one doing most of the sharing.

Looking back, I realize that the more time we spent together commiserating over our shared lot in life, the more Allie began to insert herself into my family and my life. At first, she started staying for supper, and I thought I was doing her a favour because there might not have been anything waiting for her at home. She was a couple of sizes smaller than I was, so I decided to clean out my closet and gave her my unwanted clothes. They were hand-me-downs, but Allie was thrilled to have clothes that fit and weren't ripped or faded. The friendship started when I set out to uphold my end of a bargain with God—ironically, it turned out Allie was just the person I needed at the time. She became the one bright spot in my life I so desperately craved. But I was so blinded by that need, I didn't recognize the little signs and nuances that would have told me to be careful or at least keep my eyes open.

Allie spent more time with me and my mother than she did her own. She wore my clothes. She ate at my house and slept over often. She liked the things that I liked. She looked after my mother and tended to her garden.

Then she moved into my house with all our things. She became me. It's baffling to think the one person you trusted the most could be responsible for the death of your parent, but this is where our friendship has led. I don't know if Allie forced my mother to take those pills. I don't know if she merely helped her or convinced her to do it on her own. I may not learn the details surrounding my mother's death, but I will forever wonder if I am the reason she is dead. Did I welcome this person into our home and our lives? Am I responsible for the way our lives have unravelled?

I do not trust Allie. I do not trust her to tell the truth, nor do I trust her intentions toward me. I have not spoken to or had contact with her in years. I have not been in her presence for even longer. Now I have no other choice but to confront her in her home, in my home. I need to learn about her connection to Melody Scott, and more importantly, I need to know if there is a connection between her and me. But what if I am not able to stand in the same room as her knowing it's a possibility she may have killed my mother? What if I am unable to form the words that need to be said? What if I cannot ask the questions that need answering? What if she tells me nothing but lies?

What if she refuses to say anything at all?

But what if she tells me exactly what I need to hear?

28

I awoke to the sound of voices above me. I didn't know what time it was. I looked toward the door, but I couldn't see the filtered light trickling in beneath. It must have been nighttime, or he had decided to cover the window in the hallway for some unknown reason. I had lost track of time. The days had turned into weeks, and the weeks had become months. I had been there a long time. It seemed like forever. I didn't sleep well there, wherever there was. It came intermittently and for short periods. I awoke not knowing if a new day had begun or if it was just barely past noon. I was unaware of the changing seasons and tried desperately to catch a glimpse out the hall window when he entered just to see if fall had yet arrived.

He was pacing again. He did this often. Sometimes I thought he had to work up the courage to come downstairs to see me in the basement. Other times, he came through the door angry and intent on making me pay for some unknown infraction. On those nights, I feared I might not live to watch him leave. That night, I wasn't sure what he was planning. I heard his voice above me. He seemed frustrated or angry, and I worried what came next. I thought he was arguing with someone, but he hadn't brought anyone there with him before. Yet I swore I could hear another voice. It was low, barely a whisper, but I was certain someone else was in the house with us.

"I ain't gonna do it anymore!" he yelled. "I won't."

His voice was muffled by the floor between us, but I was certain those were the words I heard. Then there was a crash, and I thought something had been thrown or broken. I might have been imagining things, but I knew for certain he was unstable and anything was possible. I had seen many indications that he was sometimes troubled by his actions but didn't know how to stop. I wished I could find the words to get through to him, but I had yet to find them. If I spoke without permission, I was punished. If I begged for mercy, I was punished. If I answered questions incorrectly, I was punished. I was afraid to use my voice. I wasn't sure it was even possible to reach him.

I found the nail tucked inside the mattress and continued working at the window. Scrape, scrape, scrape. Little by little, piece by jagged piece, I chipped away at the rotted wood. It felt like I was getting nowhere, but I couldn't stop. It was my only hope of survival, and without hope, I wasn't sure I could survive at all. I paused often to brush away the scrapings with my damaged hands. I gathered as much as I could and hid them beneath the mattress to conceal my efforts. The room was dark enough to mask the evidence, but I couldn't take the chance he might someday see what I had been up to. The thought of that made me shiver. I was sure the consequences would be unbearable.

"No, no, no!"

He was yelling again. At himself? At someone else? I wasn't certain, but I knew without a doubt that he was very upset. His pacing grew faster and faster, and his steps grew heavier as his burden swelled. I dreaded what lay in store for me that night. I hoped he could calm himself before he descended the stairs to my room. I wished that he would only come to visit and bring me food, but I knew this was wishful thinking. That night was going to be a bad one. I could feel it each time his foot struck the floor above me and sent shudders down my spine.

I heard the door closing. Was he gone? Had he left without coming to the basement? I was dreading his visit, but I missed him now that he was gone. He didn't bring me food that night, and my stomach cramped to remind me that I had not eaten in a couple of days. My water bottle was empty, and my throat was dry. I hated that he hurt me, but every time he left, I was afraid it was the last time. I wanted to scream for him to come back, but just as I opened my mouth to speak, I heard the footsteps above me resume their pacing. He had not left. The closing door must have meant I was not imaging things. There really was someone in the house with him. But who? Why? I didn't understand what was going on. I probably never would. All I knew was I was relieved he was still there, and I was ashamed to feel this way.

He continued to pace, back and forth, back and forth. He was angry and frustrated. I could tell by his grunting and his stomping. He yelled, but there was no one on the receiving end of his rage. No one but me. He was coming down the steps, slowly, as if he was forcing himself to descend. I hid the nail quickly and brushed the mess under the mattress. I cowered in the far corner of the room and braced myself for what came next and prayed I lived to see the sunshine sneaking in from beneath the door once more.

"Where the fuck are you, Helena?" he demanded as he shoved open the door with so much force it slammed into the wall behind it. "This room ain't big enough for ya to hide from me, so get ya scrawny ass over here."

The room was dark, and he couldn't see me huddling in the corner. I was frozen in place and didn't know what to do. If I moved toward him, I would suffer, I knew, but if I disobeyed and stayed out of sight, the consequence might be death or worse. And maybe, I might live through what came next only to wish I were dead. I forced myself to move and slowly rose to my feet. He lit a candle at the same time and saw me standing in the corner shaking with fear.

"There ya are. Ya can't hide from me, Helena. You should know better."

"I'm sorry," I lied. "I was sleeping."

"Well, nap time is over."

He lunged toward me, and I raised my arms in defence, but it was useless. He was so much stronger than me, and the force of his blow sent me crumpling to the floor. It took all my strength, and sheer will, not to cry out in pain. I had learned this only made him more cruel. He fed on the pain he inflicted and his urges grew stronger. Tonight I wouldn't give him the satisfaction.

"Next time, you be ready for me," he demanded. "I have to make you hurt tonight, Helena. Ya have to be punished. It is your own fault, ya know. You've brought this on yourself."

I didn't understand what I had done to deserve his wrath tonight or any other night. It was likely nothing I had done, but rather his twisted thinking and sick desires. I was lying on my back now as he straddled my waist. He pulled a roll of duct tape from the pouch of his hoodie, and I understood what came next. I had been through this before. Tears escaped the corners of my eyes, and I tried to force them to stop before he saw them. They would only make him angrier and more cruel, if that was possible.

"We are goin' to play a little game tonight, Helena. Do ya want to know what that is?" he asked, and I felt the moisture from his spit splattering on my face as he said it through gritted teeth. "Do ya hear me, bitch?" he yelled. I had not answered him, and he didn't like it.

"W—w—what game are we going to play?" I stuttered, trying to hold back the tears welling up in my throat as he pulled off a strip of tape.

"Tonight's game is called 'make the bitch suffer,'" he said. "I didn't make this game up, but I think we'll have fun, don't you? I even have some ideas of my own."

I nodded my head in agreement, unable to speak. He stopped talking and proceeded to bind my hands behind my back with the duct tape. I was already naked from the waist down, except for my underwear. My pants had been ripped to shreds shortly after I was locked in the basement. I felt his rough hands fumbling with my underwear, and he got frustrated and yanked them off with force enough to tear my skin. I felt the abrasion begin to sting immediately.

I watched as he worked the button of his jeans. He was anxious to pull them down. He stood there masturbating in front of me, trying to ready himself for sex, but it was not working and his mood was getting darker, if that was even possible. I knew that meant I would suffer even more for his inadequacy. We had been down that road before.

"Damn it! Damn it! Damn it!" he screamed, and kicked me in the legs and stomach to ease his frustrations. "It's all your fault! Ya stupid fuckin' bitch!"

I was his punching bag. He took out his failures on me, and I had no choice but to take it. Sometimes I prayed to survive, and sometimes I begged for death's escape. He dropped to the floor beside me and put his face to mine. His breath was foul, and spittle ran down his pimply chin. He had two days' growth on his face that was sparce and unattractive. He grinned at me, and his expression was eerie and twisted. He had not looked me in the eyes like that before. His demeanour was different tonight. He was wild. It was as if he had lost his battle with insanity, and I was to blame. I was afraid to breathe for fear he might snap completely.

"Are ya ready for some fun, Helena?"

He laughed and ripped apart my shirt in one quick motion, leaving my breasts naked and exposed. My nipples were erect because the basement was cold, but he misinterpreted the natural reaction for attraction and believed I was turned on by him.

"Oh, my, you are ready."

He snickered and leaned in and took them one at a time in his disgusting mouth. I squirmed beneath him, and instantly the pain seared through me as he sank his teeth into the soft skin of my breast. I screamed, unable to absorb the pain, and he laughed and bit down again, harder than before. When he was finished, his mouth was red with my flesh and blood, and I was barely able to stop the vomit threatening to explode from my body. The torture had worked, though, as he now stood poised before me with his hardened penis ready for the next level in our new game.

The pain, the torture, the intense cruelty, the games, they lasted for hours, I was sure. When he was finished, he rolled over on the filthy mattress and sighed contentedly, while I lay beside him barely conscious—and hardly sane. I was sticky with wet, red blood. My breasts were on fire and too damaged to touch. My legs were bruised and beaten. I dared not try to move for fear I would lapse into unconsciousness. I had to pee, but I wasn't sure I was able. Tonight the game was "make the bitch suffer," and he was true to his word. Tonight, I wasn't sure I would survive. Tonight, I wasn't sure I wanted to.

"Did ya have fun, Helena?" he asked, but I was barely cognizant. "That's okay. I can tell ya did. Ya played the game well. Maybe it wasn't such a bad idea, after all, and to think I didn't even want to play. How silly of me!"

I couldn't look at him when he spoke. I was afraid to move, afraid the pain would be unbearable. My arms were still bound behind my back with duct tape. They were numb. The circulation had been cut off for so long I wasn't sure they could be revived. I wanted to ask him, to beg him, to cut them free, but I was afraid to speak for fear my words would not make sense. I saw he was still playing with his thing and enjoying the remnants of his pleasure and satisfaction. I lay motionless as his hand moved faster and faster until finally he moaned loudly and released again. I wanted to scream at him to leave me alone. Instead, I watched as he rubbed his fingers through his semen and smeared it across my lips and laughed while I fought the burgeoning impulse to vomit.

I wanted him gone, and tonight I didn't care if he ever came back. I wasn't sure my body or my mind could survive another night like this. I was living an unimaginable nightmare. Tonight I felt broken. I was cold, and I shivered uncontrollably. My stomach ached from the beating and from hunger. I had not eaten in so long I might starve before I had to endure another attack. I was thirsty, and I was in unbearable pain. Tonight, I didn't care if I lived or died. Death would be a blessing.

He rose from the mattress and pulled up his jeans. He wore a satisfied grin on his ugly face, and I wished I had the power to wipe it away forever. He bent down and rolled me to my side to cut the duct tape from my wrist. I cried out in pain, unable to keep silent. He tossed me the dirty blanket at the foot of the mattress and left the room, locking the door behind him. I heard his footsteps climbing the stairs, then return shortly after. I wasn't sure I could survive any more "games" tonight, but instead he opened the door to slide in a tray. I could smell the peanut butter, but I was unable to move. I thought I would rest first.

I lay on the mattress, crying silent tears. I wished I were still a child playing games with my father. I longed to be held by my mother and hear her soft voice telling me childish stories. I thought if only I could go back and relive those days with my parents, then maybe this time things would turn out differently. I recalled all that had happened since my father's death and wondered why God had chosen me to suffer so greatly. I wondered if I would live to see the sunshine once more. And what if I did? Would my life continue on this path of hurt and sadness? Or what if I died there that night? Would anyone miss me? There was only one person in this world who wanted me in her life. What if I could find a way out of there? What if I could find my way back to her and redo just a part of my life? But after everything that had been done, did I really want to make that mistake again?

And what if she didn't want me back in her life?

What if going back turned out to be the biggest mistake of all?

29

We stay the night in a hotel along the highway on the outskirts of town. It's the first night I have spent in Deer Lake in many years, and the first night I have ever spent away from Lily. I call her before bedtime, but she has already crashed. According to David's mother, she has had quite the day. She says to call back early the next morning as they have another packed day planned to keep Lily entertained. I wake early from a fitful night's sleep, anxious to hear her voice and for the day ahead.

"Mama, Sadie and Thunder went swimming in the ocean! Sadie wasn't even scared of the waves. We had a fire on the beach and we roasted marshmallows and made s'mores. I ate two and they were really sticky and gooey," she says excitedly, the words tumbling out a mile a minute. "Mr. Jack says he's going to take me out on the ocean tomorrow and we are going to catch some mackerel. I don't think I am going to eat them, though. Fish are gross."

"Sounds like you had a fun day with the Campbells. I knew you would," I say, trying to keep the melancholy from my voice. I want so much to hold my daughter and to smell her sweet, strawberry-scented shampoo, but I have to finish what I came here to do.

"Miss Jayne said she is going to teach me how to bake cookies today. I want to make chocolate chip. They are my favourite," she informs me, and I am immediately transported back to my grandmother's kitchen. It saddens me to know Lily won't get to meet her or experience baking cookies with her own grandmother.

"Don't eat too many or you'll get a tummy ache!" I warn, but I know my words have fallen on deaf ears.

"Hello, Helena." Mrs. Campbell's voice has replaced Lily's on the other end of the line. "I'm sorry, dear, but she just darted out the front door. Jack is out there with the dogs, and she just caught a glimpse of Sadie running after the Frisbee with Thunder. She wants to teach Sadie to catch, too, she tells us. She is such a little treasure to have around."

"Thank you, Mrs. Campbell. For everything."

I tell her I don't know how I would have been able to do this had it not been for their generosity.

"No, thank you, Helena. Lily has brightened up our lives! Her energy and her sweetness has awakened our home and our lives. It is a joy to have her with us. Now, don't you worry about that little girl. Do whatever it is you and David have set out to do. She is safe with us."

"Thank you," I say, barely able to speak the words for the lump forming in my throat. Everything about this trip to Deer Lake has not turned out the way I thought it would. The memories are haunting, the regrets are weighing me down, and the insights and information are leading us, leading me, down a path I'd rather not explore. I hang up the phone just as David comes through the adjoining room door.

"Are you ready to get going?" he asks, then takes one look at my face and knows the answer is no. "First," he says, "don't worry about Lily. She is in a good place. She's safe. Second, I know this is hard, and if you want to go back home, I'll understand."

"I'm not leaving," I butt in, but he puts his finger to my lips to silence me.

"Third, if we're going to do this together, you have got to accept that we are doing it together. I am here for you, Helena. Whatever you're thinking, you've got to tell me. If you remember something, even if you think it's useless or mundane, I need you to tell me. If you have second thoughts at any time, you still need to tell me. Just remember, there's nothing you can say to me that I won't want to hear. I know what you've been through. I know how hard it was to fight your way back to where you are now. And I know you can't fully move on until we resolve this once and for all. Trust me, Helena. You know I'm here for you."

"I know," I reply, feeling guilty. "I'm sorry."

"You don't need to be sorry, Helena. Just tell me what you're thinking. You haven't said a word to me since we checked in here last night."

The silence between us lasts for a few minutes, and I feel he is about to leave my room, disappointed in the perceived lack of trust.

"It's not that I don't trust you, David . . . I don't trust myself right now. I'm too emotional and the feelings are too raw. Yesterday was hard," I begin, not entirely sure where this conversation will lead.

"I know it was," he says. "Nothing about this process is going to be easy, but it's necessary, and it will come to an end."

"No, David, you don't understand how I feel. Not really. I came back to this town, the place where my father died an excruciating death from cancer, to the place where my mother committed suicide, or so I thought, and to the place where my messed-up former best friend now lives in my old house with all my things. I thought I could waltz back in, ask a few questions about Melody Scott, and then slip right back out again, unnoticed by anyone and unaffected by all the memories that live here.

"But now I've learned that not only is Melody connected to my hometown, but she was being fostered by Allie Lockwood, my former best friend and confidante-turned-stalker. Then, add to that I hear the words, 'Your friend may have killed your mother.' David, I don't know what to think about anything right now. I don't know if I'm supposed to be looking for the man who kidnapped and tortured me and Melody Scott—and God knows who else—or if I'm supposed to find out the truth behind my mother's apparent suicide. I don't know if I should listen to what Allie has to say to me or write her off has a lunatic. David, I'm the one who asked her to look after Mom. I couldn't forgive myself if I put my mother's well-being in the hands of the woman who killed her."

"It's a lot to deal with, but you have to decide what is more important right now. Finding a monster or finding the truth."

"I don't know what to think about anything. I barely slept last night. All I kept seeing was my mother trying to spit out the vodka and pills while Allie forced them down her throat. Then, when I did manage to fall asleep, I dreamt he was with Lily. He found her, and he was taking her away from me. It's the worst feeling in the world, to think the person you love most, and who needs you to keep her safe, is in the hands of a monster. I feel like I'm living a nightmare all over again."

"I can only tell you what I think, Helena. Ultimately, you have to be the one to decide where we go from here."

"What do you suggest?" I ask, ready for some guidance.

"I think we should continue what we came here for. We have some leads to follow up on. We can see where they take us. If they are dead ends, we'll come back and you can confront Allie based on Susanna's theory. I can contact the ME's office and see if there was any indication your mother's death may have been something other than suicide, but you know if there was any doubt it would have been ruled inconclusive."

"I know," I reply sullenly.

"So, we keep doing what we're doing. We keep digging, and if the information leads us a little bit closer to catching him, then I think we should keep going until it's finished. We can come back to Allie when it's over," he suggests.

"All that sounds good, but how am I supposed to stand in the same room with Allie and ask her about Melody without wanting to choke the truth out of her about my mother?"

"I don't know, but you are a smart woman, stronger than you think, and Lord knows you are resilient. You can do whatever you put your mind to, if you truly want to."

"Thanks for the vote of confidence, but I'm not sure your trust in me is well-placed today."

"I have no doubt you can, and will, do whatever is necessary to stop this guy before he gets the chance to hurt someone else. Before he gets the chance to hurt Lily."

"All right, you win. Let's get started. Where are we going first? To Allie's or the social worker?"

"I set up an appointment with the social worker who worked with the Lockwoods last night when we stopped by. We will see him first. His name is Arthur Blackstock. He said he didn't remember the Lockwoods but would check his personal records before we come back this morning. I'm curious to find out what he has to say about Allie and her mom. You never know, he may say something that gives us more insight into Allie Lockwood's life before Melody and the reason why she wanted to foster her in the first place."

"Okay, you can drive. I'm not sure I'll be able to keep my eyes on the road today."

"First, we eat breakfast. There's a dining room in this hotel. They serve a full buffet breakfast, and I'm starving," he says, and heads for the door before I can argue.

"They used to say this place had the best breakfast in town, but that was a long time ago. A lot has changed since then."

"Maybe, but how hard is it to mess up bacon and eggs?"

"Hopefully we won't have to find out," I reply, and follow him down the hall.

Looking out the windows as we walk, I can see it will be another beautiful, early fall day in Deer Lake. I remember those well. When the leaves start to turn and the nights grow colder, everyone tries to catch the last of the backyard campfire season. The smell of woodsmoke was always a welcome scent, along with toasted marshmallows and hot chocolate. I was happy here at one time. Before our lives were turned upside down and ripped to shreds. Now the memories are bitter reminders of all the things I have lost and are gone forever.

"Smells good in here," David says, halting my stroll down memory lane.

"I'm not really that hungry," I reply. I feel like we are wasting time coming here when we could easily grab a coffee and a muffin from the drive-thru down the street.

"You need to eat, Helena. When you're on the trail like we are, we never know when the situation may change and we'll have to go. You learn to eat when you can because your next meal isn't always a guarantee. We don't see Blackstock for another hour, so now we eat."

I agree reluctantly because I know he's right. "Fine. I'll eat. I know too well how it feels when your next meal is uncertain. I'm just frustrated with how things are unfolding. I'm not sure if what we are learning is useful or just more pointless information to add to the pile of false leads."

"It's never pointless," he counters. "Whether what we learn is helpful or not, it's one more avenue we can cross off the list. But I have a feeling this time is going to be different. We are on the right track, Helena. I know it."

"I hope you're right, David. I'm not sure how much more I can take. It's been nearly eight years. That's a long time to chase a shadow and an even longer time to keep coming up empty."

We sit down to eat breakfast. Judging by the pile on David's plate, he isn't planning on eating any more today. I manage to force down a fried egg with a piece of buttered toast. The bacon was done with just the right amount of crispiness, but the smell of it is making my stomach roll this early in the morning. I sip on my second cup of coffee while I wait for him to finish eating and wonder where he is putting all the food, because surely one person cannot eat everything he took away from the buffet.

Half an hour later, we walk outside. The fall air is crisp, and the sun is just starting to rise above the tops of the trees surrounding the hotel. Our car is parked near the end of the lot, and we stroll toward it. The windshield is foggy from condensation, and the asphalt is wet with the early morning dew.

"Looks like we've got a parking ticket," I say as we get closer.

"It's not a ticket. Flyer, maybe?"

I tense as he lifts the wiper to retrieve the paper. It was years ago now, but I remember the day I moved out of my house near the college and found a sinister note waiting for me.

"What does it say?" I ask, already nervous it is a message meant for me.

He turns away from me and slips the note into what looks like a plastic baggie.

"Nothing," he answers, but he refuses to make eye contact. "It's just a lost dog flyer. I stuck it in my pocket just in case we see it."

"Tell me the truth, David," I say to him. "It's not the first time I've gotten mysterious notes on my car. It's from her, isn't it?"

He reaches into his pocket and pulls out the plastic baggie and passes it to me.

"Keep it in the bag in case it becomes evidence. Just ignore it, Helena. She's not worth a second thought."

I hold up the note and slowly begin to read, preparing myself for the message I know was written just for me. It isn't the first time I have had unsettling notes left specifically for me to find, but it has been so long since I last read one of her cautionary poems, and after everything I've been through since, the words now carry a darker meaning, and I worry what it all means.

You came home, Helena.
I knew you would.
I am so happy to see you!

"Are you okay?"

"I'm fine, maybe a little confused. It's not the first note Allie has left for me, but this one is different than the others. It doesn't feel like she's warning me about what's to come, but rather she's welcoming me home. It's just weird. I'm not sure how she found out I was here, though. It was likely Mrs. Roberts. She had nothing but good things to say about Allie. Bet she couldn't wait to run home to call her and tell her that her long-lost friend was back in town."

"Are you sure it's her?" David asks.

"Who else would it be? It's not like she hasn't done something like this before. It's not her typical string of bad poetry, but it has to be her. Who else would write me a note like this?"

"Maybe. But we came to Deer Lake looking for the monster who held you in captivity and killed Melody Scott. Is it possible he may have found you before we got the chance to find him?"

"You're saying you think *he* wrote this?" I ask, dumbfounded.

"I don't know anything for certain, but we can't take it for granted. This guy is dangerous, Helena. You know that better than anyone. Don't be so sure that Allie is responsible, that you let your guard down. Now more than ever, we have to be aware of everything and everyone around us. I think we are getting close—maybe too close. I'm going to get this tested for fingerprints and DNA. We might get lucky."

I can't believe what he is suggesting. Have I somehow put myself in his sights once again? I came here looking for him, but what if he has found me first? What if he is here, watching my every ac-tion and preparing his next move? What if, for all our planning and efforts to catch him, I end up being the catch?

What if he gets to me first?

30

The baby would be born in the spring. My doctor estimated the due date to be around mid-April, and I prayed he or she wouldn't be born early like some cruel April Fool's joke. I wasn't ready for a baby. I purchased a crib, but it was still lying in shambles on the nursery floor like pieces of a life-sized jigsaw puzzle. When I moved into this house, the bedroom had already been painted a mint green, so I'd chosen it for the baby. Green was as good a colour as any, and I had no desire to paint. So, green it was.

The previous owners had left an old wooden rocking chair in the shed. It was covered in peeling white paint, and the runners were worn flat on the bottom, but I dragged it into the house, anyway. I scrubbed off the grime and sanded away the peeling paint, then added a fresh coat of white and a yellow cushion to soften the seat. It fit perfectly in the corner of the baby's room and almost gave me a little twinge of excitement for the arrival.

Almost.

David still came by at least once a week to check up on me and to ask if I had remembered anything new. I thought he came out of duty and to ease his own guilt because he had yet to bring to justice the man who raped, beat, and tortured me for three months, two weeks, and five days. It wasn't his fault, but I hadn't told him that. I was afraid he would stop coming. David was the only person who knew where I lived. I had no one to converse with or keep me company. I wasn't sure I even wanted company. I was afraid to trust anyone after all I had been through, but I trusted David. I was coming to rely on him for more than finding the monster who had put me there.

The day I moved in, David came to help move the few pieces of furniture I had brought with me, and before he left, he installed the two chains and three deadbolts I insisted were necessary. He didn't question me about the locks or the way I made him check and then recheck each window to be sure they were secure. He understood why I was afraid and didn't try to ease my insecurities. He was more than just a police officer to me. I thought he was also my guardian angel, and maybe my friend.

He called earlier in the day to tell me he was coming to see me. Sometimes he came with information to share; sometimes he just came to see how I was coping. Today was one of those times. There hadn't been anything new to share about my case in weeks. I feared the monster had gotten away with what he had done to me. David told me I was safe because no one knew where I had gone to hide, but I would always wonder when he would make his next appearance. I was the one who got away, the girl who was supposed to stay. Someday, he would return for me. I was certain. I just hoped this time I saw him coming.

I heard David's truck in the driveway. I knew it was him because the engine was loud and distinct. Besides, no one else came to visit. I lived in the country where my nearest neighbours were a mile down the road. David thought it was too far off the beaten path and too far away from help in case of an emergency. We both knew he was worried about the monster coming back as much as I was. I told him it was the perfect place for me to be. No one knew me there, and no one cared to find out who the recluse was living a mile away. I was surrounded by fields on each side of me, and a pond separated my property from the woods beyond. If someone tried to sneak up on me, I would see them coming. Right now, everything was covered in snow, and the only way in was to come up the driveway. I paid the farmer's son next door to plow the snow. I left his payments in the mailbox, so we didn't meet beyond the initial contact, and this was how I'd like to keep it.

David knocked on the door, and I waddled across the living room to let him in. My stomach was large now, and I felt like a beach ball about to burst. I wanted this pregnancy to be over, but I was scared to death for the baby to actually be born. Delivering this baby into the world made this whole nightmare real. But had it only been a bad dream, I would not be standing there nearly ready to deliver a baby. His baby. The product of three months, two weeks, and five days of pure hell.

"Hey there," he greeted, when I opened the door. The cold air rushed in, and I hurried him inside so I could shut the door. I had decided I was no longer fond of the cold winter weather. I thought maybe someday I would move down south where it was warm and sunny every day and I could leave all my worries behind. I almost laughed at the stupidity, because I would not relax until he was in jail or dead.

"It's a cold one out today," he continued with the small talk.

"It's cold every day out here," I added, and moved to the propane fireplace blasting heat into the room. "Is there anything new?" I asked, already predicting the answer.

"I'm sorry, Helena, we haven't learned anything that will help us learn his identity, and we're running out of places to look. It's like he has disappeared into thin air. If he has grabbed another girl, she hasn't been reported missing anywhere in the province. Without more information, we don't know how to move forward." His answer was not something I didn't already know. I had heard the same reply for months now.

"I'll get you a cup of coffee."

"I do have some news, though. I'm not sure if it will matter to you or not, but I spoke to Bill Langley, the farmer who called 911 when you walked out of the cornfields."

He paused, waiting for me to respond.

"I remember his name. I still don't recall that day, though. Some things I remember so clearly I can barely breathe when I think of them. Other memories come to me out of the blue and when I least expect them," I replied.

"Well, he said the snow is nearly gone enough for him to get onto the fields with his tractor. He thinks in the next week or two he'll be able to get to the old house, or bunkhouse, as he calls it, where you were held. He's going to tear the thing down. It's in bad shape and not worth trying to repair. It's on the outskirts of his property, and he has no use for it, anyway."

"Why was it even there? It's not as if it was near town. It's just kind of sitting out there in the middle of nowhere."

"He said it's been there since he was a boy. He thinks it may have been used in his grandfather's time for the farmhands, especially during harvest time, when they worked long hours to get the crops in before the snow came. It was easier to bunk down in the field than to transport them back and forth every day. It's been vacant for as long as he can remember."

"I guess the building hasn't given any indication as to who he is or why he chose that place to lock me away?"

"No, we've checked out Mr. Langley and his two sons. They have absolutely nothing to do with what happened to you. Your captor must have somehow stumbled onto the bunkhouse on his own. We may never know how he found it or why he chose it."

"I just want to have the chance to ask him. I have so many questions I need answered. Most of all, I want to know why he picked me."

"We'll find him, Helena. I promise you, someday we'll find him."

"It's been months, David. Don't make promises you can't keep. I don't expect you to keep driving all the way out here to check up on me. You have crimes to solve, other people to protect, and your own life to live. I'll be okay. I have to be, for whomever is waiting to make his or her appearance in the next couple of weeks. We are all each other has. I have to be okay."

"Are you ready for the baby?"

"I'm not sure I'll ever be ready, but I don't have a choice now, do I?"

"That's not what I meant. You're going to be a great mom, Helena. But do you have the baby's room ready, clothes, bottles, diapers, all that stuff?"

"I have a crib."

"Well, that's a start."

"It's in pieces on the nursery floor," I say sheepishly.

I hated mentioning it. David had done more than enough for me, but I needed help, and he was the only person I trusted enough to allow entry into my home. Two hours later, I was looking at a fully-assembled crib, and my water broke. I was panicking and unable to think straight.

"It's too early!" I cried, wanting so badly for this to not be happening. "What is the date?"

"Today's date?" he asked, confused.

"Yes! Yes! Today's date, what is it?" I asked frantically.

"It's the third of April," he answered, even more confused with my behaviour.

"Thank God," I said, relieved. "It's not April Fool's."

David laughed at me, but the serious look on my face told him there was nothing to laugh about.

"It's still too early. I'm not ready. I don't know if I can do this."

"Ready or not, this baby is coming today. Come on, I'll take you to the hospital. Call your doctor and tell him you're on your way. He'll meet you at the hospital. Do you have your bags ready?"

"Bags?"

"A suitcase with clothes for you. One for the baby? Are you really not ready for this?" he asked, surprised.

I looked at him, and tears welled up in my eyes.

"I can't do this. I don't know what I was thinking! I can barely look after myself, let alone raise a baby," I cried, as panic started to take hold of my emotions.

"Don't worry about it, Helena. You've got this. And you've got me. You concentrate on delivering this baby today, and I'll take care of everything else. Okay? Are you good? Because we really need to get going. I don't want to be the one delivering your baby in my truck today."

"I don't know how to thank you, David. Or how to repay you. I know this goes way beyond your mandate as the officer in charge of my case."

"You should know by now our relationship goes far beyond that. I care about you, Helena, and I care what happens to you and your baby."

"David, I can't give you anything right now. I'm not sure I can even offer you friendship. I'm still trying to cope with what happened, and now I have this baby to care for. I have nothing left in me."

"I'm not asking for anything, Helena. Just let me be your friend. That's all I want. I don't need anything more than for you to let me help you."

I didn't know why this man had singled me out to be his friend or his pet project, whatever I was to him. I was damaged. I had a past that would make even the most hardened cop cringe. Maybe it was the mystery or the chance, albeit slim, to catch a monster. Whatever his reasons, I knew I could trust him with my life and with my baby's life. He was the only friend I had, and the only person I wanted to know my deepest, darkest secrets. What if we had met months before any of this had happened? That was a what-if

I would never know the answer to. We couldn't go back. I couldn't go back. I could only move forward, live in the here and now, and right now I was about to give birth to another human being. What if I wasn't ready? What if I was afraid to hold it? What if I wasn't capable of caring for a baby? What if I wasn't able to love him or her?

What if the baby looked just like its father?

What if he or she had his eyes?

31

I had a secret. I hadn't revealed what I knew, not even to Allie, especially not Allie. She wouldn't like what I had to say. She would be upset with me, maybe embarrassed, but mostly I thought she'd be angry. I couldn't tell her that after we stopped outside her house that one time, I grew curious. I wondered why she hadn't invited me in. I wanted to know why she hadn't introduced me to her mother. Wasn't I good enough to be her friend? Maybe she was ashamed of me and my needy mother. Maybe she was ashamed of where she came from, but Allie should have known by now that it didn't matter to me how she lived. What mattered was that we were best friends. We shared our secrets, our hopes, and our dreams. At least I did. I wondered sometimes if Allie was keeping things from me.

I decided a few days later I was going to find out for myself what Allie wasn't willing to talk about. Shortly after she left my house, I followed her. I would probably wish I hadn't, but I was willing to take the chance. She took a shortcut through the park and walked down a side path through the woods behind the school. It was hard to follow her and still remain hidden, but I managed. I ducked behind trees and hid in the bushes, and I stayed far enough behind her that she had no idea her best friend had become a snoop. She arrived at her house from the back. I stayed in the woods and watched her jump the rickety fence and go inside. I remained in the woods for at least fifteen minutes, huddled behind a big spruce tree, while I decided what to do next. I wasn't used to spying on other people, especially someone I considered my best friend, but I wasn't ready to give up and go home without learning at least something about her life when she wasn't with me.

The house was as rundown from the back as it was in the front. Tall, dried grass concealed half the fence, and tangled weeds clung to the back porch's railings. There were three steps leading up to the landing, but two of them lay broken at the bottom. It looked like the whole thing could come tumbling down at any moment. The back of the house was wrapped in faded and tattered Tyvek housewrap as if someone hadn't gotten around to finishing the back or had run out of money. I thought it odd they would have chosen this house when they moved here, but I guessed their options were limited. I noticed a back window was boarded up with plywood, and judging by the condition of the wood, it had been this way for quite a while. I felt bad for Allie having to call this house her home, and I wondered if this was what my house would look like in a few years without my father to continue with the upkeep, and my mother oblivious to the need to maintain it.

I wanted to go straight up to the back door and knock as loudly as I could to get her attention, but that wasn't a wise idea. If Allie had wanted me to know about her life in this house, she would have invited me there weeks ago. So I stayed in the woods, hidden behind the tree, swatting myself to avoid being eaten by mosquitoes. As it grew closer to dusk, I left my post in the woods and crept along the fence until I could conceal myself with the neighbour's shed. I was pleased with my move to the shed because now I had an unobstructed view straight into Allie's living room. It was exciting to act like a spy from some silly movie. I felt like I had been transported outside of my depressing reality at home into something exhilarating and fun. I settled in to watch, for what I wasn't sure, but the scene I witnessed a few minutes later left me wishing I had not come at all.

It started with raised voices. I could hear a woman who wasn't Allie, yelling loudly. At first I thought they were having an argument, until I realized the argument was mostly one-sided. Allie was sitting in the big armchair close to the window while a woman, who I presumed to be her mother, stood above her, screaming and waving around a beer bottle. I knew it was a tense situation, but what was I to do? I shouldn't have even been here. Allie's mother was a big woman, twice Allie's size, if not larger, and there she was, swinging the bottle in the air and pointing her free hand directly at Allie's face. I was scared for my friend, but at the same time, I was afraid I would be discovered slinking around and behaving like a peeping Tom. I decided to wait for a bit and hoped the situation would resolve itself. It didn't.

I watched in horror as Allie tried to rise from the chair only to have her mother force her to sit back down. She stayed seated while her raging mother continued to rant in front of her. I could hear their voices through the walls, but I could only make out a word or two. I was certain I heard the words "father" and "brother," but nothing else that made any sense. Then I watched, in shock, as Allie stood once more and pushed her mother away from her. Her mother fell. There were sounds of glass breaking. I assumed it was the beer bottle. Then came the sounds of thumping from inside the living room followed by more yelling. I was about to run to the neighbour's house and beg them to help, when the screen door opened and Allie ran out and raced down the steps. She was holding her left arm, and her face was red from crying. I almost called out to her, but instead I ducked behind the shed. I didn't think this was a good time to reveal myself. I wasn't sure there would ever be a good time to tell my friend what I had witnessed tonight. I had a secret, and so did Allie.

The dog started barking as Allie made her way out into the street and disappeared around the corner while the dog continued its howling. It was a mean-looking dog, but not nearly as mean as I was thinking her mother might be. I was about to leave and go back home the way I came, when I heard the squeaky screen door opening again. I looked up to see Allie's mother step out onto the porch. She was a heavy-set woman with dark, braided hair. She stood on the porch, smoking a cigarette, and had already replaced the broken beer bottle with another. She yelled at the dog to shut up, and it cowered instantly and ducked inside its house. She continued to look around casually as if the altercation a few minutes earlier hadn't happened. I was so mesmerized by everything I had seen and heard, I forgot I was standing in plain view of her. She turned and looked me straight in the eye and grinned, a sinister, snaggle-toothed grin. I wanted to run, but I was frozen in her sights.

"Did you enjoy our show, ya little bitch?" she asked, and I looked around, hoping and praying she was speaking to someone else. "I'm talkin' to you. Don't act like you didn't get exactly what you came here for."

I stood there speechless. What could I say to this woman who had just fought with my best friend and possibly injured her? I wanted to yell at her and tell her what a horrible mother she was to treat her daughter this way, but I didn't have the nerve. I opened my mouth but couldn't form the words. Instead, I started to back away from the shed and toward the trail, wanting desperately to disappear in the woods.

"You can run, ya little bitch, if ya want to, but ya better keep your mouth shut. Ya friend isn't who ya think she is. You might think I'm the big bad mama here scrapping with her little girl, but there ain't nothin' innocent 'bout that girl. Ya stay around long enough, you'll find that out for yourself," she yelled at me, as I hurried along the fence, anxious to get away from here and her. "That girl will surprise ya one day. I hope ya ready when it happens, 'cause it ain't gonna be pleasant."

I laid in bed that night wondering about all I had witnessed at Allie's house and everything I had heard. Why had they been fighting? Did they fight like that often, or did I happen to stumble upon a lone incident? As much as I tried to block out what her mother had said to me, the warning played over and over in my head and I asked myself, *What do I really know about Allie Lockwood?* The longer I contemplated her warning, the more I realized the friend I knew was nothing like the person her mother had portrayed. I decided Allie had not given me a reason to mistrust her. After all, she had been and continued to be my greatest supporter, my only ally, and my trusted confidante. I didn't know how I would cope without Allie, and that was all that was important to me, not these trumped-up allegations from her unfit mother.

The next day at school, Allie sat at our lunch table like she did every day. She asked about my night and how my mother was doing. It was the same trivial, yet welcome, conversation we engaged in every day. I tried to ask her about her night, and she instantly changed the subject. I wouldn't press her. I'd decided I would not try to persuade her to talk about her life at home. When she was ready to tell me about her relationship with her mother, she would. I tried to ignore the fact she was favouring her arm, and I suspected she would continue to do so for a few days. I wanted her to confide in me, to trust that I wouldn't judge, but I couldn't force it to happen. The decision was hers.

I promised myself then to take notice when she was not well. I feared it happened more often than I cared to admit. A good friend would tell someone, try to get help, but I guessed I wasn't a good friend. I was selfish. I knew that, but I needed Allie in my life too much to risk losing her. I was afraid to ask too many questions or raise too much interest for fear I would jeopardize my own needs by having her taken away from there and from me. So we would go on each day, living a lie and pushing through the crap that life threw at us. Both of us knowing there were some things better left unsaid.

I had a secret, and I couldn't tell.

When I looked down the road to the future, I wasn't able to see myself without Allie by my side. Yet sometimes I pictured myself alone, and I wondered what had happened to her and to us. I often thought about the words her mother had said to me, and while most of the time I could ignore her warning, there were moments when I wondered just who my friend really was. What if she wasn't the person I thought she was? What if I was putting my trust and my loyalty in the wrong person? What if my ignorance and selfishness came back to haunt me?

What if we were heading down a dark road, darker than the one we were already on?

32

David is driving this morning while I try to rein in the stray thoughts circling my brain. My memories and perceptions are racing all over the place as I try in vain to corral them. One minute I am wondering if I could have prevented my mother's death. The next I am trying to remember the little signs I ignored when we were kids that might have told me Allie was unstable. I know our relationship was complicated. We both had our hardships, and we both dealt with those in our own way. Sometimes that was together, but oftentimes we were very much on our own, maybe not physically . . . but emotionally? Emotionally our story is very different. I was often an open book, yet I could be selfish and centred on my own needs. Allie was very protective with her own feelings and emotions, and unlike me, she seldom did things solely for herself. Or so I thought. Maybe all this time she'd had a grand plan for how our lives were supposed to unfold. But I didn't comply, and now I have to wonder if that caused her to grow more and more unstable.

I think of my mother and how fragile she was. It was impossible for her to push back against Allie. I think of all the times she inserted herself into my life after I made it clear I was moving on. I wonder if Melody had similar experiences as I'd had with Allie. I wouldn't have dreamt in a million years that Allie would do something to hurt me, but now I am not so sure.

I continue looking out the window. We have driven over the overpass and entered Nicholsville. I always loved this side of Deer Lake. The trees are tall and majestic along the lake. You can watch the sun setting over the water with all its colours and beauty. I always wanted to live on this side of town, but my father claimed it was too far away from the centre of town and all its excitement and conveniences. I love the tranquility Nicholsville offers, but after my parents both died, I couldn't bring myself to come back here. Until now, anyway.

"There it is," David says, and points to an older two-storey house set back from the road and surrounded by tall maples and the biggest spruce tree I have ever seen. "We're a little early, but I don't think he'll mind."

Arthur Blackstock was in his backyard tending to his garden. We ring the doorbell, and a man's voice calls out and invites us to come through the side gate. It's like walking into a botanical garden. There are flowers and shrubs of every colour and size laid intricately throughout the whole area. The raised beds and various specialty gardens are lined by gravel pathways, and a fish pond sits perfectly in the middle of it all. The water trickling from the fountain is inviting, and I instantly want to sit here and forget about all the noise bouncing around in my head.

David does the introductions, and Mr. Blackstock motions for us to follow him to the porch. He offers us lemonade, and I almost laugh. It feels like we've stopped by for a friendly visit when the reality is we're here to ask questions about the woman who stalked me and may have murdered my mother.

"I remember you, Helena," he says to me. "I knew your dad. I recall him bringing you to our family picnics. You remember, the ones we held at the end of the year for all our volunteers. He was a great man. He gave so much of his time to Big Brothers and Big Sisters. It was a pleasure to work alongside him."

"Thank you," I reply. "I remember those picnics, but I can't say

I recall many of the adults I saw there. Us kids had a lot of fun running around together and trying to sneak away and out of sight."

"No, I'm sure you don't," he laughs. "Not many teenagers take notice of the adults trying to keep them under control. I'm sorry for what you went through later. You've had a hard life since those days."

"That's why we're here," David interrupts. "I'd like to ask you some questions about a former client of yours."

"I'll do what I can, but I've had a lot of clients over the years, and I've been retired for nearly three years now. I may not even remember them. Who is it you would like to know more about?" he asks.

"Do you remember a family by the name of Lockwood? It was a mother and daughter by the names of Sheila and Allie. Sheila was the mother, and Allie was her thirteen-year-old daughter. They would have come to town around fifteen years ago, maybe a little longer."

"Do you have anymore information other than their names?"

"They were new to Deer Lake, I believe," David adds.

"The father was killed in a car crash before they came," I tell him.

"Oh, now I remember them. That was a sad case, that one. Little girl was caught in a bad situation, but the mother wasn't doing anything wrong, as far as we could tell. There were no complaints about them, but I had my suspicions," he says. "I stopped by their place often. It wasn't a very habitable home, but Sheila refused to leave the house. Apparently, it was rented to them for a very low rate, and she wouldn't budge when I suggested I move them into better housing. She just wanted the monthly cheque and for me to be on my merry way."

"Allie said her mom worked hard to keep them afloat after her dad died, but she couldn't keep up," I put in.

"I'm not sure how close you were with the young girl, but

her mother didn't work a day in her life, as far as I could tell. She was fond of cigarettes and beer, if I recall correctly. I inspected that house so many times, hoping to find a reason to remove that child, but every time I showed up, the house was always in order. I checked with the school, and Allie had a normal attendance record. They hadn't seen any red flags to suggest things weren't good at home," he laments, "even though I was certain they existed. I just had no way to prove it."

"The rags she wore to school weren't enough to tell you something wasn't right?" I ask, unsettled by what I am hearing.

"I'm sorry, Helena, but my job doesn't work like that. Sometimes I wish it did. If she were beaten or malnourished, we could have done something. If there had been complaints, we could have investigated and watched them a little closer. But there was nothing, nothing but a bad feeling I couldn't quieten. I wish the rules surrounding my job were different, but I couldn't act on bad feelings alone."

"She was beaten," I say, and it's the first time I have said those words out loud, and both David and Mr. Blackstock stare at me, waiting for me to elaborate. "Well, I think her mother beat her. I saw it happen once. Allie didn't know I saw her, and I was afraid to say anything."

"You didn't mention this before. Are you sure, Helena?" David questions. He is puzzled by my secrecy, but I have no excuse for my silence other than a guilty conscience.

"I haven't told anyone before now. I couldn't even find the courage to ask Allie about it after it happened. Then, after all this time, it didn't seem relevant anymore."

"I wish you had come forward years ago, but I guess we can't go back and change the past. The young girl is doing well now, I believe, and that's what matters. I'm not sure if the information I gave you helps you any in what you're looking for, but I have some weeds waiting for me, and I'd like to get back to them, if you don't mind," Mr. Blackstock says, and I feel he has had enough of our questions.

"Just one more question, Mr. Blackstock, before we leave?" David asks.

"Go ahead, but I'm not sure what else I can add."

"What can you tell us about the Lockwoods before they arrived in Deer Lake?"

"Not much, really. They came here from a community up the coast just outside of St. Anthony, I believe. Big Brook, maybe—no, that's not it. Main Brook! They came here from Main Brook not long after the father died. They hadn't received social assistance up until then, so there wasn't much in their history. Why? Is that important?"

"We're just covering all of the bases, Mr. Blackstock. No amount of information is too much when you're conducting an investigation such as this," David replies. "Thanks for your time, sir."

"Thanks, Mr. Blackstock," I add as we stand to leave. "It was nice meeting you."

"You take care, there, young lady. You look like your father, you know that?"

"I heard that a lot when I was growing up." I laugh. "Thank you! It's been a long time since someone remembered my father. It's nice to hear."

We descend the few steps to the path leading us back out the way we came. I stop and take in the beauty of the garden once more. If it were a different time, I might just sit here and listen to the water splashing in the pond. I have not relaxed and enjoyed beauty and tranquility like this in years, not since I was dragged into that dark, musty basement. I hope someday I will be able to relax and enjoy life with my daughter, but not until he is caught or dead. We are on the other side of the gate when Mr. Blackstock calls out to us.

"I just remembered something about the Lockwoods. I'm not sure it will be useful or not. I'm not even sure I should be saying this since it's not a proven fact. But I remember there were rumours about them when I was first assigned to them. Of course, I couldn't act on what I heard because there was no proof, or you people would have been involved," he says, and looks at David when he does.

"What did you hear, Mr. Blackstock?" David asks.

"Like I said, they were only rumours at the time, but folks around here seemed to think the father's car accident wasn't just an accident."

"What are you saying? You think Allie's dad's accident was something else? Something deliberate?" I can't believe what I'm hearing.

"I don't think anything. Like I said, it was all just rumour back then, but plenty of people thought Mr. Lockwood didn't die in an accident. That maybe his accident was someone's way of getting rid of him."

"Thanks again, Mr. Blackstock," David says. "We'll be in touch if we have any further questions."

He takes my arm and leads me to the car. My head is spinning, and I can't think straight. I can barely lift my feet and put one in front of the other. This whole mystery keeps growing bigger and crazier with every question we ask. I'm not sure what, if anything, it even means for us finding the monster who held me captive and killed Melody Scott. I feel like everything is spiralling out of control and I don't know how to stop it. The mystery is like a spider, reaching out and pointing in all directions, and I have no way of knowing which leg to follow.

David pushes me into the car and closes the door behind me, then jumps in the driver's side. "What are you thinking?" he asks. I know he is concerned from the look on his face. "I can take you home, Helena, if this is getting to be too much for you. I know it's a lot to take in, but we don't know if there is any truth to what Mr. Blackstock said."

"I'm not going home. I can't. I have to finish what we set out to do. I've waited long enough to live my life. Lily has waited long enough to have her mother feel whole again. I'm not leaving. I can push through," I insist.

"Okay, then answer me. What are you thinking?" he asks again.

"I think I didn't really know my friend at all. That the girl I knew was just a character she played, and the real Allie Lockwood remains a mystery to me. I know the person I thought I knew was loyal, trustworthy, and devoted to me and our friendship, but the girl I am finding out about now was none of those things. I don't know if she just survived what she was faced with or if she was the root of all their problems. Her mother is a piece of work, but Allie takes the cake. If you believe what Susanna has to say.

"And now to learn her father's death may not have been an accident! I don't know what to say. Allie was only thirteen when he died. It's not possible for a thirteen-year-old girl to murder her own father, is it? And if not her, then who? Her mother? Is the whole family crazy or just one of them? I'm just so confused, I'm going around in circles trying to figure it all out. I don't know what to believe or who to trust. What are you thinking?"

"I think I need to speak to the officers who investigated the Lockwood accident. I've got to find out his name first."

"His name was James. At least, that's what Allie told me it was," I tell David.

"Okay. If they had any suspicions that James Lockwood's car crash was anything other than an accident, it will be in the records. I'm not sure how it fits with our investigation, either, but what I do know is the more we learn about the Lockwoods, the more I want to find out. If one or both of them are connected in any way to what happened to you and to Melody's murder, I'm going to find out what it is."

"I just don't see how they can be connected. Allie has done some despicable things to me, and she may have murdered my mother, but it's not possible she put me in that basement and did those horrible things to me. I know it was a man. At times he was just a boy, but he was a monster and still a man. Lily is proof of that."

"There are other ways she may have been involved, Helena. We'll figure it out. Right now we need to go see Allie. Are you up for that, knowing everything you've just learned?"

"I don't know if I can see her and hold my tongue at the same time. I want to strangle the truth out of her, but I also don't want to jeopardize our chances of finding the monster who brought us here. I have to see her face to face. I want to look her in the eye when she speaks. It's the only way I can trust what she is saying is the truth, or at least her version of it."

"I can make a call to the RCMP detachment in St. Anthony before we go. They would have handled the accident report for Mr. Lockwood. Maybe knowing a little more about that will help you put things more into perspective."

"Fine, you go ahead. I need some time to process everything. Stop at Joe Butt's Lookout, and I'll take some time to think while you make your call."

Five minutes later, I am sitting on the sandy beach looking out over the lake. The wind blowing in off the water is chilly today, but the coolness is refreshing. I want to wade into the water and let the waves wash over me and carry away the dirt and grime that coming back to this town has dredged up. I have been avoiding Deer Lake for years, and coming back has only reaffirmed my reasons for staying away. I long to hold my daughter and hear her sweet voice, begging for more time outside or for more ice cream. Those acts seem so mundane now compared to everything that is happening in our lives. She is miles away from me, and I am here, trapped in a spider's web taut with mystery and lies. I want to go home. I want to stay. I want to forget about the past, yet I need to know the truth. Mostly, I want this to be over. What if the lies keep unfolding? What if the mysteries cannot be solved? What if I'm stuck forever in this web of deceit, unable to find my way to freedom?

What if I can never have a normal life with my daughter?

What if this is my only version of normal?

33

Dr. Carpenter was running late. It wasn't like her to be tardy. She must have encountered an emergency. Her skills were very much in demand at the hospital. It was a sad testament to the state of our society that she was needed so badly. How many of us saw her as our only lifeline? How many of us had she talked off the metaphorical ledge? I didn't want to know how many of us she had saved from actually falling over. I wasn't sure I could have survived without her.

There were times in the first days and weeks after I escaped the basement when Dr. Carpenter was the only person who could calm my hysteria and keep me from falling into a deep depression. I was afraid he would come back for me, and I was terrified of the memories. And I blamed myself for all of it. If I was honest with myself, I believed I would always be haunted by those feelings. I was so ashamed—ashamed to have allowed myself to be abducted in the first place, and even more ashamed that it took so long for me to find freedom. And now that I was finally free, I was still living the nightmare. I couldn't sleep, and when I did, I grappled with night terrors and panic attacks. "It's normal," she told me, but I feared I couldn't get past it. In fact, I worried that even though I had escaped the basement, I would never truly be free.

My four weeks in the psych ward were more than halfway over. I was undergoing intense therapy in hopes I could somehow accept what happened was not my fault. The goal was to finally begin the process of healing, but I wasn't sure I was there yet. Dr. Carpenter wanted me to accept that even though what happened was horrific and life-altering, I didn't have to let it change me. She wanted me to believe that even though the trauma had altered me in so many ways, underneath all the abuse, the pain, and the doubts, I was still me. I was still the same person I had been before this nightmare happened. I was still good and kind. I could learn to trust again, to love again. But I wasn't sure I believed her. Right now, I was only a shell of the person I used to be. However, there was another human growing inside of me, and I had only seven months to prepare for its arrival.

Dr. Carpenter said I needed to work on accepting what happened and put it in the past, but she had no idea how impossible that idea really was. There was nothing more I'd rather do than forget he ever existed. I wanted desperately to erase the three months, two weeks, and five days he held me in that basement, but I couldn't. I wanted to love this baby I was carrying and be a good mother, but I wasn't sure how I could, knowing he was still out there. For now, I would work on putting him, and the terror he created, in a box. I wanted to be able to tuck that box away and move on, but I didn't want to forget. I wanted to be able to unlock the box whenever I felt the need. I couldn't forget him or the horror he had inflicted. At least not yet. I couldn't move on until this part of my life was over. I would never stop looking for him. I wanted to tell Dr. Carpenter this, but something told me this was not what she wanted to hear.

She walked into my room fifteen minutes late. She didn't apologize for her tardiness, but rather got straight down to business. I was happy to see her. I realized I was in awe of her and the way she was able to listen to me and her other patients, talk about such pain and heartache, yet she entered every room wearing a smile. It was as if she transformed a room just by being in it. The first thing anyone noticed about her was her wild and funky hair. I secretly called her Rainbow Brite, but I admired her confidence and her welcoming personality, much like the cartoon character she resembled. She made everyone, including me, feel at ease and safe to speak freely. I had never met anyone else like her. She truly was a marvel.

"How are you feeling today, Helena?" she asked as she got comfortable in the chair across from me.

"The same, I guess. I don't think I'm ready to leave here. I don't think I can go home yet," I blurted out. I hadn't planned on voicing those words out loud, but there they were. They had been said and I couldn't take them back.

"Why do you think you're not ready?" she asked calmly. She didn't get angry with me or frustrated with what I perceived as my lack of progress.

"Gee, I don't know! Maybe it's because I can't sleep without having nightmares? Maybe it's because he's still out there and I'm afraid he's going to come back for me? Maybe it's because I'm carrying his baby and I have no idea if I'm capable of loving it? Is that enough? Or should I go on?" I answered testily.

"We can work on ways to manage your nightmares. I've offered you the option of trying a sleep aid, but—" she began, but I interrupted her.

"I'm not taking sleeping pills. I won't become my mother," I said indignantly.

"I understand your fear, Helena, but you are not your mother."

"The answer is no, I won't take them, so please stop suggesting I do."

"Okay, then. There are other things we can try. Why don't we work on those, and maybe the other things that are bothering you might not seem so insurmountable?"

"What do you have in mind?" I asked reluctantly.

"Well, it isn't just one thing, but rather a combination of methods that when practised together can have great results," she began, and I motioned for her to continue. "You can try by enforcing a strict exercise schedule or—"

"Doc, I'm pregnant. How much exercise do you think is possible when my belly starts to grow to the size of a watermelon?" I interrupted again, thinking maybe she wasn't as great at her job as I had thought.

"Exercise doesn't have to mean running for miles or lifting weights. Exercise can mean a brisk walk that changes pace with your changing body. Exercise can be an hour of yoga that again can be modified as your pregnant body changes. There are ways to exercise while you are pregnant, Helena. You just have to find what suits you and your body."

"I used to run," I told her. "That's what I was doing when he found me."

"If running is too emotional right now, then find something else that you like doing. I promise you it can only help."

"What else? You said there was a combination of things I can do."

"Stay away from caffeine, nicotine, and alcohol, especially before bedtime, and try to have light meals well before bedtime. If your digestive system is active, and your body is stimulated by other chemicals before bedtime, your brain will have difficulty shutting off, and the risk of nightmares is greatly increased."

"I think I can manage that. Is that all?"

"No, there is one more step you can take, but this one may be a little more difficult. However, it has shown some very promising results in patients like yourself who suffer from post-traumatic stress syndrome. It's a cognitive behavioural therapy method called imagery-rehearsal treatment. It entails you remembering the event or events that are giving you the nightmares and rewriting the ending. You imagine how you would like for the event to end and try to replace it with the ending that is causing you to have nightmares. It's hard dwelling on traumatic events, but if you can change the outcomes in your mind, you are less likely to dream about them when you fall asleep."

"No offence, but that sounds like a bunch of hogwash."

"It may very well seem that way, but you will never know if you don't at least try. What do you have to lose, Helena? Right now, the only other option is medication, which you refuse to take. You are not a quitter. That is evident by your very presence here. I can help you if you want to try. Just say the word."

"The diet and exercise parts are easy," I said to her after a few minutes of silence. "It's the memories I have difficulty with."

"How so?" she asked.

"There are just so many of them," I told her. "I was in the basement for a long time. There are things about that time I can't remember because the trauma was so great, and there are things I wish I could forget. I guess those are the memories that are keeping me awake at night."

"Then concentrate on those. Take each memory, in whatever order that makes sense for you, and rewrite the ending. Take each event that caused you pain both mentally and physically, and imagine a different ending, an ending that you decide. It's a place to start. It can't hurt any more than it already does. It might just be the key to helping you move on."

"I don't know if I can move on while he's still out there. I'm afraid I'll forget all the horrific details, and when the time comes to put him in prison, I won't be able to help put him there."

"Helena, you can't have a life beyond this until you learn to cope with what has happened to you. Learning to cope doesn't mean learning to forget. It means learning to put the experience in a place in your head and your heart that allows you to move on. You have been through something most people can't even imagine. It has changed you forever, but it doesn't have to own you. You decide that. You have that power, and from what I know about you, Helena, you have the strength and the determination to overcome everything that is preventing you from moving forward."

"I hope you're right. I really do, especially now." I sighed, and my hand inadvertently moved to my stomach.

"Are you still certain in your decision to keep this child?"

"I am. Neither of us asked for each other, but here we are, joined together forever. He or she needs me, for everything. And oddly, I need it. I'm alone in this world, and even though this baby is a part of him, he or she is also a part of me, of my parents and my grandparents. I can't get rid of the only connection I have left to the people who loved me. Do you believe in nature versus nurture, Dr. Carpenter?"

"I believe there are arguments for both, but I tend to agree with the notion that a child's environment will determine if he or she becomes a good person and a productive member of society," she replied.

"I sure hope you're right, because that's what I'm depending on right now."

"Are you sure there is no one you can rely on after you leave here?" she asked. "What about the young lady who keeps coming by the hospital and wanting to check on you?"

"Allie. There was a time when I would have said she was the only person in the world I would trust to help me through this, but a lot of things have changed between us. Our friendship died long before I was abducted. Sometimes I want to reach out and invite her back into my life, but too many things have been said and done. I don't think I can trust her anymore, and I don't need that stress in my life on top of everything else I have to deal with."

"Are you certain the problems between you are irreparable?"

"They are. I left home after high school, and she had a hard time with that, especially after my mother died and I cut off contact with her. I think she stalked me for a while. I feared she was unstable. I can't open the door and let her back into my life. Not now. You know I have this dream sometimes that I'm back in the basement. I'm cold and hurt. I think he has just raped and beaten me again, and I'm floating in and out of consciousness, but I'm certain I hear yelling above me, and I swear I hear him shout Allie's name. Then I wake up, and I can't make any sense out of it because I know she wasn't there with me. I know she wouldn't hurt me like that, at least I think I know. I used to trust her with my life, but she's not the person I thought she was, and I'm not the same person she knew back then. That's the problem with us being friends again. I have too many questions and suspicions to make it work, and I don't have the energy or the heart to try."

"The mind works in mysterious ways. Maybe it was your subconscious wanting the help of your old friend. Maybe your mistrust of Allie is being projected in your nightmares. Let's work on dealing with them, and it's likely the dream about Allie will fade."

"I hope you're right. I just want to feel a little like *me* again, just to know I still exist."

"I'll be back this afternoon for our group session. Why don't you work on the imagery-rehearsal treatment? The sooner you start, the sooner you might find that, underneath all of this, are the remnants of the Helena you think you've lost."

She left the room with the same confident swagger with which she had arrived. Her long, colourful hair fell down her back and seemed so incongruous to the role she played as the confident, intelligent, and highly competent psychiatrist. I was grateful for all that she had done for me and continued to do, but I wasn't sure I could achieve what she was hoping for. I didn't know if I could bear to recall an entire memory from that basement, and even if I did, I wasn't sure that altering the ending in such a way that he ended up dead every time would be productive to my recovery. Besides, I didn't entirely know which memories were real and which memories I had fabricated.

The mind can play cruel tricks on a person when it's under extreme duress. I was sure Allie was nowhere near the basement, yet I swore I heard someone calling her name. It's likely that someone was me. Maybe I called out to the only person left in my life who might have come to my rescue. Yet there was a small part of me that sometimes wondered if my memory was real.

What if I really had heard him call out her name? Was it possible Allie really was there? What if she knew and didn't do anything? I couldn't believe she was really that disturbed.

What if I was the one losing her mind?

What if I couldn't tell the difference between what was real and what wasn't?

34

The day Lily turned eight months old was the first time she slept through the night. I awoke in a panic at seven in the morning and realized I had not fed or held her since the night before. I hadn't heard her stir or cry. It was unusual for me to sleep through the night, but I was exhausted when I went to bed, and thankfully I had not been plagued by nightmares. But now I was terrified. Had the baby cried and I not awakened? Was she okay? Was she breathing? I was more afraid for her than I ever was for myself while I was trapped in the basement. I could barely breathe, and my body trembled at the prospect of walking into her room and finding her cold and still.

I somehow found the strength to put one foot in front of the other and tiptoe to her room. When I opened the door, all I could do was laugh at how silly and extreme I was. Lily was awake in her crib, cooing and gurgling as happy as any baby could be. I pulled her close to me and wept, while she squirmed in protest. I was so relieved to find her enjoying her own sounds, it felt like the world had been lifted from my shoulders, and I realized for the first time since she had been born that I loved her more than life itself. I truly and unconditionally loved her with every cell in my body.

It was an immense relief to know that I was capable of loving this child whose father was the monster who tortured me beyond all conceivability. She was pure. She was precious. And she was mine. There was nothing about this beautiful little baby girl that reminded me of him. She had perfect, pink skin and pudgy cheeks. She had the most innocent smile and the beginnings of strawberry blonde locks. Her eyes were like chocolate brown marbles, and they sparkled every time she looked at me. She looked like my grandmother, whose name was Lillian. This was how I had settled on her name. Grandma and I had had a very special relationship, and I wanted to honour her memory by naming my child after her. Lily would be good and strong and as wise and as kind as my grandmother. I knew that every time I looked at her and held her in my arms—she would be nothing like the man who gave her life.

I had struggled a lot over the past sixteen months. First, I had grappled with the physical pain of my recovery. I had broken bones in my wrist that had begun to heal but needed to be set straight. My nose was crooked from one too many blows to the face, and I had numerous cuts and abrasions that were simmering with infection. My body temperature had been dangerously high due to the severe infections and imminent sepsis. I had been beyond dehydrated and severely malnourished, and I continued to fade in and out of consciousness for days. When my brain became clear and alert, I faced enormous mental anguish and instability. I still grappled with the after-effects of what this ordeal had done to me and what it had stolen. I had a long road ahead. I was learning to cope, but I couldn't move forward entirely until he was caught.

It was easier when Lily was awake. She needed me more than I could have ever imagined, and I needed her just as much. She was my reason for getting out of bed each day and my reason for moving forward. I loved that she was such a sweet distraction from the past. I loved to see her grow, and I watched, amazed, as she transformed into this little person with her own blossoming personality.

When I made the decision to keep her, I thought a baby would mean I wouldn't have to be alone in this world. Even though that sentiment was true, the relationship I shared with this tiny, little human was unlike any other I had experienced. For the first time since I emerged from the cornfield and ended up in the hospital, I had a purpose other than revenge. Don't get me wrong, I still dreamt of the day when he was brought to justice and I could finally close that chapter on my life, but today I had something else, someone else, worth living for.

Lily brought me the joy I didn't think I'd ever experience again. She made me laugh when I thought all laughter was lost. She allowed me to look to the future when I swore I didn't have one. I thought if I was truthful, I needed Lily more than she needed me, if that was possible. She filled a void in my heart that I thought was impossible to fill. I was, and would be, forever grateful for her. He had taken so many things from me during my time in the basement, and I feared many of those things were lost to me forever. Yet he had given me the greatest gift I could have ever asked for, my sweet Lily, who was now screaming loudly for her breakfast.

It was strange and unsettling to think of the monster who had nearly destroyed me, and then want to thank him for giving me my daughter, but that's where I was. This was where my path in life had taken me. I remembered night after night when I cried alone in the basement, cold and hungry and in pain from being repeatedly raped and beaten. I remembered hating him so much I wished he would die in the basement so I could watch the rats eat his rotting flesh. I remembered the intense feelings of relief when he'd return to me after the hours alone became too much and my hunger grew more desperate. And I remembered hating myself for wanting him to return when I knew the alternative was to die alone. Sometimes, I wished I had chosen the alternative, but in reality, the choice hadn't been mine to make.

It is difficult to reconcile your feelings when they are at opposite ends of a spectrum. Sometimes it's hard to distinguish the differences between hate and need and love. Sometimes they blend together and confuse your emotions and mess with your mental stability. I think there were days I was on the verge of insanity. I'm not sure what I would have succumbed to first—that, or the long-drawn-out mutilation of my body.

Dr. Carpenter set me on a path months before to reimagine alternate endings to the memories that haunted me. It was a relatively new method of therapy for people with PTSD to try and get past the trauma that gave them nightmares. I could attest to the validity of the treatment method. I still slept with the lights on. I still had the nightmares. Yet they came less often and were less severe. It had allowed me to function at a time when I needed it the most. Raising an infant was hard enough without having to deal with mental and emotional instability.

As part of the therapy, I was supposed to recall the memories that haunted me, then imagine them with a different outcome, one which I chose. I started out doing what Dr. Carpenter asked of me, but I wanted to do more. I wanted to be able to put those memories in a metaphorical box and lock them away until I needed them. I was afraid that by imagining different endings and outcomes I would eventually alter my memories. This was the goal of imagery-rehearsal therapy, but not entirely the goal I had in mind. So, I started to write down my memories as they came to me. As hard as it was to relive each and every torturous moment, I forced myself to remember them all and to get them down on paper. When I finished writing them down, I stored the bits and pieces of my captivity in a lockbox at the back of my closet. Essentially, I had turned the metaphorical into the literal. It gave me peace of mind knowing that no matter how much I altered the outcomes in my head, I would always know exactly how horrifically I had been treated by him, and when the time came, I would have all the evidence I needed to put him behind bars for the rest of his miserable life.

Sometimes when I was afraid I was forgetting all the horrid details, I hauled out the box of papers and notes, and I read them, every last one. I took in each word and absorbed the pain that followed. It helped to know I had not forgotten. I looked at it as practice for one day testifying in court. If it ever came to that. If I was being honest with myself, and my prayers were answered, he wouldn't see the inside of a courtroom or a jail cell. He would instead die a slow, agonizing death. Something befitting a monster.

Lily looked up at me as she sucked greedily on the bottle of warm milk. Her eyes were bright and her face so pure and innocent. I had a picture of her bundled in a soft pink blanket that I kept on top of the fireplace. There was a smaller version in an envelope sitting by the refrigerator that I almost mailed to Allie. Sometimes, I remembered my former friend, and I missed the bond that we shared. I thought maybe it was time I reached out and tried to patch things up, but then I recalled the nagging feeling that she was there. That somehow, while I lay on a dirty basement floor, surrounded by bugs and rats, my friend was above me and did nothing. I had not told David. I wasn't sure if what I recalled was even real. I tried to convince myself it was all a trick of my imagination, but sometimes I questioned that theory. I didn't want to send David on what would likely be a wild goose chase, so for now the memory remained a battle between my unconscious self and the elusive truth.

I tried to write down the words to describe what I thought I recalled, but they were difficult and not forthcoming. I struggled with the validity of the memory, and I wasn't certain I should add it to the box. But I wrote the words down, anyway, and I placed them in an envelope in the box with a big question mark on the outside. I could decide later if it belonged. For now, it was tucked safely away at the back of the closet with the rest of my nightmares. Someday, I might find a use for the scraps of truth and memories from hell, but for now I had the lid locked on tight and I chose to keep them safely hidden. They were out of sight but never out of mind.

I was learning to cope, and I was beginning to have hope that I would survive this. Together, Lily and I, we would survive, and one day even thrive. I lived with the fear that someday he would find us, but I didn't let that fear consume me. I had David to lean on and Lily to protect. Dr. Carpenter believed I was a living miracle. She told me that I was doing well, that my being here was a testament to my strength as a person. She called me the greatest fighter she had ever known.

So now when I ask, "What if he finds us?" my answer is, "I will fight him." And what if he tries to take Lily? I will kill him.

And what if he tries to finish what he started?

Then I will finish it for him.

35

David is sitting in the car, still wrapped up in the telephone call to the RCMP detachment in St. Anthony. I am anxious to learn what he has discovered. I am still in shock. To hear there were rumours at the time, suggesting James Lockwood's accident really wasn't an accident at all, sounds crazy and unbelievable to me. If not an accident, what was it? A drunk-driving incident, in which case it would have still been labelled an accident. The alternative is hard to grasp, and considering all I have learned since coming back to Deer Lake, I shouldn't be surprised to discover something else Allie wasn't entirely truthful about. I'm ashamed to admit it, but there really was very little that I knew about my friend. It makes me wonder what else I'll discover the farther we go down this road.

David puts away his cell and comes toward me while I remain sitting in the sand. "You know you're going to have plenty of sand in your shoes without burying your feet in it," he jokes as he approaches and watches as I pile mounds of sand on top of my legs and feet like I had as a kid years ago.

"You're not a fan of the beach, David?" I ask. "Don't worry, I'll dump my shoes before I get back in the car. What did you learn?" I'm anxious to hear what he has to say, yet I am reluctant to learn of yet another of Allie's lies or half-truths.

"It's an interesting case. But you're not going to like what I found out," he begins.

"I don't like anything about this, but it's where we are. I have to know what you've learned, and then we'll have to decide if it means anything to our investigation. It feels like we're searching for information about Allie and her family when we have no idea if it's useful other than to show me what a bad judge of character I am."

"Helena, when you're searching for answers, you leave nothing to chance. If that means going down the wrong path a hundred times, then that's what we do. Sometimes it enables us to eliminate suspects, and when you're lucky, it leads you straight to the prize. We've been searching for this guy for years now, and this is the most we've ever learned. I feel like we're getting closer. I know it's hard for you, but there's nothing easy about any of this."

"I know you're right. It's just that it's my life, too, that we're tearing apart. Everything I thought I knew is turning out to be either lies or illusion. I don't know what's real and what's not. I don't know who Allie was. Hell, I don't even know who I am anymore."

"You don't have to be here if it's too hard for you. I know you've insisted you have to stay, but I can do this on my own. It's my job. Go back to my parents and spend some time with Lily. They'd love to have you stay for a few days."

"Please stop suggesting I go home. It's hard for me, but I've handled harder and I've survived worse. I'm seeing this through to the end. I'll put the pieces back together when it's over. I've learned I'm good at that, too."

"Okay," he surrenders, "the Lockwood accident was ruled as such because they couldn't prove it was something other than an accident, even though they had doubts and tried to find evidence to the contrary."

"What does that mean? Allie was telling the truth?" I ask, almost relieved. Yet the look on David's face tells me there is more.

"I guess, in a sense, Allie was telling the truth. It was officially ruled an accident, but only because they couldn't prove it might have been sabotage instead."

"Sabotage? Really? This just gets crazier. Go on," I urge, wondering where this is leading.

"The accident happened in the early morning hours, just before dawn. The car was discovered mid-morning by joggers passing by who discovered the brush had been flattened going down over an embankment and then found tire treads leading straight over the edge. They climbed down and found the car on its side. They weren't sure if the man inside was dead or alive, and they couldn't reach him to find out. They called 911, but by the time paramedics got there, it was too late. James Lockwood was deceased."

"So, why the rumours about it not being an accident?"

"When the traffic accident investigators arrived, the first thing they noticed was the lack of evidence indicating Lockwood had tried to stop. There were no signs at all that he had jammed on the brakes. The accident happened on a turn, and it looked like speed may have been a factor, but it was odd that he didn't try to stop, which indicates he either didn't try to stop the car from going over the embankment, or he couldn't. When the car was checked the next day, it was discovered that the brakes had failed. There was no way for James Lockwood to stop the car from going over, even if he tried."

"What does that mean? Isn't that unusual?" I ask.

"Yes, but on the rare occasion it does happen, the brake line doesn't look like it may have been tampered with," he adds. "It appears the brake line on Lockwood's car had wear marks where it eventually broke open and allowed the brake fluid to leak out. Unfortunately, the investigators were unable to prove the wear marks were deliberate."

"Why not? Shouldn't it have been obvious to a trained investigator?"

"That's the catch. The wear marks weren't made with a knife or sharp object, which would have been obvious. It looked more like something was rubbed against the brake line so often it eventually wore through, and the kicker is they found several zip ties that were holding the line in place. It was possible that they worked loose and was the reason the brake line opened up, yet it wasn't the most likely scenario. The investigators were fairly certain someone damaged the line and put the zip ties there to disguise it, but they couldn't prove it. No one could have predicted he would go over the embankment, but maybe whoever did the patch-up got lucky when he did."

"Why would they have used zip ties in the first place? That doesn't make sense. No one holds their vehicle together with zip ties."

"According to the wife, they had been having car trouble and couldn't afford to take it to the garage for maintenance. She said her husband had tried to fix the problems himself, but he knew very little about cars. She said, and I quote, 'Guess he won't be learning now.' The officers thought she was a real piece of work, but they couldn't prove what she said was wrong, so it was officially ruled an accident."

"That's a strange story, but from my encounter with Allie's mother, I'm not surprised by her coldness. So, I guess, in a way, Allie was telling me the truth about how her father died," I say, relieved that not everything I knew about her was a lie. "Did the officer you spoke with say there was any suspicion that Allie's mother tampered with the brake line? Or was it someone else? Please tell me they don't think it was Allie."

"He didn't say for certain, but I got the impression they were leaning toward the wife having done it. Allie was just a kid. I don't think she'd have the foresight or the knowledge to interfere with the brake line. I think she was a young girl who believed the story her mother was telling. The officer I talked to did say there was a guy who kept insisting that James Lockwood's death wasn't an accident. He said he wouldn't let up for months after it happened. Even when it was officially ruled an accident and the family had begun packing up their things, he still insisted his friend was murdered."

"Did the cops look into his allegations? Was there any validity to them?"

"He said they interviewed him, but everything he had to say was hearsay and speculation. He had no proof to back up his claims, but he kept at it for a long time. Eventually he quit making noise. The Lockwoods had moved on and people just forgot about it."

"I think we need to speak to this man. I know I said we were veering away from the real reason we are here, but maybe you're right. Maybe we need to learn more about the Lockwoods. It may be the key to finally finding him. I hate to think Allie might have anything to do with what happened to me, but regardless of how this turns out, I need to know about the person I trusted for so many years of my life. She was my lifeline in high school, and I can't think I was that bad a judge of character, but it seems like I could use some work in that area."

"I agree with you," David replies. "I have to admit, I'm curious to know the reason this man was so adamant James Lockwood was murdered. Maybe this guy is a little out there, but maybe he just needs the right people to listen to him. I got his name while I was on the phone. His name is Aaron Lodge. He's sixty-three now and still lives in Main Brook. It's a four-hour drive from here. It's too late to leave now and get back again tonight. We can leave first thing in the morning or leave now and spend the night in St. Anthony. It's your choice."

"David, do you realize what this means?" I ask, and he looks at me, puzzled. "It means the girl I called my best friend, who was my greatest supporter after my father died, may be involved in more than one murder. I know she was only a young girl when her father died, but do you really think it's not possible she was the cause of his death?"

"I can't answer those questions for you, Helena. I wish I could. Maybe this trip to Main Brook will shed some light on it for us. Allie was thirteen at the time, right?"

"Yes, twelve or thirteen, at least that's what she told me. I'm not sure what to believe anymore."

"Thirteen is young to commit murder, or even engage in the actions that lead to someone's death, but it's not unheard of. I haven't met her yet to form an opinion about her, but from my experience, I think it's unlikely . . . but not impossible. You knew her. What do you think?"

"I don't know. I wish I could say absolutely not, but I don't know if Allie is capable of murder or not. Where is Dr. Carpenter when you need her!" I try to joke, but the situation isn't funny, and David understands how unsettled I am.

"I'm thinking we head to St. Anthony for the night and go see Mr. Lodge first thing in the morning," says David. "It will give us time to get back to Deer Lake tomorrow and speak to Allie. I think we should hold off on our chat with her until then. I'd like to know more about her father's accident before we ask her any questions about Melody. Do you agree?"

"You're right. We should go to St. Anthony before we question Allie, but we may be getting a little sidetracked. I know we have to follow this trail of information, but we came here to find out about Melody, and we've yet to speak to anyone who knew her besides the social worker. She must have had friends here. A guy she was friendly with or a girl she confided in? I want to know—we need to know—what was going on in Melody's life before she left for college. I'm afraid everything else we're learning is leading us in the wrong direction."

"I agree with you. I've been wrapped up in everything concerning Allie Lockwood and her family, but after everything you've told me about her—the stalking, the creepy poems, your mother's questionable death, and now her father's—I'd be a lousy investigator if I failed to follow through on this."

"I guess she is tied to Melody as well. We just don't know the nature of that relationship other than the fact Allie was her guardian. Finding out more about Melody might help us learn more about that relationship, don't you agree?"

"I do. Just don't forget that all this started with you, as far as we can tell. We need to know why, and I believe uncovering the secrets around the Lockwood family might give us the answer."

"David, there's something I haven't told you about my time in the basement. I haven't said anything because I don't know if it's real or if I imagined it while I was unconscious or delirious from the infection and dehydration—but on the off chance it was real, I think you need to know."

"What is it, Helena? You know you can tell me anything. I won't judge you or anything you have to say about that time."

"Okay, here goes." I take a deep breath, trying to gather up the courage to voice the secret I've kept to myself all these years. "I think I heard someone else above me while I was in the basement."

"What? Are you telling me someone else was there with you in the basement?" he asks, shocked by my revelation.

"Not in the basement, but in the room above me. I believe it was a woman," I continue, and I can't look him in the face as I say it, "and I think I heard him yelling at her. I was in and out of it at the time, but I swear he called her Allie or at least yelled out to someone with that name." I look up at him and see surprise written all over his face.

"Helena, this may make all the difference in solving this case and finally ending it. Why have you waited so long to tell me this?" he asks, confused, and with just the tiniest bit of anger.

"How could I tell anyone when I wasn't sure if it was even real myself? Before we came here, I still thought of Allie as a former friend. Yes, our relationship had changed, but I didn't believe for a minute she would actually do something to hurt me so badly. Now I'm not sure what I think. The only thing I'm certain of is that I never really knew her at all."

"Then let's go find out everything we can about this woman.

It's time to uncover who the real Allie Lockwood is and how she fits into this, because, Helena, I'm pretty certain she's had a big role to play in everything that has happened."

"Then let's get started. How do we find someone who knew Melody Scott without tipping off Allie?"

"I'll touch base with her social worker. She'll likely know a friend or two of Melody's who we can talk to."

We walk back to the car in silence. David stops to search his contacts for the social worker's info while I sit on a bench to dump the sand from my shoes. I look out over the lake once more. The sun's rays glistening on the water call to me as if they are inviting me in, urging me to follow the pink path to heaven. I want so badly for this to be over. It was hard before. Now the journey feels like an anchor weighing me down. My need to know the truth and to stop him is an albatross, pulling me deeper and deeper into the darkness. I long for a future when Lily and I can live without constantly looking over our shoulders, but I wonder if that day will ever come. What if I am doomed to live forever in fear? What if I leave here with more questions than answers? What if I never leave at all?

What if he, or she, is already here and watching every move we make?

36

Mrs. Roberts, Melody's caseworker, gives us the names of two individuals who she thinks might be able to answer some of our questions about Melody's life here before she left for college. David learns from the former boyfriend's parents that he's now overseas on deployment with the Royal Canadian Navy and will not be available to talk to us for at least two more months. When asked the reason for the call, his mother replies that Melody was a troubled girl and she was glad her son had dodged that particular bullet, and although she was sorry to hear the girl had died, she was not surprised it had happened.

"Doesn't sound like she was fond of her son's girlfriend," I comment. "Did she elaborate on why she disliked her so much?"

"No, nothing more than she was trouble, but we already knew she had been in trouble with the law before. She had a difficult life. I'm guessing everyone in town knew of her situation, as it was quite sensational. Mrs. Roberts did give me another name. Hopefully we'll have better luck with her. She is a former girlfriend by the name of Rachael Simon. She still lives here in Deer Lake and works evenings at the Tim Hortons on the highway."

"We can head that way now. I could use a cup of Timmie's," I answer, then add, "you know, David, I had a difficult life, too, when I was her age, but we don't all end up in trouble with the law."

"That's very true. It's all about the choices you make."

"And the people you lean on. I had Allie. Back then she was my rock, but now I have no idea who she is. It's hard to believe she could be someone other than the person I trusted so completely."

We drive in silence the short distance to the coffee and dough-nut shop on the highway. The day has been long, and processing so much information has been both trying and mind-boggling. I long to hold my sweet Lily and tuck her into bed. The only con-solation is knowing that when this is all over we will be finally free. I want to be able to show Lily the world without constantly worrying he is out there, watching us, and waiting to pounce. For the first time since this all began, I have hope that no matter how hard and disturbing things get, there will be an ending. It might not be the clean and tidy ending I was hoping for, but an ending, nonetheless.

We pull into the parking lot, and I am instantly drawn back to my teen years when all the teenagers hung out inside the coffee shop and lingered outside in the parking lot, just shooting the bull and being loud and obnoxious while doing so. I missed out on that part of my teens because I was at home caring for my mother, but I often drove by and wondered if I would have been one of the girls sitting on the hood of some guy's car had my father not died and set in motion everything bad that followed. So many things would have been different had Dad not gotten sick. Mom would still be here, and I would have gone off to college and become something other than the damaged person I am now. Mostly, I would not have befriended Allie. I would have left her sitting alone in the cafeteria and not thought twice about the badly dressed loner in the corner. Would I be here now if not for her? Is my befriending her the big-gest mistake of my life? I hope I get to find out, even if I do discover I brought this all upon myself.

"Are you coming inside?" David asks, and I realize he is al-ready out of the car and waiting for me to decide.

"Do I have a choice? We have to finish what we've started," I say in answer to my own question and close the car door behind me. "What does Rachael look like? Did Mrs. Roberts give you a description?"

"She said Rachael is a tall girl with long brown hair. I'm sure someone will point her out if it isn't obvious."

We go inside and walk up to the counter. I order us two coffees and a box of Timbits to go. The girl who serves me is short and blonde, so I look around for the person I think may be Rachael. Then I hear someone call out that her order is ready, and I realize Rachael is tending to the drive-thru window. I walk over to the side of the counter closest to her and ask if we could possibly speak to her for a few minutes.

"I don't know you, lady, and besides, I'm working," she replies abruptly.

David steps in front of me and flashes his badge. "Rachael, I'm Sergeant Campbell with the RCMP."

I realize stupidly that I should have let him approach her in the first place.

"We'd like to ask you some questions about a former friend of yours, Melody Scott."

"Can't you see I'm working?" she repeats.

"Rachael, I'm sure you're entitled to a break. It's important that we speak with you."

"My break is not for another twenty minutes. If you want to wait until then, I'll answer your questions, if I can."

"Thank you," I say, but she is already talking into her headset.

David and I take our coffee and Timbits to a table in the corner. It's hard to find privacy in a place like this, but it is the only option. Most of the tables are filled tonight. There is a group of older gentlemen gathered around a couple of tables, laughing and enjoying each other's company. There are groups of kids, both preteen and teens, grouped at different tables throughout the coffee shop. It reminds me of myself before things went bad, when I would come here with friends and teammates after our games. It was the place to hang out back then. That much hasn't changed.

David and I sip our coffee while I pick out all the chocolate Timbits and leave him the rest. "You know it's very cliché to see you sitting in a doughnut shop eating doughnut holes!" I joke.

"Ha, ha," he says. "Very funny." He looks at me, and I can tell right away that he knows my attempt at humour is nothing more than an effort to forget about the last two days and everything we've learned. "Are you okay, Helena? I know this is rough for you."

"I'll be fine. I just want this over, and the faster I can get back to Lily, the better."

"I know you miss her, but you don't have to worry. She is in very capable hands with my dad. My parents will keep her safe and provide her with the best vacation she's ever had."

"It's the only vacation she's ever had," I say. "I haven't felt safe enough to take her anywhere. I know he's out there somewhere, and I've always been afraid he'll recognize me and I won't see him. I can't risk that happening when I have Lily to think about. Maybe this time will be different."

"It will be," he insists. "Things are different this time, Helena. We're going to get him. I can feel it."

"But at what cost, David? That's what worries me." I look up and see Rachael approaching our table. "Here she comes."

"Thanks for taking the time to talk with us, Rachael. We really appreciate it," David says, and pulls out a chair, inviting her to sit down.

"I'm not sure how I can help. Melody and I were friends a long time ago. Do you know what happened to her?" she asks. I can tell by her eyes that she is bothered by what she has learned about her friend. "Is that why you're here?"

"We are here in Deer Lake trying to find out what happened

to Melody. We thought you could tell us something about her life before she left for college."

"I can try, but we stopped hanging out about a couple of years before she left town."

"Why is that?" I ask. "Did you two have a falling-out?"

"No, nothing like that. It's just she changed when she started living in that last foster home. You know she was in foster care, right?"

"Yes, we know her situation. Was there something about the foster home that prevented her from spending time with you?"

"I don't know. At first she hated it there, but then she kind of settled in. I don't know why, though, because she said it was awful there. They wouldn't let her do anything. She said one time they even made her take a cold shower because they thought she'd had sex with her boyfriend. I mean, who does that? She complained to the social worker, but she didn't do anything. She thought the Lockwoods were the perfect family for Melody, and nothing was going to change her mind about them."

"Why do you say that? The caseworker is supposed to have the child's best interest in mind when placing them in a home. If things weren't right there, it was her duty to investigate the Lockwoods," David tells her.

"Yeah, well, it seemed like that social worker really liked Allie Lockwood. Melody couldn't say anything bad about her or she'd get a mouthful from her, telling her she should be grateful the Lockwoods took her in when nobody else would. Melody got in a bit of trouble after what happened. She didn't know how to deal with what her father did. It was hard."

"Did Melody say why she stopped hanging out with you?" I ask.

"Nah, she just stopped coming out with us. She stopped skipping school, and her grades started to improve, a lot. We were in the same classes, and we always did about the same, but after she moved in with the Lockwoods, she started getting straight A's. I always wondered if they forced her to do well, or punished her if she didn't. You know, there were times she didn't eat because they wouldn't give her food. That's just not right. I told Melody to talk to someone else besides her caseworker, but I don't think she ever did. Not long after, she stopped coming around, and eventually we drifted apart."

"Did you ever ask Melody why school became so important? Did she tell you Allie forced her to do well or risk punishment if she didn't?" David asks.

"No, she didn't say that they would punish her. I just got the feeling something wasn't right. She did say one time that school was their ticket out of here. Maybe she just wanted to get away from town." Rachael shrugs, and I am reminded of my own desire at her age to use school as my way out.

"Just one more thing, Rachael, before you go back," David asks, and I can see he is puzzled about something. "When you talk about Melody's relationship with the Lockwoods, you say 'they' or 'them.' Allie Lockwood was Melody's guardian, but you act like Allie's mother was a part of the problem, too."

"Most of Melody's problems were caused by that woman. Melody said she was a real piece of work. She called her a crazy bitch most of the time. She's the one who forced her to take the cold shower, not Allie. I think she and Allie actually started to get along," she replies, then turns to go back to work.

"Rachael, you said Melody told you school was 'their' ticket out of town. Why did you say 'their' instead of 'her'?"

"Because," she answers as she walks away, "Melody and Allie were going to leave town together."

I sit there dazed by the revelation. Judging by the look on David's face, he is just as confused. If Rachael is right, Allie had intended on leaving with Melody, but for some reason, she had changed her mind. I remember when I was preparing to leave for school and Allie was adamant she wasn't ever going to leave Deer

Lake. I always thought it was her way of dealing with the fact she couldn't afford to pay for college and didn't have the support at home to offer assistance and encouragement. But what if something else was holding her back? Or worse, someone else?

"What do you make of that?" David asks, and I can tell he's trying to figure out how this fits into his theory that Allie may be behind everything that's happened.

"I don't know what to say. Everything we learn about Allie just proves more and more how little I knew about her. I can't offer insight into a person who is now even more mysterious to me."

"I think this family has a lot of secrets, and they don't all start and end with Allie Lockwood. We need to find out more about that family, all of them. I'm curious about the mother. We haven't heard much about her, but from what I've heard, it makes me want to know more. In fact, I'm certain it would be stupid and incompetent of me not to find out more about the woman at the head of this family."

"This just gets crazier and more confusing! How are we ever supposed to figure out what's real and what isn't? I feel like I'm standing in the middle of a Tilt-a-Whirl with all the bits and pieces of my life swirling around me. I want to focus on something, anything, that will help end this, but I can't figure out what it is I need to hold on to."

"Hold on to Lily and your future. This is going to work itself out soon. I promise. Let's go back to the hotel. You need some rest, and I need to sort out everything we've learned today. We can make the drive to St. Anthony first thing in the morning."

"David, don't make promises you can't keep," I tell him, knowing how quickly things can change. "Things are confusing now, but it doesn't mean we're any closer to discovering the truth. It just means he might be harder to find."

"I have no intention of breaking any promises to you, Helena Douglas. Just trust me. Things feel different this time."

The hotel is a short distance down the highway, and we arrive at our rooms in minutes. I put the key card in the slot to open the door, and I hesitate for just a moment. I almost invite David into my room, but he's already closing the door to his room. I open my door and walk in to find it freezing inside. I assume housekeeping had turned on the air conditioning, but I have no idea why she would think it necessary at the end of September. The fall air will cool the room without the use of the unit. I hit the light and hurry to switch on some heat instead. Then I notice an envelope sitting atop the desk, and I know it wasn't the maid who has been messing around in my room.

I knock on the adjoining room door, and David opens it immediately. He stands there in the opening, shirtless, and the for the first time since I've known him, I feel heat rising to my face. I turn away quickly and pray he doesn't notice.

"What's up?" he asks casually. "You need to get some rest."

"Someone has been here in my room," I tell him. "The air conditioning unit was turned on maximum."

"That's why it's so cold in here," he interrupts. "It was probably housekeeping."

"That's not the only thing," I tell him. "There's also that," I add, and point to the envelope on the desk. "It has my name on it. I haven't touched it."

"Don't. I'll get some gloves."

David returns to his room and comes back with a pair of latex gloves. He handles the envelope carefully and opens it with a letter opener. Inside is a note, and I know who it's from just by looking at the handwriting.

"It's her. It's Allie. What does it say?" I ask, nervous to hear the words.

"It's another weird poem, like you said she left years ago. I'll read it, but I'm not sure it makes a lot of sense."

The years have passed,
Time and lives have changed,
But I have not forgotten.
You came home,
To disrupt and disturb,
And to dredge up the past.
Just remember, dear Helena,
In your pursuit of the truth,
It is I who will win.
Because no one gets to leave.

"What does that even mean? Is it a warning? Is it a threat? Am I just supposed to run now like a dog with my tail between my legs? How did she even get inside my room or know where to find me?" I am shouting, but I don't know why.

"You're angry and you're scared, Helena, but we're going to solve this. And soon. I know we're looking in the right place. We are getting close. I can feel it. You just have to hang on a little longer."

"I'm not going anywhere until this is finished. I'm not afraid as much as I'm pissed off. I've had enough of her games. I need to see Allie Lockwood. It's time we had it out."

"I'm going to check in with my CO. He needs to know what's going on here. I'm thinking he'll send someone in to support us from Major Crimes. I'll also need to inform Sergeant Mackenzie here in Deer Lake. He needs to know what we've learned. We may need backup before this is over. Things are starting to heat up. I'll let you know what they say.

"I'm going to take this. I have a baggie I can seal it in. I'll take it to the detachment here in town and get it dusted for prints. If we're lucky, we'll have a fingerprint ID by tomorrow, or eventually we might find some DNA from the person who wrote it."

David leaves, and I am left here in the cold hotel room alone with my anger and my memories. I think of the creepy poems she left for me years ago. I always thought she was angry at me for choosing to go. Now it seems as if she wanted to go, too, but for some reason changed her mind. I don't know if she is pissed with me for leaving, or jealous that I did.

Maybe David is right and there is more behind these poems than I care to admit. What if I never understand the messages she is sending? What if they will only mean something to the person who wrote them? What if that person is Allie?

And what if it isn't her at all?

What if we have it all wrong?

37

I sat in the waiting room watching the clock tick away the minutes to my next session with Dr. Carpenter. I had moved away from town and into my new secluded home in the country, yet I couldn't cut ties with the woman who had helped get me there. My life would never be the same as it had been before. I would never walk carefree among strangers or run down a lonely trail on my own ever again, but I was living. I had a home. Soon, I would have a baby to share my home with. Sometimes, I thought I might have the courage to continue my college courses in the fall—albeit from home, but it was a start. I might not have been living it up, but it was a life. I would be forever grateful to Dr. Carpenter for helping me realize there was more to my life than the memories and scars left behind by the trauma I had endured. It might define me in some way, but it did not own me.

I was still recording my memories, and each time I did, I locked them in the box with the rest of the horrific details of my captivity. And each time another memory got locked away and I reinvented the ending, I slept a little better at night. I would never give up my vigilance in keeping my home—and soon my child—safe, but some days I almost felt normal, or as normal as one can after a horrific and traumatic captivity that lasted three months, two weeks, and five days.

I had a routine each night when I checked, and then re-checked, the locks on my windows and doors. It helped to ease my mind when I knew he was still out there. No one knew where I lived, other than David. I had become a recluse, but in my mind, I was less noticeable, less detectable. I wanted to be inconspicuous, even invisible. That was, until I found him. Then I wanted him to see me coming.

The long hand on the clock moved into the top position, sig-nalling it was ten o'clock, time for my appointment. Dr. Carpenter's office was designed in such a way that all incoming patients waited at the entrance to her office, while outgoing patients left by way of a second door. None of us got to see each other or witness each other's pain and successes. We knew others existed, yet we had no contact. I liked that about her office. I didn't want anyone to see me coming or going. My face was well-known by everyone. I was fa-mous, almost legendary, as the girl who went to hell and survived. My face had been plastered on television screens, magazine covers, and newspapers for weeks after I emerged from the cornfield. My story was a sensational one. My ordeal was horrific and sickening, with all the ingredients the press loved to feed on just to regurgitate later for their followers to devour.

I entered the spacious office and took a seat on the brown leather sofa. Dr. Carpenter took up her position in the armchair across from me. She had a desk with two wingback chairs in front, but I'd come to prefer the sofa and the more casual feel it emulated. I saw Dr. Carpenter every day for more than a month when I was first admitted to the hospital. She was the first person I had told my ordeal to, and she remained the only person I felt comfortable enough to discuss my darkest secrets and most revealing memo-ries. She had been my lifeline when I thought I was drowning, and my anchor when I was adrift in an ocean of trauma. Without her, I was not sure where I would be.

"Hello, Helena. How are you?"

"I'm surviving. Thanks to you," I replied.

"Helena, I'm just here to help point you in the right direction. You are doing all the work. Is there anything in particular you'd like to talk about today? Something new you've remembered or feelings you'd like help sorting out? Are you still coping at home in your new house?"

"I'm doing well, I think. The baby is due soon. Five weeks, to be exact. I'm not sure I'll know what to do with her. It's a girl. I found out a few days ago. I put off knowing for a long time. I thought if I didn't know what sex it was I could pretend it wasn't real for a little while longer, but look at me. I look like a whale, I need to pee all the time, and I can't see my feet. This is real, and I may as well face it."

"That's true. It is very much a reality. Soon you will have a little baby girl to care for. Are you ready for her and all that entails?" she asked, and I felt the anxiety creeping in.

"I don't think I'll ever be ready, but I want to try. I have so many questions about how I will feel about this baby and a lot of anxieties, but I'm going to embrace them and her. I'm hoping everything will fall into place once I look into her eyes and hold her. If it doesn't, I will deal with that, too. I'm not willing to give her up without at least trying to be her mom. She didn't ask to be born. She didn't ask for a monster for a father. She doesn't deserve to be rejected for something that isn't her fault. She deserves better, and I'm going to give it to her."

"That's good, Helena. That's all any new mom can hope for, and your desire to try makes me believe this part of your life will turn out even better than you're hoping for. Do you have someone to help you once you come home with your baby?" she asked, and I shrugged. "Helena, all new moms will need help at some point. You sure there isn't someone in your life you can count on?"

My mind automatically thought of Allie. There was a time in my life I couldn't imagine going through life without her. I always thought she would be with me for the important things, like when I graduated college, got married, had my first kid. But things had changed, and our relationship had been damaged beyond repair. I couldn't invite her back into my life after all that had happened. I had hurt her by shutting her out, and her retaliation had shown a side of her I hadn't known existed. She was a door to a part of my life I didn't care to open.

"Why don't we talk about Allie today?" Dr. Carpenter asked.

I had mentioned her name several times during our sessions. She knew we had a difficult history and an even more unsettling not-so-distant past, but I hadn't offered the details of our relationship. There were many reasons, some of which included guilt and selfishness, that I didn't want to discuss Allie and our history together.

"Why? She and I aren't friends anymore. I've told you before," I retorted. "I don't see how talking about her will help anything at this point."

"Helena, from the little you've told me, it seems as though Allie is someone who was very important to you for a long time. Why do you think the relationship cannot be repaired?" she asked.

"It's complicated," I replied. "Allie isn't entirely at fault for our friendship failing. I am to blame, too."

"I'm listening," she said, prompting me to continue.

I knew she was exploring the idea of me reconnecting with Allie. Dr. Carpenter believed I needed someone other than her to help me find my way back into society. She wasn't wrong in that regard, however, she was wrong in thinking Allie might be the person to help me do so.

"Allie started out as part of a deal I made with God to help my father when he was sick. I promised to befriend the poor girl everyone made fun of at school in return for Him saving my dad. God didn't hold up His end of the bargain." I almost laughed at how silly that sounded. "But Allie and I did form an unlikely friendship.

She was my best friend for the rest of high school, and then things changed. Eventually too much had happened for us to ever go back to where we were."

"Why do you think you can't go back? People change, Helena. You know that more than anyone. Maybe Allie isn't the same person today as she was then. Tell me why your relationship started to change."

"I left home, and as much as I felt guilty for leaving my mother and asking my friend to care for her, I went anyway. I couldn't wait to get away and start over, to live again. After all the years I spent in misery looking after my mother and tending to her basic needs, I was finally free, and I couldn't get away fast enough. Then, my mother killed herself, and deep down I felt Allie should have known she wasn't doing well. I trusted her to look after Mom, and she failed.

"I realize that I had also failed her as a friend. I knew she was living in a shitty situation, likely worse than my own, but I left her there in what was most likely an abusive home, and I went on my own without asking her to go or helping her to leave with me. I used her to ease my own guilt by making sure my mother wasn't alone. And that was only the beginning."

"You were young, then, and your own mental health was being pushed to the limits. Children aren't supposed to grow up worrying and caring for their parents. It should be the other way around."

"Yes, and children aren't supposed to grow up in fear of being beaten by their parents, but it happens. I think it was happening to Allie, but I didn't do anything to help her. I was a selfish, messed-up teenager, and I regret how I treated her. Even if I could find the courage to ask her to forgive me, it wouldn't matter, anyway."

"Why do feel so sure?" she asked.

"Because even though I treated Allie like crap, she wasn't without fault. Allie was messed up in ways I hadn't seen until after I left. She's unstable and unpredictable, and I don't need that in my life right now. I have enough going on without the worry of wondering what she's going to do next."

"Why don't you elaborate? Tell me what you think she said or did that made you believe she is unstable."

"Allie did things, said things, that normal people don't do. She stalked me after I went back to school. She turned up at a coffee shop on the first anniversary of my mother's death to ask me to come home, and here's the kicker, she was living in *my* house with all of my family's things. If that wasn't strange enough, she sent me weird poems saying how we were meant to be together and how she was going to make it happen. One time, she let herself into my house and put flowers on my table, the same flowers I had thrown in the trash the day before. Another time, she left a bottle of sleeping pills and a flask of vodka on my nightstand. It was the second anniversary of my mother's suicide. Now, you tell me who does that. No one does, not unless they are unstable," I answered, frustrated.

"That does sound disturbing. Did you confront her? Ask her why she was doing these things? Are you certain it was her who did them?"

"I didn't get the chance to confront her. Not long after her last stunt, I was kidnapped, and you know the rest. And what do you mean, am I sure it was her? Who else could it be?"

"I don't know. Was there anyone else in your life who might have done these things other than Allie? Did you have other enemies? Allie came to the hospital every day, hoping for the chance to see you, and begging the nurses to give her an update. That doesn't sound like someone who has issue with you, but rather someone who cares deeply."

"Yeah, as in stalker," I butted in. "I didn't have any other friends, and I don't have any other family. No one else would have reason to stalk me, and I didn't tell anyone how my mother killed herself. No one other than Allie knew, and she learned about it because she was the person who found her. Anyway, I've moved on. I have a new house in a new town, and no one besides David knows where I am. I want to keep it that way."

"What about Allie? Did she have someone in her life who may have wanted to scare you?"

"Allie had no one in her life besides her mother. She was a mean woman, but I don't know why she'd want to come after me when I had already left town," I replied, getting more frustrated. "She did mention a brother once or twice, but I didn't meet him. I don't even think he lived in Deer Lake. I've had enough of Allie. She and I aren't good for each other. There's nothing that'll ever change that."

"It's your decision to make, Helena. It sounds like there is a lot of history between you two, with a lot of emotions on both your parts. You may find that healing your relationship with Allie may help the both of you move on and, quite possibly, heal together. Working through the emotional guilt and the anger you feel toward her can only help you move on, even if that means Allie remains a part of your past. She is a huge part of your history, and a troubling part at that, but resolving your issues with her may make the road to a full life much smoother," Dr. Carpenter told me.

"With all due respect, I don't agree with you this time, Dr. Carpenter. We both know I wouldn't be where I am now without your help, but Allie is one subject where we'll have to agree to disagree. I am trying to move forward. I can't go backward. Allie is in the past, and that is where she needs to stay," I argued.

"Okay, then, I'll support your decision, but if you ever want to explore the idea of making things right with her, then you know where I am. Helena, you are doing amazingly well after the trauma you've suffered. I wouldn't suggest doing something that might threaten the progress you've made, but ultimately the decision is yours, and I will respect whatever you choose."

"I know you mean well, but I just can't go back. I can't let Allie back into my life."

"All right, I'll see you next week. You have your appointment schedule, have you not?"

"Yes, Rhonda gave it to me before I came in," I told her. "I'll be here. Thanks for everything." Rhonda was her secretary. She kept the front waiting room stocked with magazines and puzzle books and always made certain the tissue box was full. She knew who I was the very first day I walked into the waiting room, yet she hadn't avoided making eye contact with me even once. She was a friendly face in a place where most people were in need of a friend.

I left her office through the side exit. There was no one waiting on the other side of this door. There were more leather chairs there and a box of tissues for times when the pain was just too much and you needed a few minutes to compose yourself. I had stopped there numerous times over the last months. There had been times I hadn't been able to face the world outside and needed that extra time to decompress and leave the building. I could have called Allie during those hard days, but I didn't. I was firm in my belief that I couldn't go back. Too much had been said and done. But what if Dr. Carpenter was right? What if Allie was the person I needed to get me through all of this? What if she was the reason I couldn't entirely let go of the past? What if I was never free of the anger I felt toward her, or the guilt that rose every time I thought of her and the way I treated her?

What if the only way to move forward was to go back?

What if Dr. Carpenter was right?

38

I wake in the morning more tired than the night before. I've barely slept. As hard as I try, I can't seem to halt my brain's preoccupation with everything we've learned since arriving in Deer Lake. I'm now questioning everything I thought I knew. I came here for answers, for resolution, but I'm more confused now than ever before. I can't tell if we are closer to finding the monster who held me captive and murdered Melody Scott or if we've travelled so far off course that we're finally lost. The only thing I know for sure is coming home has been a whirlwind of surprises, doubts, and uncertainty.

"I'd ask if you slept last night, but I can tell by looking at you that you've barely closed your eyes," David comments as he enters my room through the adjoining door. "Are you sure you're up to taking the drive to Main Brook?"

"I'm going with you," I reply, while pressing my fingers into my raccoon eyes. "I can sleep on the way. It's a long drive. It's quite scenic if you haven't been up that way before. I've been several times, but this trip isn't about taking in mountains and ancient fjords. Are you sure you can't call Mr. Lodge and ask these questions over the phone?"

"Yes, I can, but I might lose the advantages of speaking with him in person. I get to see his face as he answers my questions. It's impossible to pick up on little nuances and hesitations over the phone which, in person, might allow me to ascertain how true his account really is. I don't want to believe every word this man has to say without having something to back up his theory, and if he stirred up trouble for no reason, I need to know that, too. Unless he's a pathological liar, he will show signs he's not being entirely truthful, but again, I can't determine that with a telephone call."

"Okay, let's get going, then. The quicker we leave, the earlier we'll get back. I'm still anxious to see Allie. There are just so many questions I need answers to." `

"Helena, Allie may not have all the answers you're looking for. I believe she's a big part of this whole mystery, but I'm not entirely sure she's a major player in all of this. That's why we need to know more about the Lockwood family. There are just too many unanswered questions."

"I know. Let's just go."

We walk to the car in silence. Outside, the air is cool with the approaching fall. It seems like the leaves have turned even more since we first arrived in town. Soon they will display the vibrant reds, oranges, and yellows that signal the warm and cozy autumn season. Pumpkins and hay bales will adorn front steps and porches alike, while the smells of pumpkin spice and cinnamon permeate every home and coffee shop for miles.

I recall days with my parents, wandering the pumpkin patch, looking for the biggest and most perfect specimen to carve with my father, and taking photos with the field of sunflowers as a backdrop. I remember them towering above me and being happily oblivious to how things would soon change for us. I haven't been to the pumpkin patch since. Maybe this will be the year I feel safe enough to bring Lily.

I replay our conversation yesterday and long to hear her voice, but the cell reception in these mountains and valleys is spotty at best. I will have to settle for sweet memories and hope I can catch her before bedtime. I miss her deeply and tell myself I am doing this for her, for us, so we can finally be free. Free from worry, free from fear, and free to enter the world we have been hiding from, but desperately wanting to be a part of.

And maybe we can even be free to love. I glance at David and quickly turn my head toward the window. I don't know where these feelings are coming from, and I feel the heat once again rising to my cheeks. For years I believed I was incapable of ever loving a man again, at least physically. The trauma I suffered was just too great to overcome, but I have always held out hope that, someday, I might feel comfortable enough to try. Maybe closing the chapter on this part of my life will be the catalyst I need to move on.

"Helena, are you awake?" I hear David's voice, but he seems so far away. "We're here." His voice pulls me into the present, and I realize I have been asleep for most of the trip up the coast. "Feeling better?" he asks.

"Yes, I think so. I need coffee."

"I don't think you're going to find it here."

"Let's just find Aaron Lodge and hear what he has to say about Allie's family. Where are we supposed to meet him?"

"He said he lives by the water in a red two-storey house. He told me there's a garage in the back, and he has a few old cars scattered throughout his yard that he's been meaning to work on for a while now but hasn't gotten to yet. I'm not sure if that will be enough to find him or not."

"I don't think you'll have to worry about finding him. Looks like he gave you pretty accurate directions."

It takes all of five minutes to drive through the town of Main Brook. There is really only one main road that travels through the centre of town and leads down to the waterfront, where the harbour is lined with boats of all sizes, and the sea rolls in and out with the winds and the tides. It is quite peaceful here and pleasantly scenic, but we aren't here to sightsee. Mr. Lodge's house is a red saltbox-styled home with a modern garage sitting back from the road toward the end of the property. He wasn't entirely accurate with his description, however, as there are at least a dozen vehicles littered throughout the yard and side yard. If he is a collector, it is of hunks of metal rather than actual vehicles, as his property resembles a metal scrapyard.

We pull into the driveway, and as soon as we exit the car, we can hear machinery coming from the garage out back. David tries knocking, but a welding machine drowns out the sound of our arrival. Sparks crackle and dance as Mr. Lodge continues to work on the vehicle jacked up in the garage, and the shield he wears to protect his eyes keeps his face hidden from us while we wait for him to finish.

"Sorry 'bout that, but I was needin' to get this here chassis welded back together," he says as he removes the face shield and other protective gear. "You must be Sergeant Campbell? It's 'bout time somebody took me seriously. It only took a decade."

"I'm sorry, Mr. Lodge. We're here now and would very much like to hear what it is you have to say about James Lockwood's accident. Thank you for speaking to us," David replies, showing him his badge at the same time.

"First, you can call me Aaron, and second, it wasn't an accident that killed James."

"What makes you say that? Our officers couldn't find any conclusive evidence suggesting it was intentional."

"I don't know what they found back then, and what they didn't find, but I'm tellin' you James Lockwood was murdered, and his crazy wife was the bitch who did it."

"Do you have any evidence to back up these accusations, Aaron?" I ask, interested to know why he is so adamant Allie's father was murdered.

"I don't have solid evidence like the kind you're lookin' for, but I can tell you things about that relationship that would make your hair stand up. Everyone knew Sheila Lockwood was a crazy bitch. She was a nasty woman when they met, and for the life of me I don't know why James married her in the first place, but once the girl was born—Abby or Allie, somethin' like that—well, he wouldn't just walk away and leave the kid. So, he stayed and he grew more miserable every day after."

"A lot of people live through unhappy marriages. Why do you think theirs was something more?" David asks, and I notice him watching Aaron Lodge's face closely as he answers each question.

"This wasn't just an unhappy marriage, Sergeant. Oh, no, Aaron lived in hell with Sheila. She drank, and the more she drank, the nastier she got. She called him every name in the book. He was never good enough. He was a bad husband. He was a bad father. He couldn't do anything right in his life, accordin' to that witch, and if he ever spoke up for himself, well, he paid the price for that, too."

"How so?" I ask, already knowing where this was going from my experience with Allie's mother all those years ago.

"She hit that man something awful. And he just took it. Not once did I know him to try to defend himself against her. He was good like that, wouldn't hurt a woman, you know? He figured if she took her rage out on him, she'd leave the kids alone," he answers, and his voice trails off as if he's remembering a time he'd just as soon forget.

"You said kids. Allie had a brother. Is that right?" I ask him.

"Yeah, little Jimmy. He was a handful, that one, but a sweet kid just the same. James loved those kids despite the hate their mother spewed every day."

"Why are you so sure the accident was intentional?"

"'Cause Sheila told the cops they were havin' car trouble and James did somethin' to the car as a temporary fix because they couldn't afford to fix it proper. Well, that's just bullshit. James was over here quite often just to escape his miserable life with that woman. We worked on these old clunkers together sometimes, and he knew how to keep a vehicle runnin'. He wouldn't have done what she's saying he did. It's just not right. If James had trouble with his brakes, he would have fixed 'em. Hell, I probably would've helped him do it."

"Are you certain, Mr. Lodge?" I ask, baffled by what he is telling us.

"Without a doubt, I am. You know, ol' James finally got up the nerve to leave that bitch. That's what he was doing the night of the crash. He told me a few days before he was takin' the kids and leavin' town. He said he was goin' early in the mornin' while Sheila was still sleepin' off the booze from the night before. I think she found out what he was plannin' and did somethin' to keep him from goin'."

"And you think she tried to kill him while the kids were in the car with him?" I ask.

"Nah, I'm not sure she meant to kill him, but she sure wasn't sad when he ended up dead. Her biggest worry was supportin' herself and the two kids. James was the breadwinner. She just drank most of what he brought home. If he didn't squirrel some away to buy food and clothes for those kids, they would have had nothin'."

"Allie wasn't with him when he had the accident," I tell him. "Why would he leave her behind?"

"He wouldn't have done it lightly, I guarantee it, but that poor girl was terrified of her mother. When James was at work, I think she took the brunt of her mother's rage."

"But her brother was older. Wouldn't he have stepped in?" I ask, confused.

"No, you have it all wrong. Jimmy was the baby. The girl, Allie, was two or three years older than him. He came around here with his father often. Cute kid, but shy. James wanted to take them both. I don't know why she didn't go, too."

"Aaron, was the son, Jimmy, killed in the car crash with his father?" David asks, and I believe this was why Allie had barely mentioned her brother to me.

"No, no. The boy was fine. They found him in the back seat. He was pretty shaken up. In shock, they said. He left town with Sheila and his sister not long after the cops declared the crash an accident. That bitch took the insurance money and got the hell out of town before anyone could ask more questions. Why are you two here now askin' about this? It was a long time ago. Has that bitch done somethin' else? I tell you, she's evil and she's capable of anythin.'"

"Thanks for your time, Mr. Lodge," David says. "I can't get into any details of why we are here, but you've been very helpful. Are you ready, Helena? I think we should head back. We've got quite a drive back to Deer Lake."

He takes my arm and leads me out of the garage and into the fresh air. I take in the cool air in big, deep breaths, still unable to grasp what I have just learned. "What—"

"Shh. Wait until we're back in the car," David orders, and hurries me along the driveway to our car.

Once inside the car, I cannot hold my tongue. "David, what the hell happened to Jimmy? He was just a little boy when they left Main Brook and moved to Deer Lake. How could he have just disappeared? I never saw him, not once. He didn't go to school. It was as if he barely existed!"

"I'm not sure. Let's hope there's a reasonable explanation. Maybe Sheila surrendered him to social services. Perhaps she realized she couldn't care for him and gave him up."

"You know that's not what happened. Mrs. Roberts would have discovered it when she helped them with financial aid," I fire back, "and if he were still with them, wouldn't Sheila have used him to garner more money in support?"

"I know. I'm just trying to keep you from imagining the worst."

"How can I not? My best friend had a little brother she rarely spoke of, and I've just learned he somehow disappeared into thin air the same year her father was likely murdered by her abusive mother and they moved to Deer Lake. He would have been about ten or eleven years old when Allie moved there. How could I not have known him? How could she not have told me about him?"

"Helena, there are a lot of things about the Lockwoods that Allie didn't tell you. A lot of them aren't good. This whole family is a mystery, and I know they are at the centre of everything we are trying to uncover."

We are sitting in the car discussing our conversation with Aaron Lodge when he knocks on the driver's side window, startling us in the process.

"Is there something else, Mr. Lodge?" David asks as he lowers the window.

"Well, I'm not sure it means anythin', but James said somethin' once when I was tellin' him to get out of that house and leave the bitch. At the time I didn't think it meant anythin', but havin' brought up all these old memories with you two, it came back to me again."

"What did he say?" I ask, afraid to hear any more.

"He said he couldn't get out, and when I asked him why, he said, 'No one gets to leave.' Not sure if that means anythin' to you, but that's what he said."

"Thanks for all your help, Aaron," David tells him, and closes the window before turning to me. "What's wrong, Helena? You look like you've seen a ghost."

I can't seem to form the words to tell him what I have just remembered. It seems like a lifetime ago, but those words are as clear as if it were only yesterday. I look at David as a tear sneaks out of the corner of my eye and trickles down my face. "Those are the words he said to me in the basement."

"What do you mean, he said to you?"

"When I was trapped in the basement, I begged him to let me go, and he said to me one time, 'Don't you know, Helena, no one gets to leave.' My God, David, what does this all mean?"

"It means we have to find out what happened to Jimmy Lockwood."

We head back to town a little faster, both of us deep in thought. David, I'm sure, is going over everything we've learned in the last couple of days, trying to put the pieces together. I am too shaken to think of anything other than the words he said to me in the basement. What does the Lockwood family have to do with my abduction? And if they're involved, what did I do to deserve such horror? What if the truth is even harder to accept than not knowing? What if Allie knew I was trapped in the basement all along? What if Sheila Lockwood is the mastermind behind it all? What if the monster is Jimmy Lockwood?

What if they're all in it together?

39

I leave David at the depot. He has police business to tend to, and I am a civilian, he reminds me. He asks me to wait for him in my hotel room. I think he has forgotten I am not just a civilian. I was the victim. I am the survivor. I came here looking for a monster and dreaming of closure. I will not sit on my hands now and wait for him to return with all the answers. I don't do well with waiting. My mind gets bogged down with all the questions and the what-ifs, and it leaves me feeling panicked and anxious, a cocktail of emotions I need to avoid.

I drive by the hotel without the slightest hesitation. I have decided where I am going, and it isn't the hotel. I am not sitting around waiting for David to solve the mystery and save the day. I am heading to the place I have been wanting to go since we arrived here. I want to see it for myself. I don't know if I can ever accept it, but maybe I can at least try to understand it. Yet I have no idea if any amount of explaining or rationalizing can make it okay that my best friend moved into my home with all my things right after I left it. It doesn't make sense, and now it feels creepy.

I have not told Allie I am coming. I want to see the look on her face when she opens the front door and sees me standing on her front porch. If she truly hates me enough to have me kidnapped, beaten, raped, and tortured for months, her face should express something. But what am I expecting? A show of remorse for all the pain she's caused? Will she exhibit anger at the mere sight of me? Maybe her mental instability will manifest itself in ways I have not yet imagined. Whatever happens, I can't wait any longer to find out. Allie and I need to have a conversation. I need answers, and she is the key to unlocking the mystery that has haunted me for so long. I just hope I'm not stepping into a lion's den by going there.

I park my car a few houses down the street and walk the short distance to the house. The street is much the same as I remembered. The colours have been updated, landscaping has grown and changed, and the trees are larger, but mostly things have remained the same. My house is still encased in the blue vinyl siding Dad installed a couple years before he got sick. The sun has faded the colour some, but it still stands out in the neighbourhood. I take in the shrubs and flowers in the front yard and notice they have grown immensely. I think Mom would have been happy with their success. I can still picture my father and me in the yard, practising my volleyball serve, while she ducked the stray balls as she tended to her garden. There were days I wanted to give up back then, and now I'd love nothing more than to hit that ball back and forth with my dad, or watch him teach Lily the same techniques and tricks. But I can't go back—none of us can. Time keeps moving forward, and now all we have are the memories it leaves behind.

I climb the few steps to the front porch and hesitate before knocking on the door. Should I have come here on my own? Perhaps I should have at least told David what I was planning. Before I have the chance to change my mind, I hear movement from inside the house. Someone has spotted me on the front porch. I raise my hand to rap on the door, when it opens before me and I come face to face with Sheila Lockwood.

"Hello, Sheila," I say as she greets me with a tight smile that I'm not quite sure how to interpret. "I'm here to see Allie."

She motions me inside, and I quickly realize the house is nearly identical to the day I left it. I have a nauseous feeling in the pit of my stomach knowing she has lived here all these years. Even the rug on the floor beneath the coffee table is the same. It is worn and a little worse for wear, yet it is the same print of reds, oranges, and yellows that my mother laid down years ago. I still remember the day she bought it and how she pretended to be hurt when my father poked fun at the busy pattern by telling her looking at it made him dizzy. The one noticeable difference is the smell of cigarette smoke and old french fry fat. It was the same scent Allie wore to school every day when we were friends all those years ago.

"Allie isn't here," she announces once we are inside. "I heard you were back in town. I wondered if you were going to stop by for a chat or to reminisce. Seeing as this was your home once upon a time."

I have an uneasy feeling. I wasn't sure she'd remember me, but she clearly has not forgotten. I do not trust this woman, and for a moment I wish I had waited for David.

"I didn't come here to catch up. I have a lot of questions about a lot of things. One of them being Melody Scott. I think Allie may have some of the answers I need."

"That girl don't know nothin' about nothin'. Shit happens. If you're as smart as you think you are, you'll forget about it and move on. How do you know Melody?"

"I didn't know her. But we have someone in common. Maybe you already know who it is?"

"I don't know nothin' about nothin', either. That girl was a troublemaker. Guess you two had that in common." She smirks.

"Melody was murdered by the same monster who held me in that basement years ago. He tortured and raped her the same as he did me. The only difference was I escaped and she didn't. If I hadn't, I likely would have died the same horrible death she did."

"Yeah, well, boo hoo for the both of you. Allie don't know nothin' about any of it. Coming here is a waste of your time and mine. *The Young and the Restless* is comin' on. You can let yourself out. I think you know the way." She laughs, and I feel her callousness sucking the air out of the room. "You may as well go on home. Where is home these days, anyway?" she asks, and I wonder why she wants to know.

"When will Allie be back? I can come by later."

"Don't know. She don't tell me what she's doin' or where she's goin'. Maybe she's not comin' back," she says, so coldly I am almost afraid something has happened to Allie. I have no doubt in my mind that Sheila Lockwood knows exactly where her daughter is at all times.

It makes me wonder if it's possible Allie knew nothing about what happened to Melody and me, although I find it hard to believe after all the stunts she's pulled. Yet there's something about the way her mother is acting that makes me second-guess our theory that Allie is somehow involved.

"Is there some reason you don't want me to speak to Allie?"

"Girl, I don't give a shit what you do. Just get the hell out of my house and don't come back. If you know what's good for you, you'll leave Allie alone and go back to wherever the hell you came from," she warns. The words are so casual, yet cold.

"Is that a threat, Sheila?"

"No, honey," she says casually, but her voice is so frigid it sends chills down my spine, "I don't make threats. That's a promise. Get out of town now, before it's too late."

"Fine. I'll go, but I'm not leaving town until I see Allie. There are too many things I need to say to her and too many questions that I need answered."

"Don't say I didn't warn you. You just can't go waltzin' back into town stirrin' up trouble 'cause you feel like it. This whole fuckin' world don't revolve around you. Think you would have learned that by now."

"I didn't say it did," I fire back, and turn toward the front door. "Sheila, I just have one more question before I go. Where is Jimmy?"

I feel the rage coming from her before she forms an answer, and I almost regret opening my mouth. Her face turns red, not with embarrassment, but with rage, and her whole body starts to tremble. I watch, transfixed, as she clenches her fist at her side, and for a moment I am scared of what she might do next. I expect her to charge at me, throw something, or threaten me, but instead her voice is low and steady as she looks at me with familiar piercing, black eyes and tells me, "Get the fuck out." I have no doubt in my mind then that Sheila Lockwood is as evil and calculating as the devil himself. She may not be my monster, but I am certain she has the ability to spawn one.

I walk to my car quickly, anxious to get out of there and back to the hotel. David will be furious with me for coming here to their house alone, and I wish I had waited, but it's too late. I can't go back. I fumble with the key fob and unlock the car doors just as I realize another note has been left under my wipers. Should I remove it? If I don't, it will likely blow away in the wind as I drive back to the hotel. I try to use the ends of my shirt sleeve to hold the note so as to not fudge any fingerprints, but it's useless, and I give up and grab the note with my free hand and read the words scrawled across the paper. As soon as I see the handwriting, I know this note is different. It is not like the others. The letters are barely legible and the words more threatening.

Surprise!
I am right behind you.
I told you once,
No one gets to leave.
Now it's time to go home.

I turn my head quickly, but it's too late. He is right behind me and grabs my arm and twists it angrily behind my back. I feel the muzzle of a gun forced into the small of my back, and for a moment Lily flashes before my eyes and I want to scream.

40

"Don't make a sound, Helena. Just walk across the street and get in the truck. No one here knows I exist. They don't know my name or where to find me, so makin' a scene is pointless unless you want to end up dead right here in the street. If not, keep your mouth shut and move."

I let him lead me to the old, beat-up Ford pickup across the street, but not before I manage to crumple the note he left and toss it in through my open car door. If David finds it, he will know what has happened, and he won't stop searching until he finds me. I just hope it's not too late.

He shoves me in through the driver's side and orders me to scoot over while he keeps the gun aimed steadily at my waist. He closes the door and starts the motor, and I realize this is the second time I have allowed him to abduct me. But this time is different. This time I know who I am dealing with, and this time I am not alone.

"Where are you taking me, Jimmy?" I ask, and I know I have startled him.

"Mama won't be happy 'bout that. You knowin' my name and all. But this will just make it more fun. You can call my name while I'm fuckin' ya! I can hear it now, 'Please, Jimmy, please.' Do ya still like it rough? 'Cause the rougher it is, the better I like it. We gotta make up for lost time, now, don't we?" He laughs, and the smell of

244

his breath combined with his menacing voice instantly pulls up images from the basement.

I search his face for a hint of humanity, but all I see is the same emotionless face from all those years ago. His eyes remain black holes in his acne-scarred face. His slick hair is longer, and he has aged, and time has not been good to him. Even though he is likely still in his twenties, his face tells the tale of a hard-lived life devoid of any happiness or emotion other than hate. I can't help but wonder what happened in his life after his father died that turned him into this monster beside me, and the only thing that comes to mind is Sheila Lockwood. Jimmy may be the monster I have been searching for, but she moulded this creation. What kind of a person does this to a child?

"Where are you taking me, Jimmy?"

"We're goin' home, Helena."

"Jimmy, that house was not home, and it's no longer there. The farmer who owned it tore it down years ago," I tell him.

"Ya think I'm an idiot? I know that place is gone. It wasn't really home, anyway. I'm takin' you to my home, the only place I ever felt like I belonged. You'll be happy there. It was decent, then shit happened and everything went to hell," he replies, and then turns out onto the highway, and I know where he is taking me.

"What happened to you after your family left Main Brook?" I ask him, trying to learn as much as I can while thinking of ways to let David know where he is taking me.

"How'd ya know about Main Brook?" he asks, and I am certain I see a flash of emotion cross his face, but I can't tell what it is he is feeling.

"I know a lot of things, Jimmy. I know your mother killed your father, and that's why you all had to leave Main Brook and move to Deer Lake. I just don't know why Allie got to live in the house with your mother while you ended up . . . where? Where did she take you, Jimmy?"

"I was goin' to leave with Daddy, but Allie wouldn't go. Mama always says, 'No one gets to leave,' but Daddy and me, we didn't listen. That's why he died and I got punished. Now I always listen to Mama. You always listen to Mama," he answers, and I shiver, imagining what he suffered as a child.

"You don't have to listen to her now, Jimmy," I try. "You're an adult now. You can make your own decisions. You don't have to take me wherever we're going. You can let me out here, and by the time someone finds me, you'll be long gone from here. Please, Jimmy, I can't do this again."

"Shut up! Shut up!" he yells, and I fear I have said too much. "No one gets to leave! Don't you get it? This is all your fault. If you didn't leave, Allie wouldn't have wanted to go, too, and then Mama wouldn't have made me punish you. Now you need to go back in the basement so everything will be okay and Mama won't be angry with me anymore."

I can't believe what I'm hearing. Even though I had suspicions after our confrontation, to hear Jimmy confirm that Sheila Lockwood is responsible for everything that has happened to me is still shocking. If I don't escape his madness this time around, at least I will die having learned the answer to one of the most important in my litany of questions. I may not understand, but at least I know why.

"Jimmy, I can't go back in the basement. I can't live in the basement. Please, let's just stop driving and talk this over," I plead, hoping I can somehow get through to him.

"I survived the basement. You can, too. I'll make it fun," he says, and looks at me with a smirk on his face that makes me question his sanity.

"Is that where your mother put you, Jimmy? Were you forced to live in the basement where no one knew you existed? Allie must have known. Didn't she try to help you? Why didn't you fight back together?"

"Allie is afraid of Mama. She does what she's told. Sometimes when she doesn't listen, Mama beats me as punishment, and she makes Allie watch. Now Allie does whatever Mama says so I don't get hurt. But Mama likes hurtin' us. It don't matter what we do."

"Allie was going to leave with Melody, wasn't she? She was going to defy your mother and get away from her—and you. That's why you kidnapped her and killed her. Is that what you were planning for me until I escaped? If I hadn't gotten away, would I be dead just like Melody? Is that what Sheila wanted? Did she want me dead, too? Only you failed, didn't you, Jimmy? You didn't—"

"Shut up! Shut the fuck up, Helena," he yells, as spittle sprays from his clenched, yellowed teeth. "I didn't fail. You won't be gettin' away this time."

"What are you planning, Jimmy? It's not like the last time. People are looking for me now, and they know who to look for. They know it's you," I lie. "You think your mother will protect you? She won't. She's a monster, Jimmy, and she's turned you into one, too."

I can see my words are having the desired effect on him. He is quivering with the anger seething beneath the surface. Sweat is pooling on his face, and his knuckles are white on the steering wheel. I can barely take my eyes off of the gun still pointed my way, and I pray he doesn't accidentally pull the trigger. We have driven out of town, and the road ahead is surrounded by vast wilderness. There are numerous places to dump a body on this road, and finding me afterward may very well be difficult. If I can get him to stop before we get all the way to Main Brook, I may have a chance.

I have a feeling his plans for me do not entail keeping me as his sex toy for long. It's only four hours away, and we already have a head start on David. I've left him a clue, but I'm not sure he has found it or if he even knows where to look. What if he doesn't find the note? What if he doesn't figure out where Jimmy is taking me? What if I can't fend him off long enough to be rescued?

What if David doesn't even know I'm missing?

What if it's already too late?

41

We pass the turnoff to Woody Point and continue on toward Rocky Harbour. I remember there is an RCMP detachment there, and I need to think of something to distract Jimmy long enough to grab the wheel and force us off the road. I can't think of any other way to avoid what I know he is planning. I think he is taking me to his family home in Main Brook. I don't know if someone else lives there now or if the place has been abandoned and fallen into disrepair like the basement all those years ago. Whatever the case, I have a feeling I am going to find out, and once Jimmy gets to where he's taking me, the situation is going to change, and it won't be for the better.

It has been an hour now since we left Deer Lake in Jimmy's old truck. I wonder if David has even noticed I'm not at the hotel. Does he know I am missing? Has he figured it out yet? I wish I had told him what I was planning, but I can't change what has happened. All I can do is try to keep myself alive long enough for him to find me. And what if he doesn't? I don't want to think that far ahead. I'm not prepared for a different outcome. The only one I am entertaining right now is my escape and Jimmy's capture or death. Either would be satisfying, but if I am honest with myself, I would thoroughly enjoy watching his slow, agonizing demise.

We've come to a section of highway I believe is safe enough

to survive a crash. I know it's not certain, but I am willing to try. I have no other choice.

"Watch out, Jimmy!" I yell, and quickly point to the left side of the road. "Moose!"

He turns his head quickly and hits the brakes as I reach over and grab the steering wheel and yank it toward me. The truck swerves to the right and Jimmy pulls back, forcing the vehicle to wobble and tilt dangerously, and for a second I fear we are going to tip into a rollover, but Jimmy gains control of the truck and I pay the price for my actions.

"What the fuck ya tryin' to do? Get us both killed? It might be your time to die, bitch, but it sure as hell ain't mine. Ya try somethin' like that again and you'll regret it," he warns angrily.

"I'm not afraid of your threats, Jimmy Lockwood. I know you. You're just a scared little boy afraid of disappointing his mama. You don't have what it takes to finish this game between us. I beat you once, and I'll beat you again!" I yell at him.

I see the motion of his hand holding the gun, but I'm not fast enough to ward off the blow that follows. In one swift motion, he raises his arm and comes down hard, hitting me in the temple with the butt of his gun. Pain shoots through my skull, and I instantly see stars swirling around me. I fight to keep my eyes open. I know if I succumb now I will end up in Main Brook or wherever he is taking me. I reach for the handle of the truck door. I'm not sure what I am thinking or if I am thinking at all. I just know I need to get out of this moving vehicle. Jimmy catches my movement, and a second blow knocks me out completely.

I am in the truck with Jimmy, still slumped over in the seat, yet I am looking through the windshield at myself and wondering how I got here. A few days ago I was watching my daughter playing with our dog and the sprinkler, enjoying an odd day of summer heat in the early fall. I had a life of sorts, but it was a life free of torture and pain. I had memories, but they were in the past. I was coping. How is it that I have gone back in time? Somehow, I have made one too many bad decisions, and I am back where it all started. Yet it is not the same.

The monster now has a name. Jimmy. The moniker sounds so childlike and harmless, like the kid next door. It's not the name of a monster, yet it is one and the same. My monster is Jimmy Lockwood. He is the brother of my childhood best friend. A brother I barely knew existed. He was not born a monster. Yet today he sits beside me in the driver's seat with the intention of taking me somewhere to finish the job he started all those years ago. Today he is a monster. Somewhere, somehow, he has become just a shell of the little boy he was. His soul, devoid of the ability to love, and feel, and empathize, has been swallowed by anger and hate and then spit back into the world to live out his days as a monster leaving a path of horror and human destruction in his wake.

I am one of his victims. I am the one who survived. I fought him and won, but the game wasn't finished, and now we are about to engage in round two. The day I have been waiting for and dreading, both at the same time, for eight years, has finally arrived. Today I get the chance to end this game once and for all. I stare at my slumped form in the passenger seat of the truck, and I wonder if all my posturing and all my mental preparation has been enough. Am I ready to defeat this monster, or have I fooled myself into thinking I have a fighting chance? I am not a quitter. Dr. Carpenter has told me that many times. I think I believe her. I would not be here, she says, if I was a quitter. I would be dead like Melody Scott. But I am here. I am still alive, and as long as I have a breath in me, I will fight. I will fight for myself and for the life I so desperately want. And I will fight for Lily and the life she deserves.

I feel the truck begin to slow. I don't know how long I have been unconscious. My head throbs with pain. I am certain I have a concussion, but I have to push through it. I do not stir in the seat beside him. I do not want him to know I am awake. It is a chance for me to think, to contemplate my predicament, and search for a way to survive. We turn in to a gravel driveway. The noise of stone crushing beneath the weight of the truck is telling, and I believe we have arrived in Main Brook. I am certain this is where he has taken me. I assume he has returned to his family home, to the one place he ever felt safe to be himself.

The truck stops, and I panic. What do I do now? Should I scream? I have no idea where this house is located. It is unlikely there are neighbours nearby, or Jimmy would not have come here. Do I run? I have no idea where I would run to. It feels like I'd be running back into the cornfield, where I know I have little chance of escaping. Do I do nothing and just follow him blindly to wherever he is taking me, with only the hope that David will find me to hang onto? I trust David's instincts, and I know without a doubt he will never stop looking for me, but I can't take the chance. I can't sit idly and wait to be rescued. It's not in my nature to be complacent. I am a fighter, and now is the time to fight.

Jimmy holds the gun at my side as he orders me to exit the driver's side door. He doesn't trust me to exit on the passenger side and wait for him to come around. He is right not to. I am not to be trusted to do exactly as I am told. I stumble when my feet hit the ground. My head is woozy, and my balance is off. It takes me a minute to find my footing, but I manage to stand without collapsing at his feet.

"Move," he orders, and shoves me in front of him and pushes me toward the house in front of us.

The building is barely standing. It is a bungalow that at one time may have been someone's home, Jimmy's home, but now it is being held together with a few rusty nails and a determination not to succumb to nature. The windows are merely holes in the side of the building where glass once separated it from the elements outside. Tattered curtains move in the breeze, imitating the motion of the wind that comes in small puffs. The old wooden siding is peeling its paint and has begun to rot and weather away. The brick chimney that stands at the end of the house is black with mildew and dead fungus, and the top has begun to crumble in upon itself like an implosion.

"I don't think it's safe to go in there, Jimmy," I tell him, but he isn't listening. He is focused on moving forward. He has a plan, and my voice can't penetrate the wall he has built around his thoughts. He will not allow me to cast doubts. "Jimmy, listen to me," I say a little louder, and I pull my arm from his grip and try to run, but my head is still foggy and my feet will not move like I want them to.

"Helena, don't make me do somethin' I don't wanna do. Just shut the fuck up and do what I tell ya to do," he says angrily, and tightens his grip on my arm.

"I am not going in that house, Jimmy," I tell him. "I am not doing this again!"

I somehow find the strength to kick him in the crotch and make a run for it. I don't know where I'm going, but I force one foot in front of the other and keep going. Jimmy yells out in pain, and I know if he catches me, I will pay a price for my actions. I have been down this road before. I know how it works.

"You bitch," he yells, and I can hear the hatred in his voice. "You ain't gettin' away with this."

I keep running. The world around me is swirling, and the earth seems to move in and out of focus, but I keep moving forward. I can't hear him following me, and I am hopeful, but something is telling me he will not give up this easily. A second later, I hear a bang and feel a stinging burn as a bullet passes through my skin. I cry out in pain and hold my fiery arm, but I keep going. Then I hear it again, a second shot, only this time the bullet finds its mark and stops me in my tracks. I fall to the ground and feel blood pooling around my face. I look up into the sky at the millions of stars twinkling above me, and for a moment all I feel is peace. I think it's finally over. After eight years of waiting, it's finally over. He has won. My only regret as I lay here on the ground, bleeding into the damp earth, is leaving my sweet Lily behind to find her way in the world without me. I take solace in knowing she will always have David, but I very much wanted to be the one to teach her, to guide her, and to love her.

"Now look what ya made me do, ya stupid bitch."

Jimmy is standing over me. His large figure looks down on me, and I wonder if he has come to finish the task of ending my life. He points the gun at my head, and then laughs his sick, eerie laugh, and pulls the trigger. Nothing happens, just the click of an empty chamber. He laughs louder at his cruel joke and my horror, like a child playing a game, and I realize for the first time that Jimmy has no conscience. He does not care if I live or die, or how many people his actions affect. He enjoys this. He has truly become the monster his mother set out to create.

"You ain't gonna die that easily, bitch. I've got plans for you, and it ain't takin' ya out without havin' a bit of fun first. Those bullets just grazed you, ya ain't dyin', not yet, anyway."

He laughs some more, and it scares me to witness how much he enjoys toying with me. He pulls me to my feet, and I stumble repeatedly as he half-drags me toward the ramshackle house, and for the first time I wonder if I have made a huge mistake coming after him. Maybe I'm not as strong as I think I am—or as resourceful. And for the first time since I found the note under my wipers, I think I may have reached the end.

We climb the few steps and enter the main floor of the house. It is littered with debris. Empty beer cans, cigarette butts, drug paraphernalia, and used condoms are strewn about the floor and leave a trail leading into the other rooms. Graffiti adorns the walls, and an old mattress sits on the floor in the corner, moth-eaten and mouldy. It is evident the place had been used by teenagers for quite a while, and I hope that tonight someone decides to check the place out one last time, but I know that hope is lost. It is clear the place has been abandoned by even the teens, who have now deemed it unfit to enter.

Once inside, Jimmy leads me to a doorway that leads down to the basement. The door that once separated the two floors has been removed, and the opening is black and vast and seems to lead into the great abyss. Maybe I will get lost in there and no one will find me, not even Jimmy. All those years ago, I was afraid to die alone in that basement, and I waited desperately, hoping for his return. Now all I want is to fall into the black hole and escape what I know is coming. I'd rather die alone and scared than endure the horror of Jimmy's version of fun.

He forces me to descend the stairs into the unknown. I walk slowly, trying to feel out the steps in front of me and hoping none of them are missing. We make it safely to the bottom, and it is as dark as the basement in the cornfield, and for a minute I think we are back there again. Jimmy ties my hands behind my back, and my left arm screams with the pain from the bullet that passed through the edge of my forearm.

"Can't have you tryin' to get away, now, can we," he says as he pulls the zip ties tighter and nearly cuts off the circulation.

"They'll find me here, Jimmy. Just let me go and you can get a head start away from here." I try to persuade him, but my words fall on deaf ears. He continues his task of immobilizing me and binds my feet with more zip ties. "You don't have to do this," I try again, but he isn't listening.

"Shut up! Just shut up and let me think!" he yells back, and I feel we have gone back to a time when my voice was silenced until I was given permission to speak. "Fuck! Why do you women have to talk so damn much? I gotta get outta here and think for a bit. Don't try nothin' funny. You'll regret it. I promise ya that," he warns, before taping my mouth with duct tape and climbing back up the stairs, leaving me alone in the darkness.

I am instantly drawn back to a time when the darkness was as frightening as the situation itself. To a time when critters came calling to feast on my broken body, and nightmares invaded my soul. I vowed never to be in such a predicament again, but here I am. A different basement, a different time, but the same nightmare nonetheless. What if David doesn't know where to find me? What if I spend another three months, two weeks, and five days at the mercy of this monster?

What if I let him win rather than endure the pain of fighting back?

What if he has already won?

42

There are voices above me. I hear them arguing. She is very angry, and it doesn't matter how often or how profusely he apologizes, she will not let up. Each time he begs her for forgiveness, she answers him with a smack. I hear how her hand connects with his bare skin and how he cries out in pain with each strike. I should feel bad for him, but he deserves every ounce of wrath he is receiving and more. He is a monster, but she is worse. How does a parent hate a child so deeply that they vanquish all semblance of humanity in them, until there is nothing left but an empty shell filled with hatred and a lust for cruelty? Sheila Lockwood has done this to her son. She spawned this monster.

Jimmy, in the presence of Sheila, is an eleven-year-old boy who wants nothing more than to please his mother. I hear this in their conversation in the room above me. Alone, he is a man devoid of any emotions whatsoever. So much so, I might even call him inhuman. He is intent on inflicting physical pain and emotional hurt on anyone who is unlucky enough to bear the brunt of his anger. Today, I am his outlet. I am the unlucky woman who will suffer the wrath he feels toward his mother but is unable to express to her. Today, Jimmy intends on finishing what he started all those years ago. The only difference is back then he was a boy doing what he was told. He followed the orders his mother gave him. Now he is trying to atone for not fulfilling her wishes and allowing me to escape. Sheila is here to tell him how stupid he is, but all Jimmy wants is to make his mother proud. He doesn't understand that nothing he does will ever please Sheila. She does not care. She is the devil.

I am locked in a dingy basement, dank with mould and inhabited by critters I'd rather not see. It is a different room, in a different house, and while the process is meant to be the same, the outcome is going to be very different. Jimmy has plans, and when he's finished with me, I will be dead. Unless David discovers the note and figures out what has happened and where he has taken me, I will not survive. I have been in the basement for hours, it seems. Long enough for Sheila to drive here to Main Brook. And while she insists Jimmy has made a grave mistake in kidnapping me for the second time, she will not give up the opportunity to goad me and have her last laugh.

I hear footsteps coming down the stairs. The basement is dark since the power was cut off years ago. The house in which Allie and Jimmy spent half their childhood, surviving, is nothing more than an abandoned, derelict home to stray cats, rats, and insects. If I listen closely enough, I'm certain I can hear bats in the rafters above the top floor. If I am forced to stay here all winter, I will die of exposure, but I don't think Jimmy's plans extend that far into the future. Maybe that is a blessing. I cannot survive months, weeks, or even days of horror like I did before. That is not an option, not this time around.

Sheila unlocks the door, and her large figure fills the opening as she waltzes into the room. My hands are bound behind my back, and my feet are tethered with zip ties. If I could move, I would attack her. If I had the opportunity, I think I could kill her. I hate her for what she has done to me and for what she has done to her own family. How one person could be responsible for so much pain is unfathomable, but here she is, the person who started it all.

"Well, well, what do we have here?" She snickers as she comes toward me. "I warned ya, girl, but I guess ya didn't get outta town fast enough. I told Jimmy here to wait it out, that you and your cop friend would have moved on eventually, but he didn't listen. He's not too bright, you know."

She steps toward me and pulls off the duct tape with one swift movement, and I try not to cry out with the pain as I sit up. My head is pounding from the effects of Jimmy's blows. I can feel the blood, dried and crusted, down the side of my face where one of the bullets has grazed my skull. An inch closer and I would not be here. I haven't yet decided if that was lucky or not.

"It's your fault he's the way he is," I reply angrily. "You turned him into a monster. How could you do that to your own son? What kind of mother are you?"

"You watch ya mouth, there, girl. Who the hell do ya think ya are? Tryin' to tell me how to be a mother? You don't know nothin' 'bout my life or what I had to put up with from that snivelling idiot I married and those ungrateful brats I gave birth to. He had the nerve to think he was gonna leave and take the boy with him! I told him. I told him more than once, but he didn't listen. What did I tell him, Jimmy?" she asks, and I realize Jimmy has followed her down the stairs and is standing by the door, afraid to enter without his mother's permission.

"No one gets to leave," he replies dutifully.

"That's right. No one gets to leave, and now that includes you, Helena."

"I don't understand," I say, searching for as many answers as I can before things go from bad to worse. "I am not your family! Why was I not allowed to leave?"

"You don't get it, do you? You didn't see beyond what ya wanted to see. It wasn't you I didn't want to leave. Allie followed you around like a lost puppy. She idolized you, but you never even noticed. It was always Helena this and Helena that. She knew she couldn't leave, but hangin' around with you gave her the idea that maybe, just maybe, she could go, too. I told her Jimmy here would pay the price for her leavin', but she had it in her head that Jimmy was big enough to take care of himself. If he couldn't keep her here, then I had to take care of the thing that was pullin' her away. That was you."

"So, Allie knew what you did to me?" I ask, not wanting to hear the answer but desperately needing to know. "She let you and him torture me for all that time?"

"Nah, she would have kicked up a fuss 'bout that. I made sure you'd take care of it for me."

"I don't understand. How could I have helped you?" I ask, confused.

"Girl, you are a dumb one, aren't ya? You didn't help me outta the goodness of your heart. I made ya think your best friend had gone bonkers, and you believed it," she says, laughing at her own perceived wit.

"You were the one who left the notes, and it was you who broke into my house. It wasn't Allie at all! Oh my God, how could I have believed she'd do such things in the first place? I should have known she would never leave vodka and pills on the anniversary of my mother's death. How did you know about the booze and sleeping pills?" I ask, and her laughter answers the question for me. "It wasn't a suicide, was it? You killed my mother, didn't you? It wasn't Allie who did it, it was you!"

I'm afraid to hear her confirm my theory, even though I desperately need to know the truth.

"It was quite easy, I must admit. A lot simpler than crawling under a car and messing with the brake line, and a lot quicker. At least I knew when she was gonna die. I got lucky with James. I really just meant to scare him into realizing his mistake, but the bastard died. Shit happens," she says coldly, and I get the feeling she is disappointed. "Your mother didn't give me any trouble. She really didn't put up much of a fight after I told her what I'd do to you if she didn't wash down that bottle of pills with the vodka. She was a weak woman, wasn't she? You should have been happy to be rid of the burden," she says callously.

"Why? Why did you kill my mother? What did she ever do to hurt you? You just said she was weak. Couldn't you have just left her alone?" I cry, and I want so badly to be free of these constraints.

"It wasn't her fault entirely. She wasn't the problem, as such, but she was feedin' it. Once she started feelin' better, Allie took it in her head she was gonna follow you, and your stupid mother encouraged her. She had plans to surprise you at college, so I did what I had to do to change her mind. Once I threatened to do the same thing to you that I did to your mother, she came 'round again. She wouldn't let nothin' happen to her precious Helena. Weak like her brother, that one. Dumb, too. Didn't think it'd take so long for her to realize no one gets to leave. In this family, no one gets to leave unless I decide it."

"Like you did your husband?"

"He got what he deserved. Allie was smart enough not to go then, and with a little reminder every now and then, she realized that ain't ever gonna change. She stays until I say otherwise," she says, so coldly I shiver with the thought of those kids growing up with her as a parent.

"Why did you try to make me think Allie was unstable? What was the point in that? You'd already made sure I had nothing to come home to. You killed my mother. You moved into my house. That was your idea, wasn't it?" I ask, feeling nothing but guilt for thinking Allie had been behind it all.

"I suggested it, but Allie didn't mind at all. She thought tendin' to your mother's garden and keepin' her home would somehow make up for her knowin' what I did to keep her from leavin'. Always feelin' guilty, that girl. She doesn't realize that guilt makes you weak. Right, Jimmy?" she calls over her shoulder. "Feeling guilty is for the weak. People like us, we don't feel nothin', right?"

"Yes, Mama, don't ever feel guilty. No one gets to leave. I don't forget, Mama," he says. Even though earlier he spoke like a man confident in his decisions and intent on carrying them out, in front of Sheila he sounds like an obedient eleven-year-old boy agreeing with every word his mother says for fear of reprisal.

"Why Melody?" I ask, trying to understand this woman's reasoning. "Why did you do that to her? What did she do that was so bad she deserved to die so brutally? She had already gone through so much, why take her in if you were only going to kill her?"

"Melody was a bad girl," Jimmy replies. "Allie needed to be taught a lesson."

"Shut up, you idiot!" Sheila admonishes him, and he cowers from her like a child. "Allie brought that girl home 'cause she's just as stupid as Jimmy here. She got it in her head she could save that girl, but she forgot the rules. Every now and again she has to be reminded," she says casually, as if holding a young woman captive and torturing her until she dies is normal.

"How is that teaching Allie a lesson? That's just sick! You are a monster, and you forced your own son to do the awful things you couldn't do yourself. You are the worst kind of monster. Even the devil pales in comparison to you!"

"Ha, ha. You are such a crybaby. Be thankful I didn't finish the job this imbecile screwed up. You are alive because I said so, but Jimmy here wants to make up for his mistake, and even though I told him to leave you alone for now, I think, for once, he has the right idea. It's time I wiped the earth of your presence, and Jimmy is biting at the chance to have some fun."

"You won't get away with all of this. I might not live to tell your story, but there are people who will never give up looking for me, and they are on to the both of you. It's the two of you who need to be erased from this earth and sent back to the bowels of hell where you belong."

"Ha, ha. Those are fightin' words, but too bad you're on the losin' end of this battle. I've wasted enough of my time here with the likes of you. I think I'll go home and cozy up in your mama's bed. The same one she took her last breaths in just to keep you safe. It's kinda funny, don't ya think? Think she knew how pathetic she was? Who gives up their own life to save someone else's? A weakling, that's who. That's who your mama was, girl. She was weak, just like you."

She sneers, and I want to kill her with my bare hands.

"You are the devil, Sheila Lockwood. If I ever get out of here, I am coming for you, and only one of us will live to tell the tale. I promise you, it will not be you who is left standing."

"Empty threats from a woman who will not live to see the sunrise tomorrow. I ain't a bit worried. Have fun, Jimmy!" she shouts as she ascends the stairs and leaves me alone in the basement with her son.

Jimmy waits by the door as we both listen for her to leave the house. Her car starts and she pulls away, heading back to Deer Lake, to the house she shares with my one-time friend. Allie is not entirely innocent in this long-running era of pain and torture, but she is not guilty of everything her mother and brother have done. She is a victim as much as she is complicit in their reign of terror.

If I survive long enough for David to find me here, I would love to ask her why she couldn't find the courage to tell me all those years ago, when we were just teenagers, how her mother had forced her brother to live in the basement like an animal and threatened them with harm if she should ever tell the truth. I would have told her we would find a way to save them, but what if we couldn't? What if Sheila Lockwood was smarter than all of us? What if she knew how to manipulate and scare everyone around her into doing what she wanted? But what if we had succeeded in putting a stop to her hate and abuse?

What if things had turned out differently?

What if this horror tale were just a work of fiction?

43

Jimmy stands by the door and waits until he is certain Sheila has left, then turns to me with a look I can only describe as a melding of insatiable hunger and burning hatred. He tries to smile, but the expression that emerges mimics a snarl, magnified by his jagged, rotting teeth and pale, thin lips. He is sweating profusely, and that, along with his greasy hair and acne-ridden face, is repulsive to me, and I cringe as I watch him stare at me from the other side of the room. His expression oozes with lust, and the growing bulge in his pants lets me know he is ready. Memories flood my mind from years earlier, when he wasn't much more than a boy and had difficulty controlling his urges. He is a man now and in complete control of his every action, and I am terrified.

As a young man all those years ago, Jimmy was just learning how to inflict the maximum amount of pain in return for the most basic of pleasures. There were times his attacks, while horrible and traumatizing, were also short-lived as he was unable to prolong his immense pleasure and excitement for extended periods of time. The monster who stands across the room from me tonight is not the same monster from all those years ago. This monster has grown and matured, embraced his desire to inflict pain on others, even relishes in it. The flashes of humanity I witnessed back then have completely faded, and in its place sits a human devoid of all compassion and emotion. For a moment I almost feel bad for the boy who was beaten out of this man by his mother.

Mr. Lodge had called him a sweet kid, and I wonder if it's possible that little boy still lives somewhere inside this shell of a human, and if so, whether I have a chance of reaching him, or is he scarred so deeply beneath the hopelessness and hatred that he is lost forever? I can't help but wonder what kind of person he would have become had his father's car not crashed and allowed them to escape the clutches of Sheila Lockwood. I think of my conversation with Dr. Carpenter about the merits of nurture verses nature, and I am hopeful my daughter's father had the disposition to become a different person other than the monster I see here now. This demon is the creation of his environment, an environment produced and fed by his despicable mother. I pray Lily will never see the darkness her parents have endured.

"Guess it's just you and me now," Jimmy says, as his contemptuous smile spreads across his ugly face and threatens to turn him into a caricature of a beast. "Time to have a little fun. It'll be just like old times don't ya think?"

I shiver as he stands there and laughs, and I want to wipe that sickening grin from his face. He is evil. The boy who might have at one time stood a chance is gone, beaten and forced to disappear in order to survive the only life he was allowed to live. His humanity and his compassion have been obliterated by one depraved mother. I want so much to be free from this basement just to be able to rid the earth of the likes of Sheila Lockwood.

"I forgot how much I really missed ya, Helena," he continues, as he moves closer to me. "I'm lookin' forward to catchin' up. We gotta make up for lost time. Don't worry, I'll make sure you enjoy it."

"You won't get away with it this time, Jimmy," I tell him, and it takes all my strength to hold my voice steady and pretend I am not scared to death. "They know who you are, and they will find you."

"You might be right, but it doesn't matter much to me, 'cause by the time they figure out where ya are, it's gonna be too late for you, and I'll be long gone."

"Why are you doing this, Jimmy? Is it because it's what your mother ordered you to do? Do you always do what mommy tells you to?" I torment him, and even though I can see his anger growing, I cannot help myself. "Are you afraid of your mommy, big man? Are you afraid to stand up to her? Maybe you're just afraid of disappointing her, and then you'll have to stay in the basement forever." I keep going, even though I can clearly see he is seething with rage.

"Shut ya mouth, bitch! You don't know a goddamn thing about me. I ain't no pushover, and I sure as hell ain't afraid of the likes of you. You think I don't know what ya tryin' to do? You think I'm stupid? I'll show ya who's the stupid one here, and it ain't me."

"If you're so smart and brave, why did I hear you fighting with your mother all those years ago? I heard you two upstairs, and I know she made you do the things you did to me. You were too weak to stand up to her then, and you're too much of a wimp to stand up to her now, even though you're a grown man. You can't even think without your mother's permission." I keep goading him, even though I know these may be the last words I ever speak.

"Shut up! Shut up! This is why!" he spits angrily. "You look at this and tell me I'm weak. You didn't have to survive what I lived through, so don't ya call me weak, not ever. I am not weak! I am not weak."

He stands with his back to me, only a few feet away, and pulls his shirt up over his shoulders, and I shiver at his revelation. His pale flesh has been beaten and ripped open with a strap or belt, and red scars now cover his entire back. If that wasn't enough, the words "No one gets to leave" have been seared into his skin with

266

what I think was the burning end of a cigarette. I open my mouth to say something, but no words emerge. What is there to say? I cannot feel sorry for him when he has inflicted the same level of torture on me and Melody Scott, knowing exactly how it feels to be powerless, hopeless, and in excruciating pain. Jimmy and I may have something in common, but he chose to handle his horrific experience by replicating it with his victims. He took his experience and allowed it to own him, and now he has become that which he could not defeat, his mother.

"You may have suffered, Jimmy, but that doesn't give you the right to make others feel the same pain you've felt," I say once I finally find my voice. "You could have stood up to Sheila. You and Allie could have found help, but you didn't. You stayed, and you did everything she told you to do until you became just like her."

"You don't understand. Why can't anyone understand? No. One. Gets. To. Leave!" he shouts, angrier than I remember ever seeing him before. "Mama doesn't let anyone leave unless she says so. Allie doesn't always listen to Mama, and then I pay the price. I can't let ya take Allie away, or Mama will be angry. I don't like it when she's angry."

"So, I'm right. You're afraid of your mother. You are afraid to stand up to her. You'll let her control you and everything you do rather than go against her. Be a man, Jimmy, for fuck's sakes! For once in your life, be a fucking man," I tell him.

I know I have gone too far, but I just can't stop. I hate him. I hate what he has done to me and to Melody Scott. I hate what he will continue to do to whomever his mother deems to be a threat. As long as Sheila Lockwood and her son live in this world, no one will be safe, and I am not willing to let that happen, not as long as I have a daughter to protect and the strength to keep fighting. I open my mouth to continue my tirade, but the back of his hand comes down hard across my cheek and sends me toppling over onto the floor.

The wound on the side of my head has opened up, and warm blood oozes from the gash and runs down my cheek. I cry out in pain as I hit the cold, dirty surface and land on my left side, where the first bullet passed through the flesh on my arm. My hands and feet are still bound with zip ties, and I fall hard, and now it's as if all the air has been sucked from my lungs. My shirt is wet and sticky where a steady trickle of blood leaks from the open wound. Jimmy is angry with me. I have antagonized him, tormented him, really, and now he stands over me full of rage and vengeance. I have looked this beast in the eyes before, yet this time I know, with absolute certainty, this will be the last time because one of us will not survive tonight.

"It's over, Helena. No one gets to leave, not even you. Especially not you," he says coldly, as he looks into my eyes and grins.

I instantly think of Lily and how desperately I want the chance to raise my beautiful daughter. There is nothing more I can say to Jimmy. I realize there is nothing anyone can say or do to convince him he has other options. My hope is that his final act is quick and painless, but this, too, is wishful thinking. Jimmy has a plan for me. I can see it in the way he looks at my face and my body, and I know from past experience he has no intention of ending my life without first having a little "fun."

"It may be over for me, Jimmy Lockwood," I say, as he releases his belt and begins to ready himself, "but it will never be over for you. As long as you allow her to control you with fear and the threat of punishment, it will never end. You will never escape the hell you're living, and that's the one thing giving me peace of mind right now. Just knowing you will suffer for the rest of your life and beyond makes everything I've done and endured these past few days worth it."

He opens his mouth to say something to me, but the sound of sirens in the distance surprises him, and he forgets what he wanted to say. The expression on his face changes instantly, and for a moment I see fear in his eyes. Is he afraid of getting caught? Is he afraid of angering his mother? Whatever the reason, it is immensely gratifying to witness his plans crumbling before him and to know that, whatever happens to me in the next few minutes, this ordeal will be over. If I die, I will die knowing Jimmy Lockwood will never hurt another human being again. If David doesn't make it in time to save me, it will still be too late for Jimmy.

The sirens grow louder as they get closer and closer to us. Jimmy is pacing like he does when he is nervous or trying to build up enough courage to do what he has been ordered to do. He mutters to himself as he moves back and forth, back and forth. The gun he used earlier is now by his side, and his finger is wrapped around the trigger. He is scared, and I worry how this will all play out. The vehicles pull up outside, and car doors are slamming shut as officers exit and, I assume, take up positions around the house. Moments later, I hear David's voice, and with it, I experience an intense feeling of relief.

"No, no, no!" Jimmy yells, and rakes his fingers through his greasy hair in frustration.

I'm not sure he even knows I'm still in the room, but I speak anyway. "It's over, Jimmy. You can't get out of this now." I'm certain I see the silhouette of a man pass by the broken window, and I know this will be over soon. I just have to hang on a little longer.

"I can't go to prison," he says matter-of-factly. He still paces back and forth, back and forth, the gun by his side. His forefinger dances on the trigger as he becomes increasingly agitated and anxious.

"Where did you think you were going to end up, Jimmy? You are a monster, and monsters belong in jail or dead. What do you want to do? You have a gun, Jimmy. Pick one!" I say to him callously, secretly willing him to put the gun to his head and pull the trigger. "Pick one, damn it! Jail or death?"

"I can't go to prison!" he yells at me. "I've been in prison my whole life! She put me in the basement on my eleventh birthday. She said I was bad and had to be punished, so she wouldn't let me out. I was invisible! For years, all I saw, all I knew, were the four walls of that basement. If I cried, she beat me. If I yelled out, she beat me more. She made Allie watch, and she told her if she ever told anyone about me, she would kill me, and she promised she'd do it slowly. I wish she did. I've been a prisoner. I'm still a prisoner, and I can't do it anymore!"

"Drop the gun, Jimmy," David orders. I hadn't heard him come down the stairs, but he is here and I want to pinch myself for fear I am dreaming. "It's over. Drop the gun and get down on your knees."

I watch in horror as Jimmy swings around to face David and raises the gun, and I hold my breath, waiting for him to pull the trigger, but instead he just stands there with his gun pointed at David and shaking uncontrollably. I listen as David tries to calm him down, and I want to tell him that his efforts are futile. Jimmy can't hear him. He is a boy in the basement with his psychotic mother, begging and pleading with her to set him free, all the while knowing his pleas are falling on deaf ears. Jimmy's greatest fear is to disappoint his mother and end up locked in the basement again. No one but Sheila can talk him out of this, and she is long gone.

"No, no, no," he chants over and over. "No more, no more. Can't do this anymore."

"Jimmy, put down the gun," David tries again, but Jimmy can't hear him.

"Stop talkin' to me!" he yells, but I'm not sure he is speaking to anyone present in this room. "Shut up! Just shut up!"

I watch as he points the gun directly at David, and everything moves in slow motion. I hear David yelling, and Jimmy refuses to reply, but the words are muffled as if I'm hearing them through a tin can. Then I hear the blast of a gun. It flashes in the darkened basement, and for a moment I'm not sure who has pulled the trigger, but then I see Jimmy fall to the floor at the same time I feel his blood splatter across my face. His blood is warm and thick and has a metallic scent like rusted iron, and I am thinking I should feel something. Maybe shock or relief or fear, but for a second after it happens, I don't feel anything. Then I realize it is my monster who lies dead on the floor beside me, and for the first time in a long time, I am happy. Truly happy, so happy, in fact, all I can do is laugh. I laugh loudly and heartily, and for a moment it doesn't sound like me, but then I remember it was a long time ago, before my life started down this road, when I actually laughed a lot. I laughed then like I am laughing now, with a deep belly laugh, and I think it's finally over. After all these years, it's finally over.

My laughter quickly turns to tears, and I cry with the relief of knowing this chapter has finally been written and I can close the book on this part of my life forever. David cradles me in his arms while we wait for the paramedics, who are coming down the stairs to take me out of this place. He has cut the ties securing my hands and feet, and I try to wrap my arms around him, but I can't seem to make them work the way they should.

"It's going to be okay, Helena. We got him," he says into my ear, cradling me against his chest. "It's finally over. We got him."

"Sheila," I try to tell him. "Sheila is responsible for all of this."

"Shh, don't worry about Sheila," he replies.

"But David, she—"

"Helena, we picked Sheila up while she was on her way back to town. We know all about her role in this," he tells me. "Don't worry about her. We got her, too."

The relief is overpowering. The weight that has been lifted from my shoulders is immeasurable. I have walked through life for the past eight years, waiting for the other shoe to drop, and now that it has, all I want to do is start living. Truly and wholly living. I want to hug Lily, and with her by my side, I want to embrace the world. I am ready to live a life without fear, without constraints, and without torment. For the first time in eight years, I can ask if there is a future beyond this nightmare.

What if I can finally dream without the shadow of a monster standing over me?

What if it's possible for me to trust again and be happy without questioning everything and everyone around me?

What if I can love someone again?

44

I didn't get the opportunity to talk to Allie face to face. I spent two days in the hospital receiving treatment for the damage caused by the two bullets Jimmy fired, and the severe concussion I received when the butt of the gun came crashing against my skull. When I was released, all I wanted to do was go home and be with my daughter. Lily had a wonderful vacation with the Campbells and their dog, Thunder, so much so, she still talks about it. She doesn't know anything about what happened in Deer Lake. She doesn't know how close I came to death, and I'm not sure I will ever tell her that. That will be a decision for another day, farther down the road when she is older, if I am able to convey my experiences without the hatred I still feel toward the Lockwoods.

Allie didn't try to come visit this time while I was in the hospital. David would not have allowed it had she tried. I learned later that she had been busy with the Major Crimes Unit. She has many questions to answer and a lot of explaining to do. She swears she didn't know about my kidnapping or the torture I endured, and I have chosen to believe her because it's easier than dealing with the alternative. She claims she didn't figure it out until Melody Scott turned up dead, and even then she wasn't entirely certain, and even if she had been sure, she was too scared to speak against her mother. She admitted to the officers questioning her that she had asked Sheila once if she had murdered my mother and her answer had been to laugh in her face and tell her it was her own fault. While that did not confirm her guilt, Allie was sure it was as close as she would ever get to a confession. She claims her own guilt is the reason she tends my mother's garden and maintains my parents' graves.

When she was asked about knowingly keeping her mother's secret and allowing her to force Jimmy to live out his life trapped in their basement, Allie's reply was identical to her brother's. She said repeatedly to the officers, "No one gets to leave." It seems Sheila used fear, and threats of physical abuse and torture, to keep her children from having a voice of their own. With Jimmy, she successfully erased all semblance of humanity from his soul and replaced it with anger and hatred. The little boy disappeared and was replaced with a vile human being who responded to his mother's psychotic nature by imitating her behaviour. Allie was allowed to have a life as long as it conformed to her mother's idea of how she should live. With any deviation, she was met with her mother's wrath or was forced to watch while her little brother was battered and tortured for her perceived mistakes.

David told me that even though Allie's role had not been front and centre in what had happened to me, she was not entirely innocent. Had she spoken up years earlier, none of this would have happened. Jimmy might have recovered from his trauma and gone on to live a relatively normal life. Had she confessed her suspicions about my mother's death, Sheila might have been stopped before it became my turn to suffer. Had she gotten free of her mother's clutches, Melody Scott might have been enjoying life at college. Yet even though Allie is far from innocent, no court will ever convict her of wrongdoing. She is as much a victim in this story as I am, or Melody, or even the boy-turned-monster, Jimmy.

Allie, however late she was, finally found the courage to speak up. When David couldn't find me at the hotel, he searched for me, and it didn't take long to find my car parked a few houses down the street from my old house. Inside he found the crumpled note and knew right away what had happened. He was frantic to find me, and with no idea where to start looking, he knocked on Allie's door. She was scared and afraid to talk to him, but he convinced her my life depended on her opening up to him, and thankfully, she finally let go of her fear. She told David the old house in the cornfield was the safe haven their father had chosen to take them when he had decided to leave Sheila. Apparently, James's father had spent time there as a boy while he harvested corn with his father. He knew the place was rundown, but it was shelter and a place to hide while he searched for an alternative away from Sheila. Unfortunately, Jimmy remembered the place where he and his dad were to have a fresh start, and he decided to take me there.

Allie said that when they were still kids, Jimmy would talk often of going home. He thought if they could go back to Main Brook, he wouldn't be forced to live in the basement, invisible from the rest of the world. It was the only place she could think of that Jimmy would go to feel safe. Thanks to her insight, David got to me just in time. I don't want to consider what might have happened had Allie been wrong. But I am trying not to ask the "what if" questions. Allie has a long way to go, to recover from the fear instilled by her mother. She has become a different person than the one she hoped to be, and she has a long road to recover the pieces of herself that she has lost, but at least she has taken the first steps.

I have often said that fear is many things. It takes pieces of you that you may never get back. It makes you lose control and can stop you in your tracks. But what I didn't say is that fear can change you in ways you wouldn't think possible. It can take your ability to trust, to love, and to live, but sometimes fear changes who you are. It takes your very being and morphs it into someone or something you don't even recognize. Fear can transform you into someone you despise, and make you loathe the person who you have become. And sometimes, when the fear is just too unbearable, it turns you into the monster from which you are trying to escape. Not all of us survive fear—not all of us want to. And some of us wish we hadn't.

Sheila is now in an eight-by-eight jail cell. She insists she is innocent, but her house and Allie tell a different story. David assures me she will never be a free woman ever again, and sometimes I wish we still had the death penalty. In my mind, it is a waste of fresh air to keep this woman, who created and nurtured a monster, alive. I sometimes daydream about watching a needle containing a lethal cocktail of drugs being inserted into her veins. I want to witness the fear in her eyes when she realizes she is going to hell. I wish she could see my face as I watch her die, but I will have to settle for having her rot in prison for the rest of her miserable life. Maybe someone there will take care of that which I cannot do and rid the world of the demon named Sheila Lockwood.

Dr. Carpenter came to see me twice while I was recuperating. We talked a lot about Allie and her family and the role they all played in changing my path in life. When she left my room the last time, we both knew our relationship as doctor and patient had run its course. I couldn't have made it through those first days and months without her. She kept me from sinking so far into despair that I couldn't find any hope. She provided me with ways to cope and allowed me to see tiny glimpses into the future. Gradually, those glimpses grew into hopes and dreams, and eventually, I was able to heal. Yet even though I accepted this trauma did not define who I was, I couldn't move forward, not until now. Now I can put the past where it belongs—in the past.

I still think of Allie often. It helps me to believe our friendship as two lonely and despondent teenagers was not entirely built on lies. Deep down I know Allie cared for me. I was her escape from a horrific home, and she was the rock who kept me from giving up on life. I will always feel guilty for not speaking up about her situation when I should have, and as hard as it is for others to accept, I understand why she could not stand up for herself or for her brother. Fear is a little word, yet it can reach into our lives far and deep, and its hold on us is powerful and all-consuming. As much as I hate the ordeal I suffered, I have forgiven Allie for her role in this story. I understand her plight, and I forgive her inability to act, but she is a part of a past I do not wish to revisit. Our friendship, as great as it seemed and as damaging as it was, is in the past. It is time for us both to pick up the pieces of our lives and move on. Neither of us needs to be reminded of all we have lost or had taken away. It's time to close that chapter and move on.

I look out my kitchen window to the backyard, where Lily is running happily with Sadie by her side while David pretends to threaten them with a water balloon. It has been months now since Jimmy Lockwood was killed and his mother incarcerated. I have decided it is time to live the life I have dreamed of living for so long. I have stopped asking the what-ifs. I have decided they are a waste of time. My grandmother, I'm sure, is laughing to herself at my revelation. But I finally know what she meant all those years ago. We cannot live constantly wondering what we could have done differently. The past is in the past, and we cannot change it. And we cannot live our days bargaining away our lives to ensure a perfect future. What is going to happen will happen regardless of how many times we ask what if I do this or what if I do that.

Grandma preached that we need to live for today, and I am finally ready to do what she tried to teach me all those years ago.

My story is written now. I have finally been able to tell the world the secrets I have carried for eight years. My story has an ending, and I am ready to put the whole thing behind me. As I sit here typing the last words to the final chapter, I watch as my family frolics in the yard and I realize I am finally happy. I have a daughter who lights up my life every day, and a man who is willing to love me despite all the baggage I carry. I close the cover of my laptop and pick up the box of memories that sits on the table beside me. I have printed off my last recollections of the final moments in the basement, and now the box is full. I tuck it tightly under my arm and walk toward the front door. It's a great night for a campfire, and I have everything we need in this little box to start the fire.

Acknowledgements

When I was asked if I would like to write an acknowledgement for my debut novel, I immediately said yes, and then instantly wondered what I would say. First, I have to say, it was a joy writing *Hunting Helena*, and I was quite captivated with how the story unfolded. It is entirely a work of fiction, born of my wild imagination, and in no way reflects on real people or events. If there are mistakes (and I'm sure there are), they are entirely my own.

I didn't wake up one day as an adult and say, "I'm going to write a book!" For me, this has been a dream for as long as I can remember, a dream most likely born the first time I read a Nancy Drew mystery and when I was encouraged by some very special teachers back when I was barely a teen and wrote my very first story. Mr. Jim King and Mr. Perry Hatcher, your support, your patience, and your encouragement meant the world to me and will never be forgotten.

I have to say a huge thank you to my sister, Vanessa, who has encouraged me from the beginning of this journey and without whom I'm not sure I would have finished. Thanks for listening to all my ideas, reading all my rough drafts, finding my mistakes, and convincing me to keep going when it seemed like the dream would always be just that, a dream.

To my parents, Bob and Lorna, you are the best. Thank you for always believing in me, for your never-ending encouragement, and your constant love. And Mom, just so you know, you are the reason I write stories like this. Thanks for providing me with the best serial killer library a girl could ask for!

To my family, Rick, Caitlin, Kyle, and Tyler, thank you for being mine, for supporting this dream, and never acting bored when I talk (way too much) about writing and publishing. Rick, you are my rock. Going down this road is an amazing adventure, and I wouldn't want to share it with anyone but you. Caitlin, Kyle, and Tyler, my beautiful children, I hope you know how much you are loved and cherished. And I hope you see this journey as a lesson to never give up on your dreams.

And last but not least, my team at Flanker Press. Thank you for choosing *Hunting Helena*, for believing in my work, and making my dream come true. It has been an incredible journey so far, and I cannot wait to see what the future holds!

Finally, to all you readers out there who dream of becoming writers, don't be afraid to start. If you have an idea, build on it. If you have a story to tell, write it. You're going to fail sometimes, you're going to get discouraged, and you'll want to give up. On those days, remember—we all write garbage sometimes, but that's why we edit. The fun thing about writing is you control the story, you decide how it starts, where it ends, and how to fill up the middle. Your writing journey is the same, but if you never start, you'll never know how it might end.

HUNTING HELENA

Natalie Carter-Giles has an arts degree from Memorial University of Newfoundland in English and history (double major) and has also obtained a certificate in criminology. She is an avid reader of mysteries and suspense novels and loves to spend her free time working in her extensive garden and enjoying the beauty of the west coast of Newfoundland and Labrador.

Natalie was born and raised in the beautiful island community of Ramea and now resides in Deer Lake with her husband and one of their three kids.

LEADING *the*
COMEBACK
CHURCH